This book should be returned to any Lancashire County Council Library on or before the date shown

CHINGLISH

BY **SUE CHEUNG**

ANDERSEN PRESS

This book is a fictional account based on the life, experiences and recollections of the author. In some cases names of people, dates, sequences or the detail of events have been changed to protect the privacy of others. The author has stated to the publishers that, except in such minor respects not affecting the substantial accuracy of the work, the contents of this book are true.

First published in 2019 by
Andersen Press Limited
20 Vauxhall Bridge Road
London SW1V 2SA
www.andersenpress.co.uk

2 4 6 8 10 9 7 5 3

British Library Cataloguing in Publication Data available.

ISBN 978 1 78344 839 5

Printed and bound in Great Britain by Clays Ltd, Elcograf S.p.A.

For my family,
because without them I wouldn't
have experienced life's highs and lows.
And how boring would *that* have been?!

1984

Tuesday 31st July

I've just fed boiled intestines to the local stray dog, as instructed by Dad. This has been my life up till now, completely bonkers. But I'm hoping that from tomorrow everything will become normal. That's why I've started this diary. I want to celebrate my soon-to-be completely normal life. Where do I begin? Well, my name is Jo Kwan, and at the grand age of thirteen, good stuff is FINALLY about to happen!

We are moving tomorrow, it's dead exciting. Things have been crap here – *really* crap – so when I found this empty diary while packing, I realised I could use it to write down all the good stuff that's coming. So here I am!

The first step to normality is to get out of this stinking butcher's shop, cos being constantly surrounded by raw offal and giblets is very unsettling.

The second step is to be with Simon again, who was sent off with our grandparents when I was eight and he was ten. It's unnatural to be apart from your big brother for so long. I mean, Mum and Dad couldn't have split us up any further if they tried. Our house in Hull is over a *hundred miles* away from where he is in Coventry AND I still have no idea why they did it (UR). Would be cool if he moves back in with us (as long as he has stopped wiping bogies on walls).

P.S. UR = Unknown reason. Think there will be lots of these.

Wednesday 1st August

We are in the car and heading off to Coventry. It's really happening! Dad has bought a new Chinese takeaway, although that's all I know. Mum and Dad are, as usual, not exactly being informative about what our new home is like. But I think it will be just like the old days in Nottingham, with our posh restaurant and big house – no more poky old flat above the butcher's – hurray!

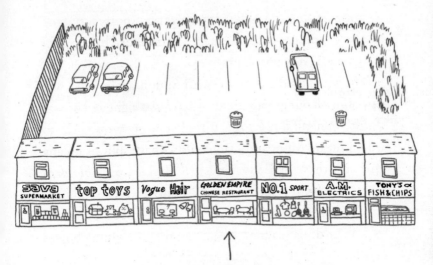

WE WERE HERE IN THE MIDDLE
OF THIS ROW OF SHOPS

Coventry will be our *third* place! The first was the Golden Empire Chinese Restaurant that Mum and Dad owned on the high street in Nottingham. They worked long hours, so me and Simon were left on our own a lot.

Being unsupervised was the best thing ever. Me and Simon could do what we liked, when we liked, and we never got told off.

. . . Apart from that time we nearly burned the house down.

It got boring eating crisps for dinner, and we thought making chips from scratch would be easy. How were we to know that lard was highly flammable?

GOOD THING ABOUT PARENTS NOT BEING HOME

BAD THING ABOUT PARENTS NOT BEING HOME

After that, Dad drafted in Grandma and Grandad, to make sure we didn't incinerate the whole place. Nothing changed much when they moved in, except we had home-cooked meals every night and a bath on Sundays.

Then my little sister Bonny came along, with her puking and pooing and crying. Grandparents must have got fed up of looking after her, as well as me and Simon, cos they moved out a couple of years later . . . and that's when Simon went with them.

BONNY AS TODDLER

PUKEY STAINS

FALLING SIDEWAYS

POOEY BOT

PARP

The rest of us moved and ended up at that bloody butcher's in Hull (UR). I've hated every second. Never made any real friends either.

Don't think any of us liked the butcher's really. So it's probably a good idea for Dad to go back to doing what he knows best, which is cooking Chinese food. Hopefully it will help him snap out of his bad moods. The less I say about those, the better.

I am strictly sticking to the good stuff in this diary.

NOTTINGHAM HOUSE

HULL BUTCHER'S

POKY FLAT →

DEN'S BUTCHER'S

GARDEN

NO GARDEN!

Anyway, I don't care about all that now cos we're off somewhere better and it's going to be TOTALLY ACE!

2.30 pm: We just took the road into Coventry. Nearly there!

3.05 pm: Arrived at new home. Have gone upstairs to take a look. It's a ONE-storey flat <u>above</u> the shop (UGH NO!), with only TWO bedrooms. That means I will have to share with Bonny. This must be some kind of mistake.

3.07 pm: Hold on, just found out there is no living room either! OK, don't panic – it's probably just a temporary arrangement till we get the big house.

7 pm: Everything unpacked. Wonder how far Simon lives from here?

Thursday 2nd August

Why has Dad bought a takeaway? Why not another restaurant? (Best not to ask while he's frantically untangling utensils). Not sure if a takeaway is any better than a butcher's, but at least it's giblet-free. It only took five minutes to have a proper look around our new home, cos this is how *tiny* it is . . .

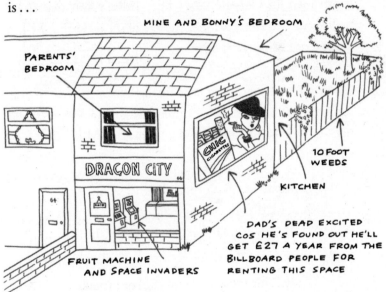

MINE AND BONNY'S BEDROOM

PARENTS' BEDROOM

10 FOOT WEEDS

DRAGON CITY

CHIC CIGARETTES

KITCHEN

DAD'S DEAD EXCITED COS HE'S FOUND OUT HE'LL GET £27 A YEAR FROM THE BILLBOARD PEOPLE FOR RENTING THIS SPACE

FRUIT MACHINE AND SPACE INVADERS

Yes, even tinier than the flat in Hull! OK, breathe. It's going to be fine . . . who needs a mansion anyway? I'm just glad we're back together again.

Simon and Grandparents came over for dinner. Simon's changed! His voice has gone all deep and he has faint stubble on his upper lip. He said, 'All right, Pongo, all right, Snotface.' He's been calling Bonny Snotface for ages but I don't know why he calls me Pongo (UR). Maybe it's a term of affection?

Mum was chuffed to see Simon after so long. You could tell by the way she was putting all the best bits of food into his rice bowl. (The bits without gristle basically.) She said, 'Eat up, mao nga lao,' and Simon cringed cos that means 'no tooth man' in Chinese. She's been calling him that since he lost his two front teeth at the age of six (UR), but he has a full set of adult teeth now.

'You two have grown so much I hardly recognise you,' Grandma said, squinting at me and Bonny. At least, it was something like that. We vaguely understood and smiled back cos we didn't know how to answer. It's difficult trying to talk in our family cos:

1) Grandparents don't speak English at all
2) Mum hardly speaks any English
3) Me, Bonny and Simon hardly speak Chinese
4) Dad speaks Chinese and good English – but doesn't like talking

In other words, we all have to cobble together tiny bits of Chinese and English into a rubbish language I call 'Chinglish'. It's very awkward. Plus we are the only ones in our family to speak Hakka – a dialect hardly anyone uses! All our relatives speak Cantonese cos that's what most other British Chinese people speak, so I don't understand ANYTHING they say.

Simon and Grandparents didn't stop long after dinner. Perhaps cos they have a house of their own to go back to now – with a comfy *living room* to sit in. Not jealous or anything!

Friday 3rd August

It's ace seeing Simon, but it will never be the same as before. For a start he doesn't live with us, and he's suddenly turned into this weird kind of grown-up – not how I remember him at all. I'm stuck with Bonny now. All right, she is eight, so there's less of the pooing and puking, but she is still complete DEVIL SPAWN. Last night she snapped all my pencils' tips by pressing too hard then put them back in the tin, as if still intact – *pure evil*!

Our bedroom is cramped (personal space = non-existent), and the only way into the bathroom is to go through our bedroom (UR). This is proving to be very stressful *and* there's a whole month left of summer holidays. Wonder if I will survive without strangling Bonny? At least I can look forward to being at the same school as Simon, the more agreeable sibling.

10.32 am: Bonny whinged about my Walkman taking up all of bedside cabinet. She said she had nowhere to put her signed photo of Gary Kemp (guitarist from Spandau Ballet). I told her he is the ugliest member of the band, and has worst perm known to man. We ended up drawing a line down the middle of the cabinet with the rule that if any item goes over, the aggrieved person can hurl it across the room.

10.48 am: Bonny hurled my Walkman across the room. (Apparently it was 'half a centimetre over'.) It flew through the open bathroom door and landed down the bog and broke. I was SO ANGRY! But had to keep it down cos Dad was in one of his moods.

BONNY BEING TOTALLY
AND UTTERLY <u>EVIL</u>!

12.03 am: Bonny fast asleep but I was still seething. I decided to chuck my cup of water over her head to teach her a lesson.

12.04 am: Bonny shrieked and sat up looking confused.

It is now 12.25 am. Can't get to sleep for laughing.

Saturday 4th August

Bonny told me she had a nightmare, which caused her to knock a cup of water over herself and now she has an itchy rash from sleeping in a damp polyester nightie. I said that was unfortunate and quickly changed the subject by pointing at an imaginary spider on the ceiling. This is justified revenge in my opinion; that Walkman cost two lots of birthday money. She swore she'd replace it and so I said, 'How? You don't have any dosh.'

'I'll get a paper round or something.'

'Er, hello? You're not old enough,' I pointed out.

Then Mum came up the stairs and said our auntie had just called, and did we want to go round and see our cousins.

They live down the road from us. Jill is the same age as me and Katy is a year older than Bonny. Their dad is our dad's older brother. Last time we saw them was four years ago at a wedding. I remember cos Mum kept saying, 'Jill and Katy speak perfect Chinese, why can't you?' And, 'Jill and Katy dress so nicely, why can't you?' So since then me and Bonny have called them our 'posh cousins', or 'Poshos' for short, cos they're sickeningly perfect. They're basically us in a parallel universe if our family had been normal.

We walked to theirs, which is one street over from Grandparents' place. Posh cousins' parents also own a takeaway but they don't live above it, instead they have a separate house like we used to.

I knocked on their spotless white front door and Jill and Katy answered in what looked like their best clothes, but was probably their everyday wear.

SUPER NEAT COIFFURED HAIR

BRIGHT EYES

JILL

KATY

FRESHLY LAUNDERED AND PRECISION-IRONED CLOTHES

ANNOYING AURA OF PERFECTION

Their house was like a show home inside; modern, light and free from loose toenail clippings. I noticed they had two living rooms (as opposed to our none): one for watching telly in and the other for 'best', whatever that means.

Posh Auntie gave us strawberry milkshakes and cheese and pickle sandwiches, which we never get, and there was no shouting, talking with mouths full, loud slurping or bits of food splattered over the table like there is at ours. There was just nice conversation – sometimes in Cantonese, but mostly in English as they know we understand that. There was a bit of Chinglish – not the rubbish sort we get at home, but the sort that makes sense. It was ever so polite and civil.

When we got back, Mum and Dad were arguing over what was a safe amount of monosodium glutamate to put in the food without poisoning customers. The takeaway is opening tomorrow and there may be dead bodies on our hands. It is an utter madhouse.

A man came to put up new signage on the shop front. It is now called 'The Happy Gathering'. I will look up the Trade Descriptions Act. I think we may be breaching it.

Sunday 5th August

Takeaway opening today. Dad said it will be open 364 days a year with one day off for Christmas – bonkers! The butcher's closed Sundays and the Golden Empire every Monday. 'So why aren't you having a day off this time?' I asked Dad. 'Ha!' he laughed bitterly, and walked off (UR). He is stressed already and we've not even opened yet.

Dad is going to be cooking in the kitchen and Mum is serving in the shop. That's a bad arrangement cos Mum's customer service skills are dire, i.e. she can't speak the lingo and she also has a habit of burping audibly in public. Well, good luck to everyone, that's all I can say.

Before opening time, some relatives came to visit and brought gifts of fermented cabbage (traditional I think). Auntie Yip is Mum's younger, nicer and educated sister and Uncle Han is Dad's younger, jollier and approachable brother. Auntie lives in Wolverhampton and Uncle in Derby, and both work as waiting staff in Chinese restaurants. (Why do all Chinese people work in restaurants or takeaways? Why can't they be teachers, plumbers or bus drivers? When I grow up I am getting a normal job.)

'Are you excited about your new home?' Auntie asked in Chinese.

Mine and Bonny's eyes glazed over cos we didn't know how to answer.

'You like it. New house?' said Uncle, helping us out in English.

We cringed and nodded. We don't really. We wish we had separate bedrooms.

Mum and Dad's bedroom doubles up as the living room. There's a bed, drawers, wardrobe, sofa, and a chair and table with a telly and video recorder on top. There's just about enough space for me to draw, which is lucky cos otherwise I'd go mad. I love art, it's the only thing I'm good at. I'm hoping to be as good as Yoko Ono one day.

6 pm: Takeaway opened. The extractor fan and woks were so noisy I had to come upstairs to draw in peace.

6.05 pm: Bonny barged in and turned the telly on loud.

6.15 pm: I turned it down.

6.17 pm: Bonny turned it up – aargh.

6.25pm: Am now in our bedroom, but the racket is even worse here cos we are directly over the kitchen . . . *and* I can smell gross garlic fumes. I can't even block it out with a pillow over my head!

Monday 6th August

Grandparents and Simon have started to come round every evening for dinner, which is nice. But whereas Simon goes home afterwards, Grandparents have to stay and help prep in the kitchen before the takeaway opens. Surely it's not fair making doddery old people work? They are ancient as hell!

Then tonight I saw Grandad sling a sack of rice over his shoulder like it was nothing and I remembered he used to be a farmer. I only know cos I found Mum and Dad's birth certificates back in Nottingham, when I was snooping about. On them it said that Mum's dad was a fisherman and Dad's dad was a farmer, in China. I guess Grandad must have had to pull cows out of ditches and grind corn with his bare hands (or whatever), so that's why he's so strong.

Grandma is pretty tough too. I swear she could chop veg, stir soup and scrub the floor at the same time. She is a proper Jedi Master in the kitchen and weirdly enough, looks exactly like Yoda. She is always criticising Mum and Dad. But they never talk back to their parents like me and Bonny do to them.

When Simon came over for dinner, he told me that when Grandparents lived in Communist China, they had to eat mattresses to stay alive and that's why their kids respect them so much. Wonder if it's true?

Tuesday 7th August

Mum made char siu and asked me and Bonny to take some over to Grandparents. We hadn't been round theirs yet, and I wanted to see where Simon was living anyway. They have a narrow terraced house like Poshos'. The door wasn't locked, so we went straight through to the back garden where Grandad was scattering prawn shells on the soil. It reeked in the heat.

'What you doing?' I asked, shielding my nose.

'It's good Chinese fertiliser,' said Grandad in Chinese.

'It stinks,' said Bonny.

'You stink,' said Grandad.

At least it was prawns. Back in Nottingham, Grandad used his own wee! When I shared a bedroom with Grandparents, I used to hear Grandad get up in the middle of the night to pee into an empty Dandelion and Burdock bottle. I thought it was cos he was too lazy to go to the bog, but one day I saw him tip the wee into a watering can and water the cabbages with it.

'UGH, we've been eating those!' I told Simon.

When Grandad served cabbage for dinner that night, we refused to go near it. So Grandma tried to end our hunger strike by giving us her dreaded spaghetti with golden syrup, which was even worse.

I gave the marinated roast pork to Grandma, then me and Bonny went upstairs to see Simon. He was untangling electrical cable but stopped to show us his brand-new, wood-veneer version Atari 2600, which I was completely uninterested in. His ambition is to be a computer engineer. He is a proper geek.

'Hey, do you know what happened to the bikes we had in Nottingham?' I said, wishing we could ride off like old times and forget about crappy computers.

'Dunno,' said Simon. 'Anyway, you were always falling off yours.'

'That wasn't me, that was the flares,' I said.

Yeah, not everything was amazing back then. Flared

trousers were death traps due to the excessive material getting caught in everything like your bike chains, under your Spacehopper, even on hedges!

HEALTH WARNING: FLARES KILL MORE PEOPLE THAN FALLING COCONUTS (BRIAN THE BRAIN AT SCHOOL ONCE SAID)

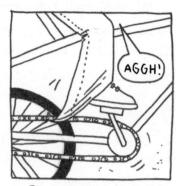

BEWARE BIKE CHAINS

BEWARE SPACEHOPPERS

BEWARE HEDGES

I prefer eighties skin-tight jeans, even though I read in *Mizz* fashion mag recently that they are the number one suspected cause of urinary tract infection.

Simon started swearing at the cables and Bonny looked

bored, so we left. As I opened the front door, Grandma shouted from the kitchen, 'Tell your mother this char siu's drier than a camel's fart. What's she trying to do, choke us?'

She might not know much about Western food, but when it comes to Chinese food, she is definitely the expert. 'OK, I'll tell her,' I sighed, then forgot on purpose.

Wednesday 8th August

9.25 am: I can forget about hanging out with Simon. I mean, he's almost got a moustache and does boring stuff with microchips. Wonder if I can forge some kind of friendship with Jill? Even though she is posh and perfect, she is still related so there must be *something* we have in common.

7.40 pm: Took Bonny with me to see what Poshos were up to earlier. Katy was practising the recorder and Jill was trying on a new school uniform, which her mum had bought from the most expensive department store in town. While waiting for them to finish, we went and gawped at their school photos. Bonny only noticed their goofy smiles but I thought they looked like Crufts' Best in Show dogs, with their bright eyes and coiffured hair. I doubted I could ever be Jill's friend cos I felt like a scruffy mongrel compared to her. I was overcome with inferiority complex, so I dragged Bonny home after our milkshakes.

'Why did we have to go so soon?'

'Just *cos*,' I replied.

When we got back, I wanted to remind myself how we looked in our school photos, so I asked Mum where they were.

'What do you want those for? You look feral in them!' she said, without once looking up from de-gibleting a chicken. Agree, we were never photogenic, especially as:

1) We always looked like we'd just crawled out of a skip
2) We probably *had* just crawled out of a skip

I could tell Mum wasn't going to co-operate. She never does when her hand's up a chicken's bum. So I went into her bedroom and eventually found the photos on top of the wardrobe in a battered biscuit tin. There was a picture of me and Simon with scarecrow hair, and one of Bonny with her mouth all wonky from where she sucked her thumb too much.

'Mum was right, we do look scary,' said Bonny, peering over my shoulder.

As I chucked them back in the tin, I spotted some crumpled black and white photos at the bottom. 'Hey, what's this?' I said. The faces looked familiar and it took a second to click. 'Oh my god, it's Mum and Dad!'

I showed Bonny. They were wedding photos from the 1960s. We hardly recognised Mum cos she was wearing one of those lovely cheongsams (traditional Chinese silk dress thing), and Dad was handsome in a slim-cut suit and Brylcreemed quiff, like a Chinese version of a young Cliff Richard. They looked so different. So . . . happy. What the flip happened?

MUM AND DAD
THEN AND NOW

BEEHIVE HAIRDO

LOOK OF YOUTH, OPTIMISM AND HAPPINESS

DAPPER SUIT

LOOK OF OVERWORKED GLUMNESS

WHAT HAPPENED?!

THOSE OVERALLS

MOULDY OLD BEANSPROUTS

Thursday 9th August

Went to inspect jungle-like weed growth in garden. It was exactly like our garden in Nottingham before Grandad moved in and mowed it. Wonder if he'll do it again for us, cos Mum and Dad won't ever.

Met an old lady taking aprons off her washing line next door. She told me her name was Mrs Burke. 'I've lived here thirty-nine years,' she said, 'and I've had half a pint of ale every day of my life. That's how I keep so young.'

She couldn't have had ale as a child, as surely it wasn't allowed? Plus she had more wrinkles than Grandma Yoda, who is virtually prehistoric.

'It gets very noisy in your shop,' she said, jabbing her finger at me as if it was my fault. 'I need my beauty sleep you know.'

'Errrrr, OK, I'll tell my parents,' I replied, wondering if woks could be tossed quietly.

I told Mum about Mrs Burke. (I try not to speak to Dad if I can help it as too much bother trying to guess what mood he's in.) She gave me a deep-fried chicken leg and raw tomato in a carton (UR), and instructed me to go round and give it to her as a form of apology.

'My mum said she'd give you this every week, for the noise,' I said, handing over the peace offering.

'It's not any of that foreign muck is it?' she asked.

'It's chicken . . . *English* chicken,' I replied. 'And a tomato, but I don't know where that's from.'

Then – didn't see this coming – she smiled and invited me in. Wish she hadn't though cos I had to spend half an hour listening to stories about her piles, while she crocheted an antimacassar.

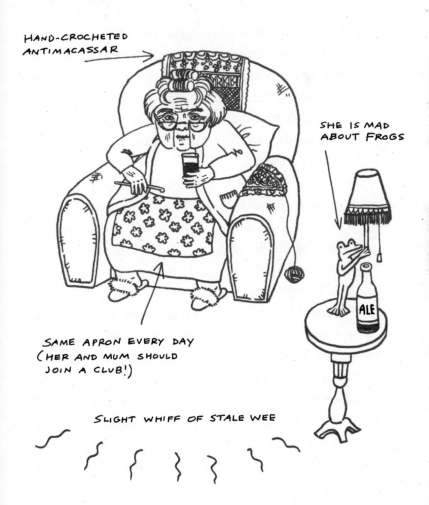

HAND-CROCHETED ANTIMACASSAR →

SHE IS MAD ABOUT FROGS

ALE

SAME APRON EVERY DAY (HER AND MUM SHOULD JOIN A CLUB!)

SLIGHT WHIFF OF STALE WEE

Friday 10th August

Had to remind Mum about my uniform today, in bad Chinese.

'I want new clothes go school,' I said.

'What happened to your other clothes?' she replied, in proper Chinese.

'My clothes go school too small now.'

'How much do you need?'

'It much resembles eighty pounds.'

'Cor, do you think I'm made of money?' she said.

'I need other stuff too, like pens and pencils and a bag,' I said, in English, cos it was easier.

'Huh?' she replied.

Gawd.

'What about Bonny?' asked Mum.

'What about her?'

'She'll need a uniform too.'

'No, Mum, she's at primary school, she doesn't need one.'

'Oh,' she replied, confused.

Mum and Dad know more about quantum physics than they do about their own kids, which is sod all. Mum once told me that when she was my age she had to leave school to stay at home and look after six younger brothers and sisters, so she never really got an education. She can't understand why we even *need* school. Dad went to school till he was sixteen, but he's just not interested in anything we do (UR). They don't even know I'm going to be at the same school as Simon, as they haven't asked. If I were them I'd want to know, and be pleased me and Simon were there for company (even if it is only at school and not at home). But they don't give a jot.

Saturday 11th August

Wowser! Me and Bonny found out Dad could draw today! I wanted to know who I'd got my talent from, so I asked Mum if she could draw and she said, 'No, but your dad's a good artist, go ask him.' Got the feeling Mum knew he was OK today, so we took the risk. He was watching snooker on the telly perched on a corner bracket behind the shop counter for the customers. It's his favourite thing on the telly. Dennis Taylor was on. I know him cos he wears special upside-down glasses for better aim – plus Dad supports him. I can see why he likes snooker, it's very calming. It's one of the very few times I feel comfortable being around him. He needs more calm in his life I think.

Me and Bonny waited till the end of the frame. Taylor won so I definitely knew Dad was in a good mood then. I asked if he'd doodle something on the order pad and he was up for it. He grinned as he sketched a head, some eyes, then claws and scales. And in only a minute he'd drawn an excellent Chinese dragon. Can you believe it? Me and Dad are *both* artists! Here's a copy I did of it.

COPY OF DAD'S
DRAGON DRAWING

ROAAAR!!!

WONDER IF IT'S
HIS INNER SELF
COMING OUT?

He didn't ask me to draw anything but I didn't mind, it was just good to see him enjoying himself for once. I thought he'd enjoy cooking, cos that's creative, in a way, but he never looks totally happy when he's doing it.

The reasons I enjoy drawing are:
1) It's fun
2) It makes me feel good
3) It's something cool to put on the wall
4) I can escape real life

Bonny has bagsied Dad's dragon drawing. It now has pride of place next to Gary Kemp.

Sunday 12th August

Asked Bonny where she'd been all morning and it turns out she has made a friend ... *before me*! And it's not Jill or Katy either. It's a girl called Mandy who lives up the road near the chippy.

'She asked for a fag and we chatted for ages,' said Bonny.

'Well I hope you didn't have a fag to give her,' I said.

'Course not, don't smoke do I?'

'How old is Mandy if she smokes then?' I asked.

'Ten,' said Bonny.

Good Lord. Don't think Bonny should be hanging around with that sort, but then again who am I to talk? I don't have a friend. I will need one soon though, before I start looking like a monumental saddo. I know there'll be loads of opportunities to make friends at my new school, but I am so crap at it I fear I may never get one.

Monday 13th August

Bonny has gone and bought a golden hamster from the pet shop, 'cos Mandy's got one'. It cost £1.99 plus free transparent exercise ball. She's called him 'Hammy'. That's the extent of her imagination. I was alarmed that Hammy's head was not in proportion with his body, but then realised he had twenty-seven sunflower seeds in each cheek, so that was a relief.

11.45 am: Bonny put Hammy in ball so 'he can enjoy a bit of freedom'.

11.58 am: Bonny went out and left Hammy unattended.

12.35 pm: Just went to use loo and found Hammy unceremoniously wedged between toilet and bottle of limescale remover covered in own droppings with expression on face that looked suspiciously like 'furious'.

When Bonny got back I had a right go at her, but she just shrugged and took Hammy downstairs to show everyone. Dad took the ball, peered inside at the poo-covered furball and chuckled. (He has a soft spot for animals.) Mum cringed. 'Dirty,' was her one-word contribution.

Then Grandad said, 'What you got that for?'

'Cos he's cute,' cooed Bonny.

'It's vermin, get rid of it!' said Grandma.

They seemed quite distressed about the whole thing. Maybe they had to eat hamsters in Communist China too?

HOW CAN ONE TEENY HAMSTER GENERATE SO MUCH POO?

Tuesday 14th August

Was concentrating sketching an oak leaf in fineliner, when I heard Bonny screaming in our room. I burst in and found her holding the vacuum cleaner, which was still on.

'What happened?'

'I've just hoovered up the hamster!' she shrieked.

I went over, switched it off at the mains and glared at her as in *how the hell*?!

'I couldn't be bothered to clean out the sawdust properly, so I took off the brush attachment and stuck the nozzle through the hatch,' she gabbled.

So I wrestled the vacuum cleaner open, pulled out the dust bag and tipped the contents on to the floor. Hammy rolled out, stiff as a board.

'Oh my god,' I whispershouted, 'you've *killed* him!'

I wasn't sure what to do (haven't been so traumatised since Hazel got shot in *Watership Down*), so I prodded the lifeless corpse a few times.

It didn't move.

'Right, well you killed him, so you can bury him,' I said.

'Can you help me?' said Bonny.

'Why should I?'

'Cos you know how to use a spade.'

'We don't even have a spade.'

'Well how are we gonna bury him then?' said Bonny.

'I think you mean, how am *I* going to bury him?'

'Yeah, that's what I said before. How are *you* gonna bury him?'

This futile discussion went on for a bit (and I was slightly crapping myself about what Dad would do if he walked into the room that second), till I noticed Hammy moving – well, more like erratic twitching really – so I made Bonny pick him up and put him back in the cage. (I didn't want to touch him as am not sure if rodents harbour fatal diseases after coming back from dead.) Then we closed the hatch and tried to forget about it, in the hope that Hammy would too. Although not entirely sure he will, considering THIS must have been the look on his face, the moment he got sucked up . . .

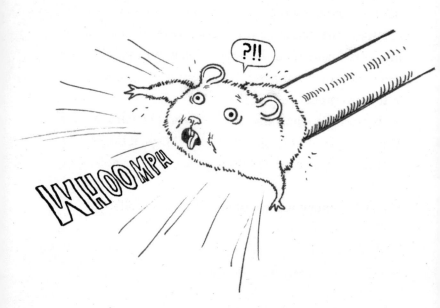

Wednesday 15th August

Jill invited me for a burger at the Wimpy in town. Thought maybe she wanted us to be best mates after all, but when I got to hers she was with *another* girl, her *best mate Sunita* as it happens. It didn't help that Sunita was extremely pretty and had thick, wavy hennaed hair. I immediately felt like a spare part and wished I was back home again.

On the bus they talked about make-up and boys. I didn't know anything about either, so for a laugh I thought I should tell them about Bonny hoovering up Hammy. Then decided not to, cos it isn't a very nice thing to do to a creature, and I didn't want them to think I was a cold-hearted murderer's accomplice. I wanted to appear normal, like them.

Jill and Sunita are both in the same year as me at school, but their stylish clothes and hair make them look older. At one point they started giggling and I thought it was about my second-hand T-shirt I got off Mum's friend. I went red and looked out the window, then realised they were waving at some boys outside.

When I got home I chucked out a whole bunch of clothes. Who wears corduroy any more anyway? Ugh. If I'm going to make friends, I have to at least not look like a spanner.

Hammy has not come out of his plastic house all day.

Thursday 16th August

Took a quid out the till (Mum won't notice, there's always loads of change in there), and bought *Mizz* mag. Checked out the fashion spreads and apparently these are the latest trends:

'Nautical'
White trousers, sailor-style cap, flirty flip-flops.
(Model cocks cap and has one leg bent back at knee.)

'Cocktail Party'
Flared mini skirt, sequinned boob tube, faux tiara.
(Model looks overly excited with both hands fanned out next to face.)

Wish I looked like that. Or at least had friends who looked like that. What are the chances though? When I looked in the mirror I decided I had zilch chance, cos who'd want to hang out with:

'Weirdo'
Spotty T-shirt, stripy jeans, teabag slip-ons.
(Model bangs head on wall and cries *'Help!'*)

NAUTICAL

COCKTAIL PARTY

WEIRDO

WHAT EVEN IS THIS HAIR?

It is very difficult for me to wear anything nice due to stunted, odd-shaped body with calves like that football player, Kevin Keegan. At present I am unable to fit into 99% of high street garments (remaining 1% = socks).

Friday 17th August

Bought new batwing-sleeve top. An article in *Mizz* says that 'wide sleeves detract from a short trunk'. Took me a while to realise they were not referring to an elephant. (Well I am *new* to the fashion world!)

Me and Bonny did Grandparents' char siu run. Simon was in his bedroom, listening to Madness on the stereo with a mate, who had bright ginger hair shaved almost to a skinhead, and so many freckles that his whole face was one giant freckle. He was also wearing a massive pair of Doc Marten boots with rolled-up jeans. Him and Simon looked totally mismatched, but then no more than Bonny and Mandy do I suppose.

'Hi,' we said.

'Oh, these are my two little sisters, Pongo and Snotface,' said Simon to his mate.

I squirmed.

'They're good names,' he said. 'I'm Smiffy.'

'He's a *bovver boy*,' said Simon.

(Note: look up bovver boy.)

I told Simon about Hammy getting hoovered up and they both laughed.

'Do you think he'll be all right?' said Bonny.

'Yeah,' said Simon. 'Hamsters come from the desert, so he would have felt right at home in that dusty hoover bag.'

Bonny seemed reassured by this information. Then we sensed we were cramping Simon's style, so went back down to say bye to Grandma, who was in the kitchen sticking an envelope down with cold boiled rice (UR).

Still no Hammy!

Sunday 19th August

Mum needed kitchen roll, so I went to the convenience store two doors down on the other side of Mrs Burke's. The sign on the outside says 'Banga Quality Foo', cos the 'd' has dropped off the end. There was a girl in there, sucking a green ice pop. She was wearing similar stuff to what I'd just chucked out.

'Hi,' she said.

'Hi,' I replied, recoiling. Her hair looked like she'd stuck her finger in a socket.

'Have you just moved in the Chinky?' she asked.

Er, Chinky?! Did she actually say *Chinky*?! I was totally offended, so answered back emphasising the correct term.

'Yes, I have just moved into the "*Chinese takeaway*".'

I could have mentioned the smell of curry in her shop, or made some other comment relating to her Indianness, but unlike her I knew where to draw the line.

'What's your name? Mine's Gurdeep,' she said.

'Jo,' I replied grudgingly.

'D'you want an out-of-date Turkish Delight, Jo?' she said, rifling around in her pocket.

'No thanks, I'll just have this.'

I plonked the kitchen rolls on the counter and handed over the money. As I hurried off, I looked back and saw her waving at me with her neon-green lips pressed against the door. Please god, don't let HER be my friend!

Monday 20th August

Bonny was getting ready to go to Mandy's, not taking a blind bit of notice about welfare of her pet, so I said, 'Hey, I haven't seen Hammy for a week. Don't you think you should take a look?'

'Meh, meh, meh,' she replied, doing childish talking-motion with her hand.

Oooh, I just want to slap her sometimes. Well if she wasn't going to do it, I would. I opened up the cage, lifted the roof off the hamster house and looked inside.

I nearly fainted. Poor Hammy was stark naked! His fur had dropped off from all the shock and he wasn't all plump and smooth either (like how I imagined a bald hamster to be), but wrinkly like a walnut! I told Bonny to call Simon for advice as he was the brainy one, but he suggested we dab him with Pritt Stick and roll him in cotton wool. So unhelpful.

Tuesday 21st August

Me and Bonny had emergency discussion about Hammy. We agreed he was about to conk out any minute, so decided to release him in park to enjoy his last days in total freedom – like in the wild.

10.30 am: Parents still asleep. Put Hammy in empty mushroom box. Left house.

10.32 am: Bumped into Gurdeep – aargh. She wanted to know what was in the box. Bonny told her it was a real-life mini E.T. that 'Wants to *go home*' (said in strangled E.T. voice). Gurdeep didn't believe us, so we showed her and she ran off screaming.

10.43 am: In park, looking for small-fluffy-rodent-home type spot.

WRINKLY AND **BALD**!

fresh
MUSHROOMS

10.52 am: Found one. Released Hammy. Said goodbye.

10.53 am: Overexcited, salivating dog came bounding towards us! Hysterical search through undergrowth ensued. Found and retrieved Hammy. Tried not to look suspicious or have heart attack.

10.55 am: Dog at safe distance. Released Hammy. RAN!!

Wednesday 22nd August

Feeling guilty about Hammy.

Thursday 23rd August

Over Hammy.

Friday 24th August

Start new school next Monday. Mum gave me money for uniform at last.

Here is list:

2 x white shirts (not blouses – too girly)

2 x grey skirts (knee length)

2 x navy blue V-neck jumpers

5 x pairs white ankle socks

1 x pair low-heeled black shoes (practical, so can run for bus and away from danger, etc . . .)

1 x black P.E. skirt

1 x white P.E. shirt

1 x pair plimsolls

1 x bag

1 x pencil case. (I want lime-green faux fur, to give impression of being both interesting and daring.)

3 x ballpoint pens (red, black, blue)

2 x pencils (B)

2 x erasers (scratch 'n' sniff banana and pineapple, going tropical)

1 x sharpener

1 x ruler

(Blazer and tie already arrived in post.)

Overspent on luminous Madonna-style string vest and Merely Musk Impulse body spray. Didn't have enough left for shoes – duh!

Saturday 25th August

Tried on new uniform, looked in mirror, despaired at ill-fitting items. Unflattering A-line skirt makes my calves look like barrels and the shirt resembles a billowing sail. I definitely will NOT make friends looking like a small ship coming into shore. And what will Simon think if he sees me at school like this? Especially if with his mates. He will absolutely die and so will I!

Consoled self by drawing my head on *Mizz* model's body and stuck it on the mirror. It will serve as a reminder that I am still waiting for elusive growth spurt (although I have a feeling I'll remain a short-arse due to Mum being only five foot one. Crappy flippin' genes!).

Sunday 26th August

Bonny brought her friend Mandy round for first time today. Was shocked to find she wore more make-up than Boy George! I couldn't believe it when she lit up a fag in the back garden – doesn't she know it's illegal at her age? I didn't dare say anything though, cos she's bigger than me and looks like she could punch my lights out.

Why does she want to be friends with Bonny, who still makes Lego houses and dresses up Sindy dolls?! Mum didn't like Mandy much.

'Ai! Ling Ling.' (Ling Ling is Bonny's Chinese name. I don't know what it means, but it makes her sound like a panda.) 'Why are you hanging around with that gai paw?' said Mum. Dad laughed out loud at this.

Blimey, I'm not keen on Mandy either, but I thought it was a bit harsh referring to her as a *prostitute*. It is times like these when I thank the Lord Mum can't speak English.

Monday 27th August

Caught Bonny nicking money out the till. I wouldn't have batted an eyelid were it not for the fact that it was a whole fiver! I mean, at least make it look inconspicuous like when I do it. 'What do you need that for?' I said.

'School stuff,' she mumbled, looking guilty.

'What school stuff?'

'Pens and . . . stuff.'

'If you don't tell me what it's really for, I'm grassing on you,' I said. Not that I will, as Dad would go berserk.

'I'm lending it to Mandy.'

'Lending? Yeah right.'

'They can't afford bog roll so they have to use newspaper. You wouldn't like that would you?' she said.

I shuddered at the thought and let her off, but told her that next time maybe Mandy should swap her fag money for bog roll, or save some dosh by wearing one ton less mascara.

God, I am starting to sound like Mum!

Tuesday 28th August

Went out in garden hoping weeds had been hacked down by magic helper gnome, i.e. Grandad, overnight, but it looked worse than ever. Then I heard a voice shout out, 'Do you want Turkish Delight?!'

I looked over Mrs Burke's fence. It was Gurdeep across the other side. Her hair was like a bird's nest. I tried to work out why it looked like that and came to the conclusion that it just needed a good brushing.

Offer of more stale confectionery was tempting, but perhaps not basis for friendship. Just to get rid of her, I said yes and seven bars came flying over. Six were lost in a tangle of ivy and one hit me on the side of the head. I managed to recover all but one. I hope no one saw us. I don't want anyone thinking me and Gurdeep are associated in any way. (The Turkish Delight was dead nice though.)

Wednesday 29th August

Heard knocking at eleven this morning and went downstairs. It was Gurdeep again! She was peeking through the letter box, even though the whole door is completely see-through glass.

She asked if she could play the Space Invader and gave me a crumpled pack of potato puffs in return. I didn't want her standing in the doorway where the whole street could see us, so I told her to come in and be quiet while playing cos Mum and Dad were still in bed. Instead, she screamed all the way through four levels. Thankfully by level five, she got exterminated.

Thursday 30th August

While we were having dinner tonight, Gurdeep barged through the back gate straight into the kitchen, totally uninvited, with her jumper on back to front and inside out, so that the Woolworths label was flapping under her chin. 'Hi, Jo, I got you Mars Bars,' she said, handing them over.

'Who are you?' said Dad.

Oh no, was he about to get angry?

'I'm from Banga's,' said Gurdeep.

'Ah, from Indian shop. You Indian?' said Dad in a friendly tone.

Phew, he was all right about it.

'Yeah,' said Gurdeep.

'Why you bring Mars Bar then? Why you not bring samosa, eh?'

I thought for a second Gurdeep might think he was being racist, but then I thought how can one racist know when another racist is being racist? Hmm.

'OK, I'll bring some next time,' said Gurdeep obliviously, then left.

'Is she simple?' asked Mum in Chinese.

'Ha ha, Gurdeep's your friend!' said Bonny.

'That girl, your friend?' asked Dad.

'No, I . . . I . . .'

Then everyone laughed. Great. Now everyone thinks she is my mate. I wanted to tell them I would never make friends with that green-lipped dope in a million years, but I could only have said that in English, so no one would have really understood, apart from Bonny, who was laughing so much she was choking on her pak choi. Good, served her right.

Is it too much to ask to have friends like *Mizz* models?

Sunday 2nd September

First day of school tomorrow. I will have to face being saddo new kid with no friends *yet again*.

Tried on uniform hoping, by some miracle, I didn't look like a tool this time, but I did. Then Bonny walked in and shouted, 'Ha ha! You look like a tool!' I told her to shut it then she started crying, which wasn't like her.

Turned out she was worried about going to school tomorrow as well. I keep forgetting Devil Spawn is only eight years old. It's a shame there's five years between us, otherwise we could get on loads better like I did with Simon. Maybe I should try harder to be a more responsible sister?

To make her feel better I pointed out that her school

was only five minutes' walk away, while mine was a stupid, massive trek across town, AND she didn't have to wear a crappy uniform. That did seem to cheer her up, but unfortunately, *I* am still dreading it.

Monday 3rd September

First day of school. Woke Bonny, brushed teeth, put on uniform, then we tiptoed downstairs so as not to wake Mum and Dad. There was no cereal for brekkie cos I'd forgotten to buy any, but I found some digestive biscuits and we had them instead.

'Don't be late for school,' I said to Bonny, then took some change out the till and walked to the bus stop to meet Jill and Sunita. I wondered if Bonny would be OK. Katy is at a different school so Bonny wouldn't know anyone at all. At least I know Jill and Sunita. Anyway, there was nothing I could do about it now.

The bus came on time, but we had to change on to another one halfway there. What a palaver, it took almost an hour to get to school! We split up at the gates cos we were in different tutor groups. The place was massive and I got lost straight away. There are six two-storey blocks, one five-storey block, a main hall and P.E block. Eventually I found the room where I was supposed to be, walked in and sat at the back, where no one could see my hideous uniform, or hear my stomach rumbling. (Note: buy proper brekkie!)

We did timetables most of the morning (double art on Wednesdays – yessss!), and I spent breaks wandering about on my own, trying to look as if I was going somewhere important but just wishing the bell would go. God, I thought those breaks would NEVER END. Jill and Sunita said I could hang around with them, but I didn't want to cos that would have made me look even more incapable of making friends of my own.

Kept an eye out for Simon so I could run for cover in case he saw my uniform and/or noticed I was on my own like a saddo. Thought I'd spotted him at one point and panic-hid by placing hand over my face, but it was a different Chinese lad.

When I got home Mum and Dad didn't ask me how school was. I didn't expect them to and anyway, they were busy defrosting squid rings. I went upstairs where Bonny was watching telly. 'Hey, how was school?' I said.

'All right, I suppose,' she mumbled, comfort-eating a bag of fudge.

'Don't you want to know how mine was?'

'How was your daaay?' she said, as if it was too much effort.

'Crap,' I replied, then went to Banga's for cornflakes.

Tuesday 4th September

Aargh, forgot to buy milk! So we couldn't have a single flake of cornflakes, and Dad had eaten all the digestives. Felt bad sending Bonny to school with no proper breakfast two days in a row. 'We could have moon cakes,' I said.

'Ugh gross!' replied Bonny, fake-puking.

I agreed. Only an idiot could come up with the idea of a cake filled with salted egg yolk encased in what looks and tastes like wallpaper paste. We get a ton of these dumped on us by friends and relatives at 'mid-autumn festival' this time each year. Apparently, it's when Chinese people 'worship the moon god for bringing peace and prosperity' or some other twaddle. That's what Grandad told me back in Nottingham anyway, when he used to put moon cakes and joss sticks out on a table in the back garden for the god. It hasn't worked. There has been no sign of peace or prosperity in our family so far.

Went to school starving again, but actually I didn't feel like eating, cos being the saddo new kid makes you lose your appetite. Got direct bus to school this time instead of faffing about changing, but had to walk ages to find the bus stop. It turned out I'd just missed one too, so I was late for English due to miscalculation of transport timings.

I sat at the only empty desk next to a scary-looking girl with crimped hair and eyeliner. Wasn't sure about her at first, but she offered me bubblegum, which was cool. I didn't risk chewing it in class like she did, so she probably thought I was a right square, especially as I was dressed like one too.

BORING LIMP STRAIGHT HAIR

BACKCOMBED, CRIMPED DYED BLACK HAIR

COLOURING NAILS WITH PENCIL TOTALLY MAD!

COOL BUTTON BADGES

READS SMASH HITS ON THE SLY

FLAT SENSIBLE SHOES

BLACK SUEDE PIXIE BOOTS

COOL BAND PATCHES ON SATCHEL

FURRY, GREEN PENCIL CASE (MY MOST ANARCHIST POSSESSION)

Wednesday 5th September

Had first art lesson today – dead exciting! My teacher is called Miss Waterfall. She is twenty-something, wears magenta-rimmed glasses and knows everything there is to know about art – I think I love her already. We spent the lesson drawing a still life of three pine cones, a broken wing mirror and rusty kettle on a ruched satin tablecloth.

Some boys moaned it was boring and asked if they could draw laser guns and jet fighters instead. Miss Waterfall explained that the key to being a good artist is to master line, shape, form and texture, then she came over and commented on how accomplished my work was in front of the whole class. I smiled smugly at whinge-bag boys.

Saw scary cool girl at lunchtime, sitting on her own by the science block listening to her Walkman. Guessed she was waiting for friends, so carried on past. She saw me and waved!

Noticed Gurdeep doesn't go to my school. Also great news.

Overall, most excellent day.

Thursday 6th September

Was on my own at lunchtime again, so did a detour around science block to see if scary girl was there. She was, sitting in the same place as yesterday. Why was she on her own again? I went past casually, caught her eye and feigned surprise when she waved.

'Oh hiya! Didn't see you there,' I said. She motioned for me to come over.

'All right?' she said.

'Yeah, you?'

'Yeah.'

I sat down and noticed how alarmingly thick her eyeliner was close up. 'What you listening to?' I asked. 'New Order,' she replied. I'd never heard of them so she let me listen to a bit (which I liked!), then we chatted till the bell went. Her favourite bands are The Cure, Siouxsie and the Banshees and Cocteau Twins, she has a black cat called Luna and her favourite subjects are art and maths. Apart from liking maths, she is so cool. (Shame we're not in same art class though.)

Her name is Tina, short for Christina, but she hates that, just like I hate Joanna – ugh. We arranged to meet at the gates at home time. By lucky coincidence she gets the same bus as me and lives in the same street as Poshos. This is fate. I have potential friend – *yessss*!

Friday 7th September

Told Bonny about Tina but she didn't believe me and said, 'Bring her round and show us then.'

No way!

For a start, Mum and Dad do not know how to conduct themselves in a civilised manner AND I do not want her knowing I live in a flippin' takeaway. (I know Bonny isn't bothered about Mandy seeing our not-normal parents and not-normal home, but Mandy uses newspaper to wipe her bum with, so she's seen it all.)

'Yeah, maybe I'll bring her round one day,' I said.

'See, I *knew* you were making it up!' sneered Bonny.

'Oh shut up or I'll tell Mum you're giving Mandy money out the till.'

'Lending,' she said.

'She won't pay you back,' I said.

She ignored me and carried on sticking her Howard Jones poster on the wall. (Why does she always go for the frizzy-haired freaks (UR)?)

I have decided to cut down writing in diary every day from now on cos of homework. Plus the whole point was to write down all the GOOD stuff that's been happening. So far, Coventry has been more average than average.

Wednesday 12th September

Me and Tina cracked up in science today when the teacher sliced open a bull's eye and it squirted all over the girls in the front row. Tina was surprised I didn't flinch, so I told her I used to play marbles with pig's eyes at the butcher's in Hull.

'Whaa?!' she said.

'It was Dad's idea, not mine,' I explained, quickly.

'Oh.' She seemed quite impressed.

'He's a bit weird like that,' I carried on. 'Anyway, it was no good cos they stuck to the lino.'

I asked how come *she* didn't flinch and she replied, 'Cos I'm a Goth ain't I?' As if that explained everything. Anyway, we have bonded over eye juice.

At lunchtime we sat on the bench outside the Mini-Mart and ate pasties. (School dinners are disgusting, it's all greasy chips, shrivelled sausages and burnt burgers.) 'Do you like it here, at your new school?' she asked.

'S'all right,' I said. 'Do you?'

'Not that bothered.'

'Where's all your other mates then?' I found it odd she seemed not to have any.

'I prefer being on my own,' she said. 'People have a go at me for the way I look, so I keep myself to myself.'

I was shocked. I thought only people like me got picked on. Sometimes I get flashbacks of the kids at primary school running up to me at playtime, calling me 'Chinky', while pulling their eyes into slits. I didn't get it. I'd go home and look in the mirror and think, But my eyes are nothing like that, they're almond-shaped.

'Bullies are idiots,' I said.

'Cretins,' Tina agreed.

It's nice to know I can share the experience of being bullied with someone who understands. So glad I have a friend now! (Other than Gurdeep, who's not really friend at all, of course, just half-witted neighbour.)

Wednesday 19th September

Was harvest festival assembly this morning. It's that time of year when destitute pensioners in the community get the pleasure of receiving other people's dented cans and out-of-date perishables. Hope I don't get picked to deliver the parcels, it's so dull talking to boring old biddies. I am already forced to do it with Mrs Burke every Sunday!

Tina was bringing in a Fray Bentos steak and kidney pie. In an attempt to join in I decided to bring something too. Unfortunately, there was little choice cos everything we have in our cupboards is either:

1) Foreign
2) Catering size (ten times bigger than normal)
3) All of the above

I plumped for a giant tin of bamboo shoots, which stuck out like a hedgehog in a nudist camp next to the custard creams and Cup-a-Soups on the display table. Tina asked where I'd got it from and I had to lie cos she's not supposed to know I live in a takeaway.

'Off my gran,' I said. 'Wish I hadn't brought it though.'

'Why?' said Tina.

'Cos it's too . . . *foreign*. No one'll eat it.'

'Don't matter,' she said. 'Those wrinklies aren't bothered about the grub, they just want someone to whinge at about rationing during the war.'

After assembly, a teacher asked me to take the bamboo shoots back, as it wasn't practical. When I got home, Mum went spare cos she uses the tin for standing on when she can't reach the top shelves. So the teacher was wrong. It is VERY practical – ha!

Sunday 23rd September

I know we live in a Chinese food establishment but I wish Mum would sometimes make us English food. It's not as if she doesn't know how to cook it, cos there's English food on our menu, like steak and chips and mushroom omelette. I'd be just as happy if she gave us the 'pretend' Chinese food on the menu, especially the spare ribs, crispy noodles and spring rolls. Apparently it's pretend cos it's been 'designed to suit the Western palate', Dad says. I bet if customers ever ate *proper* Chinese food, the sort we have to eat, they'd spew their bloody heads off.

For instance, tonight Mum made chicken's feet, which means boiling them till the gristle turns gelatinous enough to chew (UR). But whenever me and Bonny complain, we're told that English food and pretend Chinese food don't have any nutrients like proper Chinese food. How can chicken's feet be nutritious? They're the bits that normally get chucked away!

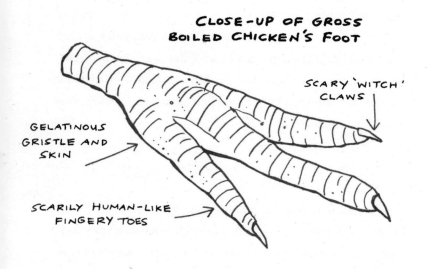

CLOSE-UP OF GROSS
BOILED CHICKEN'S FOOT

SCARY 'WITCH'
CLAWS

GELATINOUS
GRISTLE AND
SKIN

SCARILY HUMAN-LIKE
FINGERY TOES

Tuesday 2nd October

Was in English class wondering whether to rhyme antelope with cantaloupe, when out of the blue, Tina asked where I was from.

'Eh? Uhhhh, Nottingham.'

'Nooo, where are you *really* from?' she said.

'Errrrrm . . . my mother's womb?'

'Stop messing about, you know what I mean.'

'I don't.'

'Well . . . are you like Chinese or Japanese, or from round there somewhere?'

I was insulted at first, cos she was mixing us all together in one big oriental lump, but then I felt I had to let her off, cos even *I* find it hard to tell us apart sometimes. My favourite artist Yoko Ono is Japanese, but I couldn't tell which country she was from just by looking at her. I did grow up in Nottingham though, not the Far East, so maybe that's why I didn't know.

'Oh riiiiiight!' I said. 'My parents are from Hong Kong.'

'Hmmm, sounds exotic,' she said, nodding thoughtfully.

'It's about as exotic as cheese and pineapple on a stick,' I replied.

If only she knew.

Anyway why was Tina asking me where I'm *really* from, as if I couldn't possibly be from here. I always thought I was from here. Can't I just be from here?

Wednesday 3rd October

Recreated 'cocktail party' look from *Mizz* in art today. Nicked some aluminium takeaway cartons and cut them up for sequins. Miss Waterfall put the finished piece up in the corridor, in full view of the whole school. Tina said it was brilliant and neo-modernist. No one's ever been interested in my art up till now (not even Dad, who can secretly draw), so I was dead chuffed. Yoko Ono is kind of neo-modernist, and I look a bit like her.

At lunchtime me and Tina did each other's portraits in the art room. As I shaded in her single crucifix earring, I thought how lucky I was to have someone so cool as my friend. But I couldn't help feeling insecure at the same time. I was nothing like her, so why would she want to hang out with me? She is interesting, quirky and rebellious, while I am just, well . . . non-descript, really.

Later on at home Mum shouted up the stairs, 'Yenzi! Yenzi!' My Chinese name, on my birth certificate. It means 'swift', as in the bird (UR why they called me that). Then we get English names too, to make it easier for English people to remember. Why not just stick with the English name? It would be much simpler.

'What?' I shouted back.

'Do you know why some of our cartons are missing?'

'Oh yeah, I turned them into a neo-modernist cocktail outfit,' I said in English.

62

'Huh?' she replied.

And that, sadly, is how most of our conversations end.

Tuesday 16th October

A Chinese man came into the shop today. I saw him waving a leaflet so I went out to see what he wanted. He was a stranger, which I found surprising, cos I thought every Chinese person in the entire country knew each other.

The leaflet was for Mum. It was mainly in English so that was an oversight on his part. I tried my best to translate it for her. 'English lessons with the Coventry Chinese community, every Tuesday six to seven pm, Eastgate church hall. Ooh, Mum, you should go.'

'When will I have time for that?' she whinged. 'When I'm stuck here stuffing spring rolls every day!'

Mum's integration into British society is hindered by a beansprout-filled pancake.

Thursday 18th October

Was on my way to French when I bumped into the two whinge-bag lads from art class. One of them said loudly, 'Ugh . . . I can smell something horrible, can't you?'

'Yeah, like . . . *soya sauce*,' said the other, just as loud.

'It's coming from over there.' They sniggered in my direction.

WHAA?! I looked around. There was no one else. Yep, they meant me.

Oh god. All those stinky cooking smells from the kitchen must have penetrated my clothes without me knowing! I sniffed them discreetly but could only detect Merely Musk spray, which was a relief.

I was still gutted for being picked on though. Will apply extra body spray from now on, just as safety measure.

Friday 19th October

7.50 am: Can't believe those stupid idiots thought I smelled of soya sauce! It's been bugging me all night. I bet they're just jealous of my artistic prowess.

When I got to school this morning, I immediately asked Tina if she thought I smelled of soya sauce. 'No,' she replied, 'but go easy on that body spray, you smell like my nan's loo freshener.' Which didn't help.

Saturday 20th October

Got paranoid and shoved every item of school uniform in the wash today, and doing the laundry is not easy when you don't have a washing machine. I mean, who in this day and age DOES NOT own a washing machine? Flippin' US, that's who! Even our grandparents, who live in the Dark Ages, have one. Apparently, there's just no room for one in our gigantic, industrial-size kitchen.

So I am the mug who has to make the trip to the launderette every fortnight with the entire family's sweaty socks and pants. OK, it's only five minutes up the road, but it's the most agonising five minutes, like walking over hot coals but with nobody cheering you at the end. I dread bumping into Jill and Katy, or worse, Tina! It's bad enough hiding secret of takeaway, but no washing machine either? Double cringe.

Today, while putting clothes in the washer, I noticed Bonny's Smurfette top stank of fags. Hope she hasn't been smoking! Dad would kill her if he finds out. Then later, when I transferred stuff into the dryer, I discovered Mum's overalls had turned all my new school socks blue. Ugh. No choice though. CANNOT have school uniform smelling of stir fry.

Monday 22nd October

7.45 am: Bonny has a black eyeliner from Mandy that she keeps hidden in her drawer. While she was in the bathroom, I used it to make my eyes like Tina's (but less heavy). Was amazed at how much bigger they looked! Almost like Western eyes.

Showed Bonny and she handed me a pair of what looked like scissors but with funny curved bits at the end. 'They're eyelash curlers,' she said and demonstrated by trapping her own eyelashes in between each curvy bit. Her eyes looked massive! Then I realised Jill must do her lashes like that cos her eyes look less Chinese than mine. Maybe that's why she doesn't get bullied (not that I know of anyway).

Went to school with new curly lashes. No one accused me of smelling like soya sauce today. Think the eyelash thing worked! Did mini air punch at final bell, but the R.E. teacher noticed and asked what the matter was, so I had to make out I was chuffed with my tracing of Jesus healing a leper. Everybody heard and started sniggering, which didn't help my attempts at appearing normal (oh why was I born with no weirdo off-switch?). Wish Tina could be in all my lessons, to shield me from the cruel, cruel world.

Had a nose around in Bonny's drawers tonight to see if I could find evidence of her nicotine habit. Found none. She is ever so sneaky.

Wednesday 31st October – Halloween

Chicken's feet for dinner (again) – gross, but to be fair, Halloween is entirely appropriate for Mum to serve this monstrosity.

Gurdeep wandered into the shop wrapped head to toe in bog roll dabbed with ketchup.

'Are you supposed to be a mummy?' said Bonny.

'Good guess! Here's your treat,' said Gurdeep, plonking a bent Curly Wurly on the counter.

'Hold on, aren't we supposed to give *you* one?' I said. I offered her a chicken's foot, which she squealed at, then hobbled off.

'Ha ha ha! Your friend very stupid,' said Dad, in English. Bonny sniggered.

'She is *not* my friend,' I reminded them.

Am starting to feel sorry for Gurdeep. It isn't nice to be picked on (I should know, from getting it at school . . . and Dad). Still no way I'd be Gurdeep's friend though, she would annoy the heck out of me. If only my family could meet Tina, then they'd see I already have a friend and stop trying to pair me up with Gurdeep. Problem is, there's no way I want Tina to meet them – especially when I never know what sort of reaction I'll get off Dad.

Monday 5th November – Bonfire Night

Me, Simon and Smiffy chipped in for fireworks. Smiffy is fifteen, same as Simon but looks older cos he wears bovver boy gear. (Tina told me bovver boys are lads that go around causing trouble, but Smiffy seems decent enough to me.) Even though he is underage, he buys cider from Banga's all the time, so we sent him there for our rockets and sparklers. Then Mandy and Bonny arrived, so we all took turns lighting, except Mandy, who claimed she had pyrophobia, which was rich coming from someone who sparks up at least twice a day!

Mum came outside later and said, 'Hey, you wan somefing eat?' in English. We said yes and she fried chicken balls for us and Mrs Burke, who was watching over the fence supping a glass of ale. I was dead chuffed, cos Mum was acting like a proper mum for once, and for a millisecond it felt like we were a proper family.

Before Bonny was born, Mum and Dad used to take me and Simon to the cinema sometimes. I'd fall asleep in the stack of dirty tablecloths chucked behind the restaurant bar (not sure where Simon slept), and at closing time around midnight, Mum would dig me out. Then Dad would drive us to the Nottingham Odeon, where the Chinese community organised late-night showings for those who could only go out after their restaurants and takeaways shut.

Bruce Lee was in most of the films, but sometimes there was a bouffant-haired comedienne called 'Fei Fei', which means 'Fatty' in Chinese, and she was my favourite. I couldn't understand half of it, but I didn't care, cos I had a whole box of Fruit Gums and the family to myself.

I was thinking about this while the fireworks were exploding and we were munching away, and for a moment it seemed almost possible for Tina to come round and meet the family after all. Then Dad came trotting out. 'There's a customer needs serving!' he shouted at Mum, who obediently returned to her duties, then the memory fizzled out – just like Banga's cheapo sparklers.

'Why can't Dad do it?' said Simon, aggravated. 'He's the one who speaks frickin' English.'

'I don't know,' I replied blankly. I don't think anyone knows except Dad.

Saturday 10th November

Mum made me go to the chippy for a deep-fried pizza (UR)! She never leaves the kitchen so how did she even know they existed? Plus she is always going on about eating nutritious food and that sounded like pure lard *and* it wasn't Chinese.

When I ordered it, the bloke in the chippy looked at me as if it was the last thing a Chinese person would eat. 'It's for my mum,' I said, as if passing on the blame would stop me being incriminated. I looked on in horror as he got the pizza out the freezer, tore off the cellophane and whacked it straight into the deep fat fryer.

Just as I collected the pizza and turned round to leave, two girls from school walked in and one said, 'Ugh, look who it is.' It was Julie and Sam, the girls me and Tina laughed at when they got bull's eye juice squirted all over them in science.

Crap.

'What you got pizza for? I thought you only ate dog,' said Sam with the blonde perm. Then they both cracked up thinking it was the cleverest comment anyone had ever made. Idiots. I swerved past them out the door while they weren't looking. Phew! That was close.

When I got back I handed Mum her late-night snack, dripping with grease.

'Isn't it a bit unhealthy?' I asked, grimacing.

'It's my only treat in life,' she said.

'I wouldn't call coronary artery disease a treat.'

'Huh?' said Mum.

Lord help us.

STEAMED CABBAGE

PIG TROTTER SOUP

FISH WITH HEAD ON

RICE

FLIPPIN' CHICKENS' FEET

DEEP-FRIED PIZZA GOODNESS!

Sunday 11th November

Bonny came into the shop with Mandy, who looked like she'd walked straight out of Billy Smart's Circus with the amount of blusher she had on.

'Whaa you wan?' said Mum, in English.

'Do you want to buy any of these for Christmas presents?' said Mandy, arranging face creams and nail varnish on the counter. 'Good price for you, Mrs Kwan.'

I could tell they were nicked, plus didn't she know Mum DOESN'T DO Christmas presents? Bonny could have told her that. Mum wafted her hand at the items saying, 'No good, no good!'

Mandy, who is very thick-skinned (from all that foundation I expect), got the message and muttered, 'Come on Bonny, let's go,' then scooped everything back into her handbag and left.

I am worried about Bonny, but at the same time pleased she has found fellow Devil Spawn to share evil pastimes with.

Went to deliver char siu to Grandparents on my own. Smiffy was there with Simon. I told them about the bullies in the chippy and what they said about eating dog. I nearly fell over when Smiffy said, 'I thought you *did* eat dog?' I turned to Simon for back-up but he just replied, 'Yeah, we do.'

'WHAT? Course we don't!' I spat.

'Not us, you spanner. Some parts of China do. No one would dare eat dog in the UK.'

'Ugh, that's disgusting!' I said. 'I can't believe anyone would eat their pet!'

'No, they're farmed, like lambs are here.'

It made me think about all the different types of animal people ate and why some were acceptable and some weren't. Basically, unless you're a vegetarian, you've got no right to say which animal you can and can't eat. So Julie and Sam can bloody well sod off.

Monday 12th November

Told Tina about the dog thing. Turns out she didn't know anything about Chinese people eating them, so it was all a revelation to her.

I was dreading having to face Julie and Sam again, but to my utter horror Tina went up to them at break, looked them straight in the eye and said, 'Do you eat meat?'

'Whaa?' said Julie.

'Cos if you do you're a hypocrite.'

'What you on about?' Sam sneered.

'For your information Jo doesn't eat dog, but you eat pig, lamb and chicken and they're kept as pets, so what's the difference?'

The bullies went silent. Then Tina grabbed me by the arm and stomped off with a smug grin on her face.

I think she gets some sort of enjoyment out of beating the bullies.

'Oh my god, they're really going to kill me now,' I muttered.

'Nah, they won't mess with you while I'm around,' she reassured me.

That's all well and good, but what happens when she's *not* around?!!!

Monday 19th November

Was totally crapping pants about seeing Julie and Sam in science today, but they left us alone! Tina's rant worked – she is a genius – it is a miracle – hurray!

Tuesday 20th November

The Wongs came to visit tonight. They are Mum's friends and have a takeaway on the other side of Coventry (which is closed on Tuesdays – lucky sods). They have a son called David who is five years older than me, is short, has greasy hair and picks his spots. Our mums joke about marrying us off to each other, but I would rather stick drawing pins into my corneas.

Mum doesn't have time to do proper parenting so the life guidance she offers me and Bonny comes in the form of barked orders like, 'Ling Ling, stop hanging around with prostitutes!' and 'Yenzi, get married so I have one less thing to worry about!'

Ominously, that's what she barked shortly after the Wongs had gone.

'I'm not marrying David Wong,' I said firmly.

'Why not?'

'Cos he's got a face like one of your deep-fried pizzas,' I said. 'Anyway, no one has arranged marriages any more.'

'Me and your dad was arrange,' said Mum unexpectedly, in bad English. 'We marry in New Territories, Hong Kong, my village.'

Wow!

Arranged?

That explains a lot, cos they never seemed a good match to me.

Dad was outside emptying the bin, but she lowered her voice as she went on . . .

'Kwan Yun wanted more pretty girl in village, but me and him, arrange.'

My skin prickled.

Mum could have been someone else!

I wonder who she was, the 'more pretty girl'? Did Dad love her and not Mum? Why did he have to marry Mum? Would my life be different now – better? But then I guess this marriage of convenience makes more sense of everything: why Dad resents Mum so much, why he's angry all the time, why Mum lets him boss her about . . .

We never talk much, let alone share secrets, but now Mum has given away a HUGE one – and I don't know what to do with it. She has suddenly confessed to being second best. What am I supposed to say to that? I wouldn't even know the right words to say it with. If only she'd bothered teaching me Chinese. Anyway, I will never know the truth of why they got married, and what happened to the more pretty girl.

Saturday 1st December

Was dead cold today. Dad sent me to Banga's to buy a tin of Irish stew for his lunch, so he could eat it while watching the snooker. Porridge and Irish stew are Dad's favourite Western food – warms you up in winter I suppose. Not sure how he got into it, but he let me try some once and even though it smells like dog food, surprisingly it tastes all right. He heats it up in the wok. It's weird seeing Irish stew in a wok.

Banga's have put their Christmas decorations up already and covered their windows in fake snow. Gurdeep wasn't around. 'Hi, Mr Banga,' I said, 'I didn't think Indians celebrated Christmas?'

'We don't, we celebrate *profit*,' he said, cutting a snowflake out of newspaper.

'Do you celebrate Christmas?' asked Mrs Banga, who was stacking cans of baked beans in a golden sari that looked way too extravagant for the job.

'Not really, but we are closed for the day.'

'Then you celebrate Christmas!' cheered Mr Banga, shaking out the snowflake. 'Christmas day is busy for us, so we don't close.'

Whaa? That means they are open *every single day of the year*! Wow, and I thought Dad was nuts.

Sunday 2nd December

Told Bonny we might get chicken's feet at Poshos' for lunch today.

'What you on about?' she said.

'Jill told me they eat chicken's feet sometimes AND she loves them,' I said.

'Shut up.'

'Ask her.'

'But they're like *so* English. Why would they?'

'It is one of life's eternal mysteries,' I said.

I thought about dog meat, which we don't eat, and chicken's feet, which we do – but which was actually the most disgusting? No wonder British people get confused about what Chinese people eat.

We got egg mayo sarnies in the end, so we needn't have worried. Poshos have got their Christmas decorations up too, posh ones of course. There's a real holly wreath on the front door and a real tree in their 'best' living room. They are the only people in the world I know who have a real tree.

Jill and Katy were making a table centrepiece they saw on *Blue Peter*. They get on sickeningly well. If that was me and Bonny, we'd have glued each other's heads to the table by now.

Afterwards we went to see Grandparents, who never put decorations up. Their house is as bare as a Stone Age cave.

'Mum says come round for Christmas dinner,' I said to Grandma.

'Tell her the meat better be moist or I'm not eating it,' she replied.

Nice to see they have *some* standards.

Monday 3rd December

Was freezing all day, so spent lunchtime in the art room with Tina mucking about with paints. She asked if I wanted to go Christmas shopping one Saturday. 'Then you can come over to mine after,' she said.

Oh god no.

I do not want to go to Tina's house, cos then she would want to come back to mine, and she is not supposed to see my not-normal house and my not-normal family.

'Hmm, I can go shopping but I've got to do homework after,' I said.

'OK, maybe next time then?'

I hated lying but what else could I do? Anyway, weren't lies invented for moments such as these?

Sunday 9th December

Mrs Burke's got her tree up. It's a fake one with fairy lights and a star on top.

'That's nice,' I said, quietly envious cos now *everyone* has a tree except us.

'Have you got yours up yet?' asked Mrs Burke.

'Mmm, no, we never have one.'

'Don't the Chinese do Christmas?'

'Some do, not us,' I answered, wondering how I'd reached my teens without really knowing why (UR).

Come to think of it, Grandparents did make a special effort to put trees up when they lived with us in Nottingham, which was thoughtful, considering the whole idea was alien to them. They must have felt sorry for me and Simon cos of the whole absent parents/neglect/malnutrition thing.

Later, when Dad was frying rice in the kitchen, I went up and said, 'Why don't we have a tree, or decorations? Everyone else has them; the pub, chippy, newsagent, Banga's, even the launderette, and I'm the only one who ever goes in there.'

Then Bonny chirped up, 'Yeah, why can't we have decorations?'

Dad stopped tossing the wok. '*DECORATIONS?!*' he said, glaring at us as if he was about to blow his top. Then a sense of dread filled me. I'd misjudged his mood. He started swearing in Chinese – which is always a bad sign. Bonny backed off and went out the door, leaving me to face the wrath. Dad shouted something in Chinese about wasting money and bashed the wok. That's when I knew I should make myself scarce too, so I quickly edged out the door.

Me and Bonny hid in the alleyway for a while, afraid to go back in. Instead we thought we'd do Dad a favour by getting the cheapest paper-chain kits from the newsagent, which looked almost as nice as tinsel.

When we knew Dad had calmed down, we sneaked back in, made the chains and taped them across the shop ceiling. Gurdeep came and gave us some leftover spray snow, so we finished the look by doing the bottom corners of the window. Hopefully, it will cheer Dad up a bit. It has certainly cheered me up cos our shop isn't the odd one out any more.

8.35 pm: As only good things are going in this diary I can report that Dad has not reacted to the paper chains yet. That must mean he's OK and not angry about them – phew!

Monday 10th December

Wanted to give something special to Tina for Christmas, so I made her a Goth-themed card with a black tree covered in black glitter baubles. On the front I wrote 'I'm dreaming of a black Christmas' in black felt tip. It couldn't have been blacker if I threw a bucket of tarmac over it. She will love the festive irony.

Speaking of which, Mum and Dad have not even noticed the paper chains . . . or snow. What is the flippin' point?!!

Saturday 15th December

Went Crimbo shopping with Tina. Have been taking a few coins out the till here and there to save up. Mum and Dad haven't noticed yet *and* I've been doing it since the Golden Empire, only then it was out of the tip tin.

Mum and Dad get a pressie off me every year, but I've never had a single one off them ... actually that's a lie. When I was six, I woke up and found a huge, gift-wrapped box downstairs with my name on. It wasn't signed but I thought it was off Mum and Dad. I was so excited to get my first-ever present from them I thought I was going to burst. *They do love me after all!* I was thinking. Inside was a little chair shaped like a fluffy yellow teddy bear. It was so amazing I sat in it for hours. Then when I went down the next day, it had gone.

THE CHRISTMAS GIFT I HAD FOR A DAY !!!

Like.

Totally.

Disappeared (UR).

When I asked Mum and Dad where it was, they replied, 'Teddy Bear? Chair? We don't know what you're talking about.'

Whaa? Then had I just imagined it? I couldn't have, cos I remember unwrapping it and everything. But at the same time why would they lie to me? I didn't understand. Where the hell did it go? Am traumatised to this day, but as I'm such a kind and generous person (traits not passed down by parents), I am keeping them on my gift list:

Mum — chicken recipe book (lots of pictures, no feet)

Dad — tin of Irish stew, packet of porridge oats

Bonny — cuddly hamster toy (cannot be killed)

Simon — pen with name on (except couldn't find 'Simon'
              so got 'Simone' and Tipp-Exed out 'e')

Grandparents — proper garden fertiliser

Tina — black lace fingerless gloves

Cousins — can't think what to buy girls who have everything?

Mrs Burke — crochet hook

Gurdeep — hairbrush

Moi — a brand-new Walkman at last — YAY!

Monday 17th December

Gave Tina her blacker than black Christmas card. I have never seen anyone so happy over something so un-jolly. She gave me a card. It had a cartoon reindeer on saying 'I've got a mince pie stuck up my bum' and another reindeer saying 'Don't worry, I've got some cream for that'. HA HA HA! It's so ace that Tina knows me so well!

Monday 24th December — Christmas Eve

Was chaos in takeaway today. Customers staggered in drunk as soon as we opened, including a 'choir' of five Talbot car factory workers, singing 'Jingle Bells'. I asked Mum if we could give them anything, as I'd read in the *Sun* newspaper (which we get for the customers) that some of them were going to be made redundant due to Maggie Thatcher trying to close down the factories.

Mum chucked two bags of prawn crackers at them and yelled, 'Shut your mouf!' Compassion has never been one of her strong points. She is quite forceful when she wants to be though – why can't she be like that with Dad? Oh yeah, the 'more pretty girl' thing.

Later on, Julie and Sam walked past outside. They saw me stacking cans of Fanta on the shelf and banged on the window, mouthing threats. They had tinsel on their heads and were sharing a can of cider – morons. I ignored them but got ready to sprint into the kitchen just in case they came in. This constant living on edge is not good for my blood pressure.

I suggested Dad should close early, but it had the opposite effect of him opening an extra hour so he could relieve the drunks of their hard-earned cash. Shouldn't they be with their families the night before Christmas?

NO TREE! ⟶

Tuesday 25th December – Christmas Day

Woke up bursting with excitement!

Huh, as *if.*

I wasn't getting any presents off parents and even if I was, there'd be no tree to put them under, so why *would* I be excited? Bet Tina, Jill and Katy got loads of pressies under their trees this morning. I did have three gifts under my bed though: a lip gloss off Bonny (nicked by Mandy probably), a box of Maltesers off Gurdeep (within sell-by date!) and a sketch pad off Tina. When Simon came over he gave me a *Now That's What I Call Music* double cassette compilation for my new Walkman, which was totally ace! Felt bad about his boring pen, but I know it will come in handy, cos all he does is write endless essays.

Whenever you see families celebrating Christmas on the telly, they are singing songs, pulling crackers and eating turkey. We're not like them. We don't do songs or crackers, and instead of turkey we have lobster (UR). Christmas is just like any other day in fact . . . but with a giant crustacean.

The lobster comes in a polystyrene box, still alive with its claws elastic-banded together. Then instead of Buckaroo! or Operation, we play 'Who's stupid enough to take the laggy off the lobster before it goes in the wok?' This year it was Simon.

After he'd survived the annual near-death experience, we all stood back as Mum chucked the lobster into a boiling wok of water and clamped the lid on to stop it climbing out.

For years I swore the lobsters were screaming, but later learned that it is actually the steam escaping through their shells.

'Happy Christmas one and all!'

BONNY ADDING TO MAYHEM

Wednesday 26th December — Boxing Day

Christmas break over. The woks are crashing and doing my head in again.

Been getting into more fashion and make-up stuff lately so I drew in my new sketch pad most of the day. It's A3 so I can do loads of big, frothy stuff like ballgowns in it – cool! Later I called Tina to see if she wanted to go to the sales. When she answered I did my usual *'All roight, Tiaana!'* in a dopey Brummie accent, but it was her mum who picked up, which was well embarrassing. There was an awkward silence, then she asked if I was looking for Tina. I replied, 'Actually yes, thank you very much,' in a strange, posh accent that came from nowhere. It turned out Tina was at her big sister's in Rugby.

Hardly anyone came to the takeaway tonight due to staying at home to eat gross turkey curry. Was bored so I delivered Mrs Burke's bonus festive chicken and tomato (or chomato as I'm calling it from now on) along with her crochet hook Crimbo gift. She told me she was on her own yesterday and had roast turkey, which she couldn't finish. If I'd known I would have invited myself over! She asked how my dinner was and I lied and told her we had turkey too. It was easier than explaining the lobster.

She shuffled over with a parcel and said, 'I've got something for you too, love.'

Wow! A Christmas present, for me?

'Thanks, Mrs Burke,' I replied gratefully.

It felt like a wad of bank notes. I thought maybe she was secretly loaded, and that it was a reward for delivering her chomato every week. And if it was all fifty-quid notes, I'd give it to Mum and Dad towards that house we still haven't got.

'Whassat?' said Bonny, as I burst into our room to open it.

'A million quid I hope!' I said, tearing it open.

I pulled out the contents and Bonny cracked up. It was only the flippin' antimacassar Mrs Burke had been crocheting for the last four months. AAAAAARGH!

WHAT AM I SUPPOSED TO DO WITH THIS ?!!

Saturday 29th December

Dad reckons New Year's Eve is going to be twice as manic as Christmas Eve, so he's asked Uncle Han over to help. I like Uncle, he is nothing like Dad, he is more like Grandad: bald, rotund and jolly. And – get this – he actually pays attention to us kids. Weeiirrd!

When I was seven, he taught me how to trap birds, like he did as a boy in Hong Kong. Three doors down from the Golden Empire was a chippy that kept a bin full of scraps, which Uncle used as a trap like this:

1) Find a stick about six inches long
2) Prop bin lid up with it
3) Tie a long piece of string to bottom of stick
4) Unravel string and hide halfway down the car park behind another bin

DUMB BIRD

TASTY STUFF (NOT A TRAP HONEST)

STICK

STRING

Eventually a sparrow, or starling, would sniff out the contents and perch on the edge of the bin. Sometimes the birds got spooked and flew off, but if you were patient enough, one would hop in and as soon as that happened ... *wham!* We'd yank the string, the lid would fall and it was caught.

I'd run over and slowly open the lid, while Uncle slipped his hands in to grab the bird. Then we would tie a piece of string to one of its legs and fly it like a magic, self-propelled kite!

It was dead cruel but I didn't know any better. Maybe Uncle didn't know it was wrong either, cos when him and Dad were young lads, they caught a monkey and tied it to a tree as a pet. I am guessing that tying up various animals was the main source of amusement for kids in Hong Kong back then. Thank god someone invented telly, that's all I can say!

Monday 31st December — New Year's Eve

Was looking forward to seeing Uncle but as soon as he arrived, Dad ushered him straight into the kitchen and shoved a wok in his hand – what a welcome!

When the usual drunks arrived, I made myself scarce and went upstairs to finish off colouring in a ballgown and listen to Eurythmics on my new Walkman. Everything was fine till Bonny came barging into the room and pulled off my headphones.

'Hey, I was listening to that!' I said, tugging them back off her.

'There's shouting downstairs!' She looked worried.

'What? There's always shouting.'

'No, it's really bad,' she said. 'Go see what's up, will you?'

She was probably overreacting, but just to shut her up I went downstairs and peered through the curtain into the shop. There were a dozen blokes crammed in and one of them, an ugly guy with a crew cut, was having a go at Mum.

'There's not enough chips in here!' he said, stabbing at

his brown paper bag and showing Mum the contents. Mum always puts way too many in, so he was talking out of his backside. 'You lot are always ripping us off, I want me money back!'

What did he mean by 'you lot'? As in 'Chinese people', as if we were the enemy? Mum glared at him, stuck for (English) words. Not one of the others tried to stop him cos they were:

1) Too drunk
2) Couldn't be bothered
3) Were enjoying the free entertainment

My heart was thumping like mad. I wanted to throw a bottle of chilli sauce at his stupid thick skull, but was afraid I'd miss and make things worse. Or not miss and make things worser than worse.

'What's up?' Uncle called from the kitchen, sensing something was going on.

'Someone's complaining about his chips,' I said, glancing at Dad, who was pretending not to hear by tossing the wok too loudly.

'Gis me money back!' yelled Ugly.

'You sha up!' Mum yelled back, finding her words.

Oh god, no one was backing down. Who was going to stop it? Not Dad, he was too busy cowering in the kitchen. Ugly scrunched up the bag of chips into a lard-sodden ball. One of his mates went to stop him but it was too late.

92

'No one tells me to shut up, *Chink*,' he scowled, and launched the chips at Mum, who got hit square in the neck.

'You dirty pig dog!' she shouted at him, in Chinese.

Then Uncle pushed past me, holding a meat cleaver.

Huh? What was going on? What was the zen-like bird trapper doing?!!!

'Come on then!' the drunk goaded, while all the other blokes ran out the shop.

I was hoping Uncle was just trying to scare him off, but instead he vaulted over the counter and chased him out the door and down the middle of the road into oncoming traffic! Cars screeched to a halt and blasted their horns, while Uncle and Ugly skidded about. I think Ugly got away with all his body parts intact. I think he probably got the message too.

Ha! There I was trying to make us fit in by decorating the shop with paper chains, then Uncle goes and does a Bruce Lee in full view of the street! Typical.

I will be slated at school if anyone finds out about this.

1985

Tuesday 1st January

New Year's resolutions:

1) Stop being bullied!
2) Tell Tina I live in a takeaway!
3) Grow!

Uncle Han came for dinner as he's going back to Derby tomorrow. He gave me a tenner as an early birthday pressie – cool! Mum made special occasion Spam and Dad praised him for chasing away the 'kaizi' (hooligan). Bonny had seen all the drama from the bedroom window and thought it was 'brill'. She wishes Uncle could stay and protect us forever. So do I, but not with a flippin' meat cleaver. Am dreading school next week.

Monday 7th January

Saw Tina for first time since before Crimbo holidays. It was so good to see a friendly face! But my delight soon wore off as we walked through the school gates.

'Hey, Kwan, is your uncle Bluce Ree? Hai ya! I chop your head off!' It was Julie and Sam. They were with whinge-bag art class boys.

Great.

'What they going on about?' asked Tina.

'Oh nowt,' I said quickly. 'They're just being morons.'

'SHUT YOUR FAT GOBS!' Tina shouted back at them.

Why is she not scared of them? Maybe she knows her Gothiness looks intimidating. Or maybe it's just cos she's white, and the bullies find it harder to slag off someone who's not a 'second-class citizen'.

'Shush, they'll come over,' I hissed.

'They won't, they haven't yet have they? Anyway, why they going on about Bruce Lee?' she said.

Oh god. I couldn't keep the takeaway secret any longer. I took a deep breath and gabbled, 'They're talking about my uncle. He chased a drunk out of our takeaway with a meat cleaver on New Year's Eve. And yes, I live in a takeaway.'

There.

I said it.

Tina was now going to be ashamed of me like I was of myself, for having a family who moved to England and instead of becoming more English, decided to open a takeaway and become even more Chinese! No wonder I got bullied. Tina would probably ditch me.

'I know you do,' she said.

'What?' I gasped. '*How?*'

'I have got eyes and ears you know.'

'Well, why didn't you . . .?'

'Cos I knew you didn't want me to know. Look, you could live in a Chinese takeaway in Chinatown in China for all I care and I still wouldn't give a crap.'

Wow. She didn't give a crap. She is a true friend. I nearly cried.

Tuesday 8th January

8 am: Sounds stupid but am a bit nervous about seeing Tina today, even though she knew about the takeaway all along. What if she wants to come round, like friends do? Am dreading her asking. And if that day ever comes, which I hope to god it doesn't, Dad better be in a good mood.

At lunchtime me and Tina sat in the art room. I showed her my sketch pad, which was supposed to be for practising perspective in, but secretly I'd been using it for fashion designing – mainly items I dream of wearing if only I had the body for it. Miss Waterfall walked in. 'Oh hi, Jo and Tina,' she said fetching paintbrushes out the cupboard. 'Getting some extra work done are we? That's what I like to see.' I quickly shut the pad.

'Yeah, I was, er, just showing Tina what we've been doing in class.'

'And that is . . .?' Miss Waterfall asked, testing me.

'Using vanishing points and horizon lines to create three-dimensional perspectives.'

'Great!' she said, smiling and walking out again.

'That was jammy,' said Tina.

'Good job I remembered,' I replied, sweating slightly.

Tina changed the subject. 'Anyway, what's it like living in a takeaway then?'

Oh no, she was hinting at coming round!

'I bet you get to eat some right nice grub.' She beamed at me.

No she wasn't – phew!

'Ha, yeah,' I lied. Funny how everyone assumes we eat what's on the menu, when really we're chomping on fish heads and chicken's feet, which Tina would think was just as bad as dog, so I didn't let on. Instead I told her that we once had a posh restaurant and house in Nottingham, then a flat over a butcher's in Hull, and how I now shared a shoebox with Devil Spawn at the takeaway.

'The places get tinier each time. It's mega crap,' I said.

'Well you can always escape to mine if Devil Spawn starts doing your head in,' she said, trying to cheer me up. 'And hey, it's your birthday soon. What you doing?'

'Nothing much.' I shrugged.

'Are you having a cake?'

'Don't be daft.'

'Why not?' asked Tina.

'Cos we don't do birthdays.'

' . . . Or Christmas,' she added.

'Ha ha, yeah. We don't do anything fun.'

'God, and I thought I was the one who's supposed to be a miserable Goth!' she laughed.

Friday 11th January — My birthday (age 14)

Bonny gave me a woolly Rudolph hat, i.e. blatant unwanted Christmas gift, a hazard of being born in January, and at school, Tina brought in a chocolate swiss roll.

'Happy birthday!' she said, presenting it on a piece of tissue.

'Oh wow! My very first birthday cake, thanks,' I said.

She gave me a hug. I am not comfortable with hugs, so I just kind of patted her back. Then she gave me a can of Rock Hold hairspray, which is the stuff she uses – ace!

When I got home I had another surprise. Mum gave me one of those Chinese marbled egg thingies. She said they symbolised wealth and prosperity. (Why does everything Chinese have to do with prosperity?) From what I could see, she must have boiled it, cracked it carefully all over, then steeped it in soya sauce to make the marbled pattern on the inside when you opened it up. Thanks, Mum, I'm sure that must have taken up some of your precious time to make! Birthday significantly improved by cake and egg. Then Gurdeep came round and spoiled it all by giving me a nativity-scene snowglobe.

Wednesday 16th January

Took my Rock Hold hairspray into school today so Tina could show me how to do my hair. It's amazing what you can achieve by vigorously combing it the wrong way round and smothering it with what is effectively glue. I ended up with a flippin' gigantic knot that we nearly had to chop off with a blunt craft knife. Rather than end up bald, we agreed to rescue my hair by rinsing the spray out with water, so lunchtime was spent with my bonce in the sink in the girl's bog. Great.

Monday 4th February

Chinese New Year starts today. It is the year of the Ox. I put the telly on and they announced it on *Blue Peter*. It's the only way I ever find out, cos Mum and Dad never tell me these things. It gets on my nerves when people at school ask me what Chinese year it is, cos my source of information is the same as everybody else's. 'I dunno, watch *Blue Peter*,' I tell them.

After *Blue Peter*, *Take Hart* came on. It's my absolute favourite show of all time, presented by my absolute favourite TV presenter, Tony Hart, who can make a picture out of anything: pastel, charcoal, collage, even old bits of junk he finds in his shed! The best bit of the programme is the Gallery, where your art gets put up on display if it gets picked. Imagine the whole nation seeing your work. It's a fast track to fame and fortune for budding artists like me I'm sure.

Forgot to make it one of my English New Year's resolutions, so I'll make it a Chinese one instead (if they do that sort of thing).

Chinese New Year resolution:
Find fame and fortune via *Take Hart*'s Gallery

Might be tough though – in the last three years I've sent in thirty-seven pictures and not a single one has been picked (UR). The person in charge of submissions must be partially sighted. I feel compelled to write in and complain.

Thursday 7th February

Wrote complaint letter to *Take Hart* that went like this:

Dear Sir or Madam,

Having been an avid and loyal follower of your quality children's art programme since it started broadcasting, I am disappointed to say I have been very let down in recent times.

The reason being that I have not had a single one of my thirty-seven pictures displayed in your Gallery. Each week I look forward to seeing my work on display and each week I switch off the television set with a heavy heart.

I deem myself to be a naturally talented artist and have been drawing since I could pick up a crayon without eating it, so I find it perplexing that you have never considered me.

Please find enclosed picture thirty-eight. I eagerly anticipate it being up in your next Gallery.

Yours regretfully,

Jo Kwan (aged 14)

P.S. I will readily accept original artwork signed by presenter/ artistic genius, Mr Tony Hart as compensation.

The letter is in an envelope along with a self portrait of me as Yoko Ono. They are bound to put this up knowing how disgruntled they have made their most number-one fan. Then all I will have to do is sit back, get talent-spotted, become rich and famous and buy a proper house for us all to live in – hurrah for me!

Saturday 23rd March

Nothing much has happened for ages, then today Simon got caught stealing a pair of trousers in the department store . . . down his trousers! Ironic. And shocking for an upstanding citizen like him. Well it just goes to show he is still feral at heart, just like when we were back in Nottingham.

I was calling him about borrowing a tape when he told me he'd nicked a pair of beige chinos, which he has wanted for ages but couldn't afford. Posh Auntie had to go and fetch him from the police station, cos Grandparents don't speak English and Mum and Dad won't deal with any non-takeaway related business. Simon was glad Mum and Dad didn't pick him up. They would have only caused a scene and been dead embarassing, he said.

Thought Dad would go mental, but him and Mum haven't mentioned it once (UR). Maybe they didn't want to kick up a fuss in front of Posh Auntie, who has brought her kids up oh-so-proper.

I first got caught nicking at junior school. I'd shoved a Ladybird book called *The Enormous Turnip* up my duffle coat as we were leaving at home time. Then stupid curly-haired Scott, who was standing behind me, puked into my hood. All the other kids ran off screaming. The teacher insisted on taking off my coat to clean it. 'No, miss, it's all right,' I said.

'Take it off!' she hissed, yanking at the toggles.

ACTUAL TURNIP

Then it happened. The book slipped out.

It might as well have been an enormous turnip, the way it thudded to the ground.

'Well,' said the teacher, examining the crime scene. 'What have you got to say for yourself?'

'I completely hate Scott,' I replied.

Back home I got a hiding off Grandad, not for stealing, but for ruining a brand-new coat. Twisted or what?

Me and Simon have been stealing ever since we discovered the tip tin at the Golden Empire. It was too easy and no one ever pulled us up for it, so we have just carried on. And Bonny's at it now too. Wonder when she'll get caught?

Monday 1st April

Chicken's feet for tea. That's April Fool's covered then.

Saw Bonny with Mandy in the alleyway. They both had too much orange lipstick on. They looked like they were sharing a fag but I couldn't tell, so I banged on the bedroom window. Bonny turned to me and stuck her twos up – charming.

What could I do even if she was smoking? Call the police? Maybe I will get a leaflet from school outlining the dangers of lung disease and yellow teeth (which would clash horribly with their orange lipstick).

Take Hart had better get my letter, cos my future is in their hands.

Saturday 6th April

Mandy bought a new hamster for Bonny's birthday. It's not a golden one this time, but a grey Russian Dwarf. Simon said it looked like a malnourished rat. (Dad hadn't even noticed Hammy had gone.) Mum and Grandma shouted over each other at Bonny to get it out of the kitchen. My only concern was making sure it didn't end up like the last one, so I laid down some rules:

1) Do not hoover hamster
2) Do not leave hamster in ball covered in own excrement
3) If hamster dies, I will play no part in its disposal

Bonny has surprised everyone with hidden powers of imagination by naming him Cedric Quentin Horatio Bob (UR). I suggested 'Bob' for short but she insists on the full version. Conversations about her pet hamster are now truly tedious.

Went to Poshos' as they had birthday presents for

Bonny. She got a purse and handbag set off Jill and Katy. Great, just right for stashing all that cash she's been nicking out the till for Mandy. Bonny told them about her new hamster.

'What happened to your other one?' asked Katy.

'Oh, that one died *aaages* ago,' Bonny replied.

'How?' said Jill.

'Well . . .' Bonny gesticulated, as if we had to listen very carefully to what she had to say next. ' . . . I accidentally hoovered him up, and then . . .' I punched her in the arm to stop. She glared at me and carried on. 'He was still alive but went bald from shock, so we set him free in the park, but then he nearly got eaten by a dog so we had to rescue him before letting him go again and then we ran off.'

Jill and Katy were speechless.

After a while Katy said, 'That's, er . . .'

'Awful!' Jill filled in. 'And a bit cruel, don't you think?'

'Which bit?' said Bonny, genuinely curious.

'Anyway,' I butted in, trying to save the day. 'It lived its last moments wild and free, which is more than can be said for most pets.'

Then I quickly said goodbye, while dragging Bonny out the door.

Sunday 14th April

Mum took us to McDonald's for Bonny's late birthday treat. I was surprised cos:

1) She never remembers our birthdays
2) She never takes us anywhere

But today she had planned ahead and fried the pork balls early in order to have a couple of hours off. I was dead chuffed she'd made the effort, but then had a mild panic about her going out in her saggy overall. She opted for fuchsia velveteen jogging pants with elasticated ankles instead. Which was a relief.

Mum invited the Wongs (great), but Dad stayed at home cos he doesn't like going out unless it's on his terms (UR).

The Wongs, who are normally as loud and brash as Mum when they come round to visit, were surprisingly civilised. Even David refrained from picking his spots at the table. It must have rubbed off on Mum cos she didn't burp too loudly, fling food about or mention marrying David once. In fact, nothing happened until halfway through the meal when, without warning, she felt compelled to take off her shoe, plonk her foot on the table and shout out in Chinese:

'LOOK AT MY BUNION!!!'

Everyone looked as ordered, and tried not to choke on their gherkins. I shrank in my seat, hoping nobody else in the restaurant had witnessed it.

'Enjoying your birthday?' I said to Bonny, wincing.

But she had put a McDonald's bag over her head and couldn't hear me.

Tuesday 16th April

Received letter from *Take Hart*:

Dear Jo,

Thank you for expressing your concerns. Unfortunately, due to the amount of submissions we receive, we are unable to guarantee that every one is shown.

We do value our viewers' contributions, so please keep sending in. Hopefully you may see your picture in our Gallery very soon.

Yours sincerely,
Fiona McFarce
Submissions Assistant

What?!

It was just a stock letter sent to every poor sod who wrote in, with my name filled in at the top! Called Tina to tell her of injustice and she said, 'They wouldn't know talent if it slapped them in the face with a wet fish.' She is a true friend, but sometimes I don't have a flippin' clue what she's on about.

Damn! How will I become famous artist now?

Thursday 18th April

Went to Banga's for Dad's Irish stew. Gurdeep asked if I wanted to go to kung fu lessons at the Talbot car factory social club across the road. At first I thought she was being racist again, but then she said, 'You could be cool, like your uncle,' so she was actually being nice . . . I think.

I can't work out if the Uncle Han thing was good or bad. On the one hand, 'doing a Bruce Lee' is such a cringy Chinese cliché, but on the other hand, no one would dare mess with him again – and yes, that IS cool.

I mean, what if the bullying at school got worse? What if I got into a fight and Tina wasn't around? How would I defend myself then? Maybe I *should* learn martial arts, cos I'd rather be Uncle than Dad in a situation like that, any day.

'When is it?' I said to Gurdeep.

'Next Monday.'

'OK, why not?' I said.

Then she did a silly little jig and knocked a pyramid of Alphabetti spaghetti over. The girl is a liability.

Asked Tina if she wanted to come, but she said no as she didn't want to ruin her hair.

Monday 22nd April

Kung fu night.

6.55 pm: Arrived at club with Gurdeep. Smiffy was also there … wearing a kimono (UR).

7.06 pm: 'Steel' the instructor (ha ha! No way was that his *real* name) demonstrated moves and explained sparring.

7.17 pm: Steel asked if anyone would like to get up for a 'one to one'. No one volunteered.

7.18 pm: Steel pointed at Smiffy and said, 'You, the one wearing your mum's dressing gown.' Then Smiffy got up with an angry look on his face and started sparring with Steel.

7.21 pm: Smiffy lost it completely. He was punching like a windmill. (Due to public humiliation about his kimono/dressing gown probably.) He seemed intent on killing Steel and was actually foaming at the mouth. Steel grabbed him by the scruff of the neck, dragged him to the swing doors and hurled him out head first. Unfortunately that door was bolted to the floor. There was blood everywhere.

7.23 pm: Smiffy zigzagged out of the unbolted door. 'AND DON'T COME BACK!' Steel yelled after him.

7.30 pm: At home recovering from shock. *I* am never going back, never mind Smiffy!!!

Tuesday 23rd April

Told Dad about the snooker tables I saw at the social club last night. (Yes, I noticed snooker tables amongst the mayhem.) Thought he would be interested cos he is still watching it on the telly before the shop opens, plus it might be something for him to do outside of the takeaway.

He might even make some friends – improve his moods? Anyway, it's looking good. He got excited about the snooker and this does not happen often. Mum looked pleased that Dad was pleased, so I was pleased that they were pleased. Well done, me!

Thursday 25th April

Dad has bought a snooker cue off Kev, Mandy's brother, who is nineteen and ten times dodgier than Mandy. He was so chuffed that after dinner he got it out for me, Simon and Bonny to look at, as if we'd be bothered about a glorified wooden stick! He screwed it together and showed us how to put chalk on the tip to give a better grip when hitting the balls. It's not very often we get Dad's attention, so we did our best to look interested.

Afterwards, I told Simon about Smiffy getting whacked by the instructor at kung fu.

'Do you reckon he'll be all right?' I asked.

'Yeah, he's pretty hard,' Simon chuckled. 'He wanted to be a boxer once, but he's got weak knees.'

Gosh. There's more to Smiffy than meets the eye.

'If he stays out of trouble he'll do well for himself,' Simon went on. 'He's not going to uni though. He thinks it's boring.'

'Fair enough,' I said, thinking I might as well take the opportunity to come out with something I'd been planning for a while. 'Not everyone needs to go to uni. I'm going to art school.'

'What? Why don't you get a degree?' he asked, frowning.

'Why should I?' I said, frowning back.

'So you don't end up stuck in the frickin' takeaway like Mum and Dad.'

'I won't.'

'Art school won't guarantee that.'

'How do you know?'

I thought *I* was the only one bothered about our parents owning a takeaway, especially when I'm the one having to live in this damn place, but Simon seemed really touchy about it.

I have discovered that Simon is actually very angry about a lot of things deep down. Mostly at Dad, but Mum too, for taking his side all the time. I wonder if Simon knows why he got sent away to live with Grandparents? It probably wasn't the time to ask.

'They work like twelve hours a day,' Simon said, ignoring my last remark. 'Seven days a week, three hundred and sixty-four days a year,' he said. 'Sod that for a laugh.'

'Yeah, sod that.' Had to agree with him there. I can't think of anyone doing the same hours, not even Mr and Mrs Banga, cos they do shifts with various family members.

But I'll never get marks at school like Simon does – all I can do is draw. So if being an artist isn't a proper job, what else can I do?

Monday 29th April

Bonny was shouting at Dad when I got back from school. I crapped myself cos it's always dodgy territory getting into an argument with him.

'What d'you do that for?!' she said, as loudly as she dared.

'I give it fresh air,' said Dad.

He sounded guilty, but mildly amused at the same time, so I could tell Bonny wasn't in any danger. I let her carry on.

'They're not dogs, they don't just come running back when you call them!' she said through clenched teeth.

It transpired that Dad had taken Cedric Quentin Horatio Bob for 'a walk' in the garden (UR), where he wandered off under some weeds and vanished (Bob, not Dad). Bonny is not having much luck with her little rodent pals.

DAD SHOULD HAVE PUT THE HAMSTER ON A LEAD!

At least this one lasted a record three weeks, Hammy only lasted one! When I told her she could always get a new one, she thought for a second I meant Dad, not Bob, and perked up. So I corrected her and she started sulking again – ugh.

Saturday 4th May

Dad was up early today (11 am), jangling his car keys at us. He was in one of his chirpy 'eccentric' moods.

'Want to come?' he said, grinning.

'Where to?' we asked.

'The farm,' he replied (totally UR).

Me and Bonny looked at each other quizzically, then decided to be brave/adventurous/stupid and got in the car. When we got to the farm, we followed Dad to a pen full of kids (young goats, not children, Dad less keen on *those*!), where they were holding an auction. We stood and watched and felt right out of place, and before we knew it Dad had bid and bought two of them! One was black and white, the other brown and white. It took all three of us to shove them into the back of the car, where Bonny had to squeeze in alongside.

'Why have we got goats?' I asked. (Valid question, I thought.)

'Bonny hamster gone, so now we get goats!' said Dad.

Oh right, he was making up for losing Cedric Quentin Horatio Bob.

'What we gonna to do with them?' said Bonny.

Dad looked at her in the rear-view mirror and said, 'We put them in garden and they eat all the weeds, isn't it?'

Unlike other dads, who would have gone down to the local hardware store and purchased a lawn mower, ours has gone and bought a couple of cloven-hoofed ruminants.

Just brill.

Sunday 5th May

We are now owners of two weirdy beardy creatures trit-trotting about in our back yard. Dad has fenced off a part of the garden and built a wobbly hut with some spare wood Grandad gave him. Simon brought the wood round and he thought the goats were 'mad'. Mum didn't bat an eyelid. She is probably used to Dad's antics by now, but I still wonder what the heck goes on in his head.

The brown one is a girl, so I've called her Baarbara (ha ha! I crack myself up, I do), and Bonny got fed up with having to say Cedric Quentin Horatio Bob the whole time, so she has returned to form and called the boy goat Billy (phew!).

Dad made me go to Banga's to buy cabbage, Weetabix and Jammie Dodgers for them. Those flippin' things get fed better than we do! They have cleared a third of garden already though, so Dad's crazy scheme has actually worked.

Called Tina to tell her about the goats. She thinks my family sound 'utterly amazing!' and now wants to come meet them all (crap! I was hoping this wouldn't happen). I value our friendship so this must *never* happen.

'They're not, you don't know what my parents are like,' I warned her.

'How bad can they be?' she replied, doubting me.

'VERY,' I said.

'In what way?'

'They're just a bit . . . well, shouty and stuff.' I winced.

'What and I'm not?' she laughed.

She had a point. Maybe she could handle meeting Mum and Dad? I don't know, it's too cringey to think about.

Sunday 12th May

Mrs Burke asked if we were going to put the goats in the chop suey! I thought she was joking, but she looked deadly serious. Why does everyone think we eat anything that moves? I put her excuse down to being old and senile. I turned it into a joke and told her, 'Nah, they'd be too tough, so they'd be more like chop *chewy*.' She didn't get it.

I asked if she had any old newspapers for a papier-mâché project at school. She gave me a pile of *Coventry Telegraphs* to sift through and I spotted an ad in one of them. It said:

ART CLUB

All levels welcome.

11 am Saturday mornings.

£3 for two hours and full use of equipment.

84b, Corporation Street, Coventry.

Cool! This is just what I need to help get me into art school. (And restore confidence after the slap in the face from *Take Hart*.) I felt bad not inviting Gurdeep to come with me after she'd asked me to kung fu, but she once showed me a portrait she'd done of her mum with a moustache and thirteen fingers, and it was not a good look.

Friday 17th May

Decided to improve my image in preparation for Art Club. Was not going to backcomb my hair again, not after last time when I nearly had to cut the whole lot off! Thought maybe colour might make it look more arty. So went to Boots and bought bleach and pillar-box-red dye, with hope of looking like one of Bananarama as result.

7.15 pm: Took bleach out of pack. Ignored instructions. Instructions are for non-artistic conventionalists. Slapped it on willy-nilly.

7.48 pm: Rinsed bleach out, stared disconcerted at orange fringe.

7.59 pm: Got dye out. Ignored instructions. Splodged on fringe.

8.45pm: Rinsed dye, squirted in mousse, dried hair. Looked OK considering didn't have clue what I was doing.

8.52 pm: Fluffed and sprayed with the Rock Hold hairspray Tina gave me.

8.59 pm: Just been downstairs. Mum said I 'look like a chicken's arse'.

CHICKEN'S ARSE

What does she know about being trendy? She wears elasticated-ankle jogging bottoms, for crying out loud. And why does she wear them anyway? All her female friends and relatives manage to dress smart. Then I remembered about her being second best to the 'more pretty girl'. Did she resign herself to being the frumpy one after that? Hmm, no. It's probably just impossible to look good when you're permanently covered in a film of grease.

Saturday 18th May

Art Club day. Managed to tame hair thank god. But Bonny still took the mickey, as clothes-wise I had gone for the second-hand Oxfam look. I told her she didn't understand enough about the alternative art scene to comment, which shut her up. I did notice she had a new ra-ra skirt on though, which she could never have afforded.

'Where did you get that from?' I asked.

'Mandy gave it me,' she answered shiftily.

Hmm, nicked it for her, more like. Anyway, I was late and didn't have time to argue, so I left it and went to catch the bus.

As I walked into class I immediately realised that all efforts to update my image were entirely pointless, as everyone there was over fifty. Great. Am looking forward to conversations about bladder problems and composting, then.

The teacher introduced herself then went into boring tirade about the crime of leaving lids off paint tubes. I sat next to an old codger called Roy and found it extremely hard to concentrate, cos his nostrils kept whistling every time he breathed out.

We did a life drawing of a wrinkled pensioner in a toga. Roy didn't. He started drawing the Starship *Enterprise* using pointillist technique. He'd only done the flight deck by the end of class. Blimey, twenty-third century interstellar exploration vessels will be a thing of reality by the time he has finished.

Monday 20th May

Tina loved my new hairdo but thought it was too New Romantic, so she backcombed it (despite fending her off), till it looked like I'd been attacked by bats.

'There,' she said, 'Gothy is best. Now you're Siouxsie Sioux and I'm Robert Smith.'

'But Robert Smith's a bloke,' I said.

'No, he's androgynous, so he's not a man or woman really.'

Tina knows so much cool stuff. She reads the *NME*, so she must get it from there. I tried reading it once, but there's too many hard words in it like 'existentialism' and 'zeitgeist', which make my brain hurt.

As Tina was putting the last touches in, Julie and Sam walked past. 'Look at the state of them witches!' Julie said to Sam. Then Tina turned to them and blurted loudly, 'Yeah? Well at least we're not BITCHES, like you!' I thought this was quite clever and nodded in agreement (from behind Tina). They couldn't think what to say back so they just sneered and walked off. That's the thing with bullies, they're not the smartest bunch.

David Wong and his parents came round with a box of moon cakes, even though it's the wrong time of year and they are gross (yes, the moon cakes *and* David Wong). The dads talked about how gristly the wholesale beef was lately, while the mums joked about me and David getting hitched again. I am fed up with it. Up till now David has never said a word to me, preferring instead to talk to the adults in Cantonese while looking at me occasionally in a creepy way – well either that or he was just born with the face of a stalker. Tonight though, he came right up to me with the moon cakes and said in English, 'Lotus paste with lard crust.' Oh my god! Was this to be the first of many advances? I sensed the mums gushing as I took the box off him. Then I made some excuse about homework and sprinted upstairs to slam my head in the wardrobe door repeatedly.

When they'd gone, Bonny asked if I would actually marry David Wong and I replied by chucking a moon cake at her. Despite what Simon says, I am determined to be an artist and not the wife of a takeaway proprietor, like Mum.

It took half an hour to brush the knot out of my hair tonight. Now I know what it must be like for Gurdeep.

Wednesday 22nd May

Told Tina I was desperate to avoid Wong situation. She laughed and told me not to be so melodramatic! It's all right for her, she's not being threatened with arranged marriage, or takeaway inheritance.

After art class, Miss Waterfall called me over. She had my sketch pad in her hand and said, 'I've just been going through this and there's no classwork in it. Just pictures of corsets and kaftans and jumpsuits, why is that?'

I searched frantically for an excuse, but in the end I owned up.

'I . . . I just really like fashion design.'

'Your enthusiasm's great, but this pad is for classwork,' she said, looking slightly concerned.

'Sorry, miss.'

'If fashion design's what you want to do, I can help look into it for you, find out what colleges do what courses and so on. But you still need to pass your art O level to get in, and I can't do that for you.'

Gasp! Miss Waterfall is going to help me!

'Thanks, miss! Sorry, miss. I'll make sure I do my classwork from now on.'

Then I thought it was a good time to ask, 'So, do you think they're any good then . . .' I glanced towards the sketch pad, '. . . my designs?'

'You have a natural talent, there's no doubt about that,' she said. 'But . . . *focus*,' and she tapped the side of her head with her finger, smiled and handed back the pad.

After she left, I sat there on my own, taking it all in. Wow, I thought. I have natural talent. An art teacher, not any old art teacher but Miss Waterfall, said that to *me*. I felt a strange warm glow inside, then a sudden realisation hit me . . .

Yes, that's it!

I am going to be a FASHION DESIGNER – HURRAH!

Friday 31st May

Since deciding to become a fashion designer I've been experimenting with my image in a serious way. I was happy with my hair but my make-up needed sorting out, so I tried to add height to that unsatisfactory attachment to my face, a.k.a. flat nose, by doing some clever shading and highlighting. I followed *Mizz*'s instructions by applying a lighter strip of foundation down the front and darker down the sides, but it has made me look distictinctly badger-like. It's not easy trying to 'polish a turd' as they say.

BADGER SNOUT

(I AM <u>SO</u> OVER RESEMBLING COMEDY ANIMAL PARTS)

Saturday 1st June

Went to Art Club with new nose make-up to see what the reaction would be. No one noticed cos they're all geriatric and more interested in crab paste sandwiches.

Everyone drew a bowl of apples, except me. I designed a

new winter clothes range. My plan is to send some ideas to *Mizz* and see if they will offer me a job when I leave school. Perhaps I'll get valuable contacts through them, etc. Then I can watch Simon weep as I overtake him on the ladder to success.

Roy can't understand my fascination with stick-thin women in massive shoulder pads. He doesn't get fashion cos he is nearly sixty and wears sandals and a cravat. Anyway, he has just developed repetitive strain injury from doing too many dots on his Starship *Enterprise* – maybe he should have stuck to the Granny Smiths instead.

Monday 15th July

First day of summer holidays – YESSSS! Been looking forward to this for weeks.

Up till now, I've been trying to squeeze fashion design in at Art Club and between homework. Now I can really get stuck in. Am going to get one of those professional cases to put my work in, *portfolio* I think it's called. I've seen them in the shops in town, but they're dead expensive. I spent the tenner Uncle gave me for my birthday ages ago and it would take me months to save up by nicking coins from the till. Where the heck can I get the money from?

Caught the goats gnawing the fence. They have almost got through a whole post.

Saturday 20th July

We were told in Art Club today that Coventry Central Library are running an art competition and the first prize is a £50 WHSmith voucher – talk about coincidence – if I win I could get a portfolio! Actually if I win, I wouldn't even *need* a portfolio. I would simply inform *Mizz* of my accolade and they'd hire me on the spot. GASP! This could be my big break!

The rules are open; any subject in any media, so I drew Grace Jones in a lycra ballgown and flicked silver paint on for a futuristic effect. Roy said he wished he'd thought of that technique, which made me feel like some kind of creative pioneer. I am bound to win now. Roy is submitting his Starship *Enterprise*, which he has finished at last. Good luck to him, but really, who is going to want to look at a silly spaceship thingy?

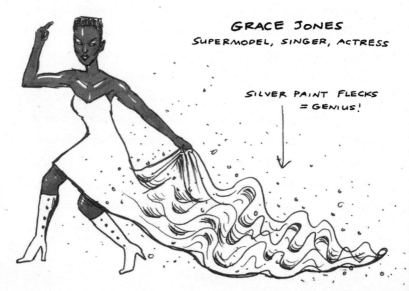

GRACE JONES
SUPERMODEL, SINGER, ACTRESS

SILVER PAINT FLECKS
= GENIUS!

Monday 22nd July

Filled in art competition entry form, packed it with the picture and took to post office. Couldn't think of anything to do after that (except await my inevitable success), so I called Tina to tell her about it.

'Excellent, good luck with that!' she said. 'You up to anything later?'

'Mm, not really,' I said.

'Can I come over and see your goats?' she asked.

I wasn't expecting that. Damn.

'No,' I replied firmly.

'Why?'

'Cos my parents will be there and I don't want you to meet them.'

I wasn't ready for her to see them or the hot, noisy, stinky takeaway yet. Ideally, she would never see them EVER.

'Awww, go on,' she said. 'I know you keep saying they're mad, but I'm friends with you aren't I? And you're the maddest person I know.'

'Ha ha!'

'Go on,' she pleaded.

I'd hinted about Mum's shoutiness and Dad's unpredictable moods before, but I think she thinks it's the average type of aggro all families have to deal with. She doesn't know how serious it is in ours, how much we're screwed up by it, and how it sometimes turns nasty. How can I make her understand when I don't understand it myself?

Anyway, I'm not going to go into all that here cos this diary is only for good stuff and Tina's only going to hear the good stuff too. I want her to think I'm normal.

But normal is also inviting friends round, and I bet she'll be wondering why I wasn't. I can't do nothing.

Tuesday 23rd July

Was chatting to Tina on the phone about the Simple Minds interview in *Smash Hits* when she started going on about coming round again. 'Pleeeeeeease,' she begged. I groaned. She was doing my head in.

'Oh . . . *all right* then. If you really *have* to.'

So that was that.

I am about to sacrifice best friendship ever by bringing Tina back to meet my mentaloid parents. I had to, otherwise she would have started asking questions. I will have to pray Mum and Dad are on best behaviour when she comes round.

Then Tina told me she was off to Majorca with her mum soon, so it will have to wait. Good. Hopefully that will give me enough time to change my identity, pack my belongings and move out.

P.S. Tina's mum must be very rich if she can afford to go abroad?

Wednesday 24th July

Poshos told me and Bonny that they are going on a break to Grimsby. That's near Hull where we used to live! Not where I'd expect them to go on holiday. But at least they are *going* on holiday, unlike us. When I asked Mum why we couldn't go she said, 'Go and stay with your Auntie Yip in Wolverhampton.' *Wolverhampton?* I wouldn't send my worst enemy there. I know for a fact Auntie has sprained her ankle three times in the last year tripping over all the discarded cider bottles.

Tuesday 30th July

AARGH! Had to deal with maggot infestation in outside bins today! Why me?

Bonny uncharacteristically asked if she could help, but I think she was bored cos Mandy's away at her nan's in Leicester. Bonny swept the maggots into a heap, while I chucked boiling water over them (Dad's suggestion), but they kept crawling away and Bonny kept screaming. It was the stuff of nightmares. Afterwards, I had to scrub the yard with bleach but we didn't have enough, so I went to Banga's for more. Gurdeep wasn't there. Her dad said she's gone to Delhi with her mum, to see relatives. 'Why is everyone on holiday except us?!' I complained to Bonny.

'We've never been on holiday,' she reminded me.

'Yeah, but there's always a *first time*,' I said.

'No, that's just a *saying*, stupid,' she replied.

We are poor deluded souls.

Thursday 1st August

Poshos are back from holiday and they came round unannounced to look at our goats! It was their first time over since we moved here. I wilted when they saw our hovel compared to their show home. But it turned out they weren't interested in our hovel, or even our goats really. All they did was brag about Grimsby. They went on and on about the arcades, candyfloss, donkey rides and even the flippin' bidet in their en-suite. When they finished, they gave me and Bonny a photo of themselves with a monkey wearing a fez (UR).

Saturday 3rd August

AARGH! Missed Art Club cos maggots went berserk and broke loose in the goat pen. Grandma went outside to put something in the bin and found the goats lapping them up. I would have happily let them carry on, but Dad was worried they'd get ill, so he left me and Grandma to clear up the mess. What about *me* getting ill?

Got postcard off Tina. The picture on the front was a beach scene. It looked nice apart from the beetroot-coloured fat blokes in skimpy trunks – ugh. I put the postcard on the shelf where we could all see it at dinner. Me and Bonny decided to refer to it at every available opportunity, in the hope parents would give in and book a holiday through sheer pressure. A bit like a modified Chinese water torture.

Sunday 4th August

Tina is back – hurray! She called to say she'd spent most of her holiday nursing sunburn, as she'd forgotten how her translucent Goth-like skin was totally unaccustomed to that kind of heat. 'I'm like Dracula,' she said. 'I sizzle like bacon as soon as daylight breaks.' Nice.

She asked what I'd been up to and I told her I'd been designing stuff to go in my portfolio, when I get it. (I didn't mention the maggots.)

'It's the summer holidays!' she said. 'Give yourself a break.'

'How am I meant to get to Majorca?' I said.

'No, you plum, just like, enjoy being off school. Look, my mum knows a woman who works at a riding school. She's asked if I want to go and said I could bring a mate. Will you come? It'll be a laugh.'

Hmm, Tina was right, I hadn't had any fun since the summer holidays started. But then questions flared up in my mind:

1) Was it safe to go near an animal with teeth like paving slabs?
2) Would I get hoofed in the skull by their giant metal shoes?
3) Won't the hats interfere with our hair?

But on the other hand I was intrigued. Horse riding is one of those hobbies only white girls normally do, along with Sunday school and ballet and Brownies. It will be dead interesting to see what the fuss is all about.

Tina didn't mention coming round. Perhaps she's forgotten. Bloody hope so . . .

Thursday 8th August

Thought I was a gonner today!

Me and Tina got the bus to Bedworth and walked to the stables from there. Tina's mum's friend, Carol, took us to the ponies (horses, ponies, same thing), and told us not to stand behind them in case they kicked us in the head (I *knew* it, I just *knew* it!).

Tina got a chestnut one called Star, and I got an old grey nag called Harold. Had a bad feeling about him, he looked well doddery. Anyway, after almost dislocating my neck getting on, we trotted off down the field.

11.15 am: Went riding along river. Presumably so if ponies did buck, we would have had a soft landing in water.

11.37 am: Harold stopped. I thought he might have been going to the toilet.

11.38 am: Harold's front legs buckled. Then his back legs went. Then he rolled over on top of me and trapped my left leg.

11.39 am: I was so winded no sound came out when I called for help, so I mouthed 'help' instead, while circling finger around problem area.

11.40 am: Carol came over (taking her sweet time).

'Well,' she said. 'Looks like he's had enough for the day.'

'Yeah, he's not the only one, Sherlock,' I wanted to reply, but couldn't as I was still winded.

NEVER again.

Saturday 10th August

Tina called to see how I was coping after the ordeal.

'I got steamrollered by a horse,' I said. 'What d'ya reckon?'

'I bought you a box of Quality Street to say sorry . . . kind of,' she said. 'Shall I bring it over?'

Damn! She had remembered about coming round. But I still wasn't ready, I don't know why. I mean, when Poshos came over they didn't care about the state we lived in, so why should Tina? This was different cos she was my mate. The best one I've ever had. What if Mum and Dad make a scene and scare her off? What will she think when she sees I don't live in a house like hers and Poshos' – we don't even have a living room for her to sit in!

I got angsty and replied, 'Er . . . thanks, but don't worry about it, honest. I'm off to Art Club now and won't be back for a good few hours.'

'Oh, OK,' she said. 'Well let me know when's a good time and I'll try not to scoff your chocs while you think about it.'

At Art Club I couldn't stop fretting over Tina coming round. It's bound to happen sooner or later. Roy was trying to show me his new drawing of a *Star Wars* Stormtrooper but all I could think about was Tina. What would she think if I kept on making excuses? That I'm ashamed of her in some way, when really I'm afraid she will be ashamed of me?

' . . . and they wear an impressive range of survival equipment, including this blaster rifle . . .' Roy droned on.

His nose was whistling louder than usual today, which only added to my irritation.

Tuesday 13th August

11.35 am: Oh my god! Oh my god! Excited and hyperventilating. All our whinging about holidays has paid off! Parents did most of the prepping for today last night and they have got up early to take me and Bonny out! Have they gone mad? They never do this. We haven't been told where we're going (UR), but it doesn't matter cos everyone loves a wonderful, magical mystery tour, right?

12.05 pm: We are in car. Excitiiiiing!

12.35 pm: We have stopped halfway down the motorway to grab lunch at service station café.

1.10 pm: Me and Bonny wolfed food down. Couldn't wait to get back on the road!

1.20 pm: Am looking out the window. Hmm . . . buildings look familiar.

1.21 pm: GAAAAH! We're heading back home!

That had been our holiday. Pie and chips at the Little Chef on the M1 motorway (sob).

When we got back, Billy had eaten a wasp. His face was blown up like a balloon and he was baa-ing like a maniac. Mrs Burke was shouting over the fence about the noise waking her up. It was two in the afternoon, the lazy cow! Didn't she know what a bad day *I* was having?

Went to Banga's for a comforting bag of Wine Gums. Gurdeep was back from holiday and seemed strangely different. She was wearing sparkly bangles, a pretty dress and had brushed her hair. It was ever so silky. She told me how amazing Delhi was, and even her voice sounded more refined! Wow, her holiday must have been good.

Lucky for some.

Saturday 17th August

10.35 am: Results of art competition are being announced today. If I win, I might even ditch the portfolio and put the fifty-quid voucher towards a proper family holiday instead (if it will stretch to that).

3.40 pm: After lunch I went to meet Tina at the library to check results of competition. Was sure I was going to win something. But when we got there, we discovered Roy's Starship *Enterprise* had a gold sticker on.

WHAA?!!

Roy had been given first prize . . . for a load of stupid dots! Is there no justice in the world?

Second prize was a watercolour of Coventry Cathedral and third was a manhole cover in pastels! I didn't even make it to third! What about my incredible fashion-trend prediction, the lycra ballgown? Has nobody got taste?

Tina bought me a milkshake to cheer me up, or calm me down, whichever, but I felt like turning Roy's painting into a Jackson Pollock with it. Am now boycotting Art Club.

When I'd finished ranting, I could see Tina had been waiting for a chance to ask me her eternal question . . .

'Hey, can I come over and see Billy and Baarbara next week?'

Ugh, she had caught me at rock bottom. What did I have to lose?

'Yeah, suppose so,' I sighed.

'Yesssss, I'm going to see the goats!' she screeched, sploshing her ice cream float about.

Lord help us.

Wednesday 21st August

Tina is coming round today. DREADING IT.

Popped into town for some pencils and met Tina outside the hairdresser's. She'd had cornrows put in as an experiment! It looked dead different, but she has the kind of face that suits any style. She wants to be a hairdresser when she leaves school. I think she'll be ace at it.

On the bus to mine Tina said, 'Can't wait to see your goats, I bet they're a right laugh. Bet your parents are too. They could teach me how to fry rice and stuff.'

'You'll be lucky,' I replied. 'They hardly have time to fart.'

I was trying to be funny, but really I felt sick. This could all go wrong. Excruciatingly wrong. It was the first time I'd brought a friend home since I was six, and even then I made sure the parents weren't in.

Before going into the shop, I reminded Tina exactly how insane Mum and Dad were. She told me to keep my knickers on. Thankfully Bonny wasn't around to add to the insanity. As we walked into the kitchen, Dad was frying prawn crackers and Mum was slicing beef. They both looked up. I kept calm, took a deep breath and announced, 'Mum, Dad. This is my friend, Tina.'

Mum pointed at Tina's cornrows. Oh no, here we go, I thought.

'HA HA HA! YOUR HEAD ROOK RIKE ONION!'

Excellent.

And that's why I'd never brought a friend home. The stupid thing is, Mum wasn't even taking the mickey. She'd just said the first thing that came into her head, as *always*.

There was an awkward silence. Then Tina burst out laughing. 'Ha ha ha ha ha ha!'

I looked at her quizzically.

'Yeah, Mrs Kwan, you're right,' she said, prodding her cornrows. *'Onion head!'* And they both started cracking up.

I couldn't believe it. Mum and Tina were actually getting on! Even though they could only communicate by pointing and prodding and saying 'onion' a lot. I was relieved, and a tad envious. I mean, when was the last time *I'd* had a laugh with Mum like that? I can't remember. Maybe cos whenever Mum says anything like that to me, I take it as an insult, whereas Tina took it as a joke. Mind you Tina doesn't have to live with the madwoman. She'd have a different opinion then.

'Cor, your mum cracks me up,' said Tina.

'Glad *you* think so,' I replied, ushering her out into the safety of the back yard.

'Oooh, we going to see the goats?'

'Yes,' I said. And I must admit, I'd never been so pleased to see their dopey, buck-toothed mugs in all my life.

Billy and Baarbara trotted over as soon as we appeared. It was feeding time and I'd forgotten their Jammie Dodgers. They didn't look disappointed though, cos goats only have one expression and that's 'dumb'.

Just as I thought we'd escaped from my parents, I heard flip-flops padding up behind us. It was Dad. (He's the only person I know who wears flip-flops all year round, even in arctic conditions.) I panicked as I didn't know what mood he was in. It would have made no difference if I'd told him about Tina's visit beforehand anyway, cos he flips one minute to the next. You take pot luck with Dad – and live with the consequences.

'Hey, goats hungry!' he said, shaking a bag of cabbage at Tina. 'You feed, go on.'

Phew, he seemed OK today. Or so I thought.

Tina was super excited. She dangled a leaf over the fence, which is the wrong way to do it, as goats have not yet evolved to distinguish vegetable matter from human flesh. I was showing her the correct way, which is to chuck the leaves as far away as possible, when Dad opened the gate and walked into the pen. Oh no. He looked in one of his 'eccentric' moods.

Dad crouched down and motioned for the goats to come over. Then Billy climbed on to his back and positioned his front legs over Dad's shoulders. Er, sorry, had I missed something? Had Dad been teaching the goats to do acrobatics in secret? Were they about to form a human/goat pyramid?! Dad hoisted himself upright, then holding on to Billy's back legs, started sprinting up and down the garden.

Right. OK. He was giving Billy a piggyback ride.

BAAAAAA
BAAAAAAAA

(Or a goatyback ride I guess, in this case.) Tina couldn't get enough, while I quietly died inside.

'Baaaaaa! Baaaaaaa!' Billy bleated.

'He seems to be enjoying it,' said Tina, between hysterics.

'Or it could be cries for help? It's hard to tell,' I suggested.

After a few laps, Dad let Billy hop back into the garden. I detected a slight wobble as Billy wandered off. Wonder if this counts as animal cruelty in the RSPCA's eyes?

Tina said it was the best day of her entire summer holidays, but I am in bed still recovering from shock.

Friday 23rd August

Tina was not at all phased by Mum and Dad. (Either that or she is a very good actor, plus good job Dad was being sociable, if you can call it that.) She wasn't even bothered about the greasy kitchen, or that we didn't have a living room. She is truly true friend. I am so flippin' relieved! Even Bonny couldn't get on my nerves tonight.

'Hey, Mum said your mate's got a head like an onion,' she said. 'Has she really? Bring her round again so I can have a look. I've never seen an onion head before.'

'Yes that's right, Bonny,' I replied flatly, 'she is a scientific human-stroke-vegetable hybrid wonder.' Then I went off and got my art stuff out for the first time since losing the art competition. I am literally back to the drawing board, but that's OK cos right now, life is pretty damn ace.

Designed some turban-style headwear and wondered why they weren't looking quite right. Then realised it's cos they looked like giant onions on the models' heads.

Monday 26th August

Me and Tina went into town to buy some stuff for school. New term starts next week – booo! Needed a new jumper but instead got a Talking Heads T-shirt just cos it looked cool. Oh, and a tube of electric-blue mascara, much to Tina's disgust. Bonny likes it though! It's the first thing we've agreed on for ages.

Simon has passed all his O levels. Seven grade As and a B for geography. Simon blamed the B on Smiffy 'nutty dancing' around the room to ska music, while he was trying to revise. I blame it on Simon not knowing everything he claims to know. He will be going to sixth form to do maths, physics and computer science A levels while Smiffy learns to carry a hod (cos he's just started a bricklaying apprenticeship).

Me and Bonny got a box of chocolates from Banga's to congratulate Simon. He offered them to Mum and Dad and said, 'I've passed my exams.' Dad looked at him blankly and carried on blanching noodles and Mum, recognising the word 'exam', said, 'You're wasting your time mao nga lao. Why not work here and start earning? You can buy your clothes then, instead of stealing them.' Mum has never been tactful, so her comment wasn't a complete surprise. It was still mean though.

Simon hid his disappointment by stuffing a caramel barrel in his gob. Bonny sifted through the chocolate box pretending she didn't hear, but I felt bad for him. No other parents I know would just shrug off their kid like that. Simon worked his socks off for those results. He was dead proud, but they couldn't care less. Maybe Dad was jealous that his son had found a way to a better life? And I'm sure Mum doesn't even know there *is* an option for a better life. But in the end I put it down to them both being emotionally stunted, as always.

He must feel so dejected. It's like they can't be bothered with him, ever since he got sent away to live with Grandparents.

As I chewed on my hazelnut whirl, I suddenly panicked. At least his plans for the future were going like clockwork. I have already failed an art competition. Must crack on with fashion designing. At least I have Miss Waterfall's help if I need it now.

Monday 2nd September

First day back at school – ugh. I am in fourth year seniors and still haven't grown into my uniform.

Bumped into Miss Waterfall at break and told her about losing the art competiton. She told me, 'There will be other opportunities. You've got to learn to take the rough with the smooth.' I took that as meaning success doesn't come overnight and that I've got to keep on trying. Then I thought about the parents, who have been trying for decades and they're still overworked and poor. Is rough with the smooth really the answer?

Simon has started sixth-form college and Smiffy is two weeks into his bricklaying apprenticeship. He comes to the takeaway for his tea now he gets paid. Tonight he arrived covered in dirt.

'All right, Mrs Kwan, I'll have beef chop suey and chips,' he said to Mum.

'Hey, where's your woo yin see?' Mum asked, pointing at his grubby face.

'What's she say?' said Smiffy, looking at me, baffled.

For a moment I thought of lying, but I knew Smiffy wouldn't mind so I told him.

'Woo yin see means "fly shit". It's Chinese for freckles.'

He looked bemused.

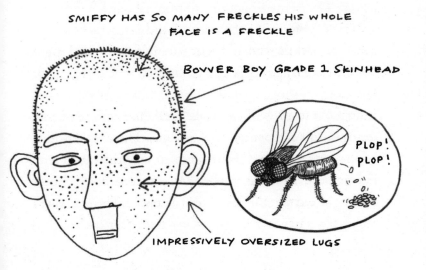

SMIFFY HAS SO MANY FRECKLES HIS WHOLE FACE IS A FRECKLE

BOVVER BOY GRADE 1 SKINHEAD

PLOP! PLOP!

IMPRESSIVELY OVERSIZED LUGS

'Oh yeah, right, ha ha ha. Fly shit!' he said to Mum, laughing.

'Yeah, fry shi!' said Mum, comprehending.

'Chinese no have fly shi?' asked Smiffy, suddenly talking like Mum, as if she would understand him better if he did so.

'No, just you Engerlish. You red hair!' Mum answered, gesturing at her own hair.

And for one actual second, I swear I was witnessing Mum having a full-on conversation (of sorts) with an English person – there's hope for her yet!

Wednesday 18th September

Tina has invited me round for lunch. Not sure how I feel about it. I would have avoided it before, just so I didn't have to invite her back in return. But she has seen the takeaway now, so I guess there's nothing to worry about.

Tina's mum is a social worker . . . and a single parent. I've never met anyone with only one parent before. Mind you, I don't know many people. I find it odd. Who does her mum talk to when she has problems? And who does she go out and have a laugh with at weekends? Then I remembered our mum doesn't have any of that anyway. So why do people bother getting married at all? I guess having two wages helps. But that doesn't make sense either, cos we have two wages coming in and we still can't afford a house . . . or holidays to Majorca.

Tina's mum and dad split up when she was eight. He lives in Manchester now. She doesn't see him much, maybe once a year. Tina's older sister moved out a year ago, she's a single mum too. Actually, I'm intrigued now. I think I will meet Tina's mum.

P.S. At least her mum will be normal.

Thursday 19th September

Told Tina I am happy go round hers any time. She was dead pleased (I think going round to each other's houses somehow validates a friendship). She said she'll make sure her mum puts on a 'nice spread'. I've never been to an English person's house for lunch before, so I'm really looking forward to seeing what will be dished up.

Saturday 21st September

Went to Tina's today. I assumed her mum would be cool like her, so I wore my Talking Heads T-shirt, skinny jeans, black eyeliner and blue mascara.

They only live five doors down from Poshos. Their house looked the same as theirs from the outside, but inside they had not-very-nice flowery wallpaper and swirly carpet. Apparently Tina's mum had put off decorating for ten years in favour of a continental holiday.

She was standing in the kitchen eating toast and jam. Strange, as I thought she was going to make us food. She is about the same age as our mum, with long, wavy, dyed red hair, and she had a multi-coloured striped jumper on.

'Hi, Mum, this is Jo from the takeaway,' said Tina.

I was hoping she didn't twig it was me who called her that time with the stupid Brummie accent. She smiled. 'With the goats?'

'Ha ha, yes, Mrs, I mean, erm, Miss Roberts,' I replied. She hadn't twigged, but I was embarrassed about the goats and what to call her.

'Call me Jane,' she said. 'Where you from?'

Great. Four seconds in and I was already being asked that age-old question.

'Nottingham,' I replied, not trying to be clever but just stating a fact.

'Ah, that explains why your English is so good.'

Will there ever be a day when I meet someone for the first time and they don't mention anything about my Chineseness?

'Where are your parents from then?' she asked, letting Luna the cat lick butter off her toast.

Ugh, our mum would have beat it with a ladle if she saw it do that.

'Hong Kong.'

'Oh, *konnichiwa*,' she said, grinning.

JANE SHARING HER FOOD WITH THE CAT — SO UNHYGIENIC!

'No, that's Japanese, Mum!' said Tina.

'Sorry, what's "hello" in Chinese then?' asked Jane.

Suddenly I felt hot. I didn't know. I didn't actually know how to say something as simple as 'hello'. I tried to think of the times our family greeted people, or each other. But I couldn't work out any specific words that meant 'hello'. I went bright red and wilted.

'I dunno,' I admitted.

'So you don't speak Chinese then?' said Jane, looking bemused.

God, the whole thing was ridiculous. How do you explain you don't speak Chinese when your parents are Chinese, you look Chinese and you live in a Chinese takeaway?!

Even Tina looked baffled.

'Anyway,' Jane said, sensing that I wanted to run away and hide in the broom cupboard. 'Sorry I can't make lunch, I'm off to my mate's. She's teaching me how to play guitar. I got you Pot Noodles though. Nice meeting you, Jo.'

'Soz, I didn't know she was off out,' said Tina after she left. 'You're probably sick of noodles as well. I'll do some toast.'

Whaa? When will the Chinese stereotyping ever end? Plus I thought English people ate proper meat and two veg meals, not Pot Noodles and toast. Yeah OK, now I'm being presumptuous.

P.S. Tina's mum is kind of cool, but she is not normal.

P.P.S. Asked Mum what 'hello' was in Hakka and now I know why I was confused! Mum and Dad say 'Oi' on the phone, but I always thought it was the same as the English 'Oi' – I mean, what a stupid word for hello! And when greeting in person it's 'Ni hao'. But we only ever have the Wongs round and they never say 'Ni hao' to them! So I've forgiven self for own ignorance. (But Jane will always think I'm a dunce.)

Monday 23rd September

On the bus this morning Tina apologised about her mum asking all those questions.

'It's all right,' I replied. 'It's a bit weird though, cos I always feel Chinese when I'm with English people and English when I'm with Chinese people. It's never one or the other. It's a bit crap.'

'Well you're English to me but just happen to *look* different,' said Tina, adding to my confusion.

'Your mum seems cool though. I can see where you get it from,' I said.

'No way! I'm nothing like her, she's an old hippy!'

'She's better than my mum.'

'Dunno what you're on about, your mum was fine when I met her. Your dad was too. Well he was the day I went over anyway.'

'Yeah, he's been OK lately.' I pondered. 'I think the goats have cheered him up.'

'Oooh, when can I come and feed them again?'

'Whenever you like,' I answered confidently, for the FIRST TIME EVER.

Wednesday 25th September

A new boy has just started in my year. He's called Warren and is from South Africa (somewhere hot with zebras in, I think). The girls are going hormonal over him. Even Tina giggles every time he walks past. She has turned super odd.

He's *okaaay* I suppose, if you like tall, good-looking, tanned, floppy-fringed types. In fact he looks a bit like my guilty pleasure pop idol pin-up, Nik Kershaw, if you leave out the tall and tanned bit.

WARREN X

After school Tina phoned to tell me she was in love with Warren – *what the?!* She wanted advice on how to ask him out. She has clearly gone mad.

'But you're a Goth and he's like . . . *dishy*,' I pointed out. 'You don't exactly have much in common.'

'We're both into Bowie,' she said eagerly. 'I saw a sticker on his geography book.' Wow, she sounded desperate.

'I know,' I said, being facetious, 'I've got a David Attenborough video I can lend you. If you watch that, you can impress him with your knowledge of African wildlife.'

Her face lit up. 'Yeah, maybe that'll work. Never know unless you try eh?!'

Oh dear. Her sense of humour has been clouded by a fog of lust. Also, I couldn't help feeling a tiny pang of jealousy, cos Tina is MY best friend, she can be no one else's.

Started drawing Cindy Crawford in a zebra-print jacket. My collection of designs is coming on v. well.

Thursday 26th September

Was searching through our videos for Tina when I found half a pack of Benson & Hedges concealed in Bonny's *Here are the Smurfs* case. So she *has* been smoking, the sneaky git! She wasn't around, so I put the anti-smoking leaflet I got from Health Ed at school into the case alongside it and put it back on the rack. Hopefully she will get the hint, stop smoking and all this will 'blow' over (ha ha!).

Later on Bonny came storming down the stairs. 'Did you touch my fags?' she whispered, so Mum and Dad couldn't hear.

'No, I didn't *physically* touch them,' I said.

'Well, they're not mine. I'm looking after them for Mandy.'

'They're bad for you, Bonny, and so's LYING!' I whispered loudly back.

'I'm not lying!'

'Oh, and are you still nicking out the till for her as well?' I said, while we were on the subject.

'Get knotted!' she hissed, then stormed out the shop and slammed the door behind her.

Situation handled perfectly then, I reckon. Anyway, why should I be the one to tell her what's right and wrong? That should be our parents' job, not mine, not that they ever will. Poor Bonny. She's going to end up more messed up than me or Simon, I know it.

I have more important things to think about anyway. Continued with Cindy's jacket.

Friday 27th September

Tina has started hiking her skirt up so the hem falls mid-thigh – it's totally out of character!

We bumped into Warren at break in the library. Tina got his attention by 'accidentally' dropping a stack of books all over the floor like a helpless simpleton. It worked though, cos he came over and helped pick them up, what a gent!

Tina went to say something, but nothing came out and she went bright red and flustered. I have never seen her like that before. It was most bizarre. Then Warren saw the copy of *Practical Goat Keeping* I'd been reading and was trying to hide behind my back. He said, 'Do you have goats?'

'Er, yeah,' I replied, knowing I must have looked like the biggest weirdo ever.

'We used to keep a herd of them in South Africa. They're great aren't they?'

'Er, what? I mean yes, ha ha!' I said, going red myself.

Why was *I* blushing? I certainly didn't fancy him, although close up he did have the most dreamy emerald-green eyes.

Anyway, after he'd gone I gave the video to Tina – the nature programme about African mammals – which she is going to watch and memorise. It's the most keen she's ever been about any kind of homework. I remain sceptical.

Cindy Crawford does not have emerald-green eyes, but that's the colour I made them anyway.

Monday 30th September

Tina's plan was to stalk Warren in the dinner hall today. I went with her, to make sure she didn't do anything silly, then watched aghast as she wrestled a couple of first years to the ground, so she could stand behind him in the queue. She is possessed! When Warren got to the serving hatch, she tapped him on the shoulder and said, 'Hey, Warren, have you ever seen a pangolin?'

Uh-oh, I thought.

'No, I don't play any musical instruments,' he replied, mystified.

'What? No . . . er . . . Oh right, no, not a mandolin, a *pangolin*,' Tina explained.

At which point Warren was asking for an extra sausage, so that was the end of that.

'Oh god. I must've looked like a right idiot,' she said afterwards.

I had no sympathy. She'd brought all this on herself.

'Well, anyone using *pangolin* in a chat-up line *is* a right idiot,' I replied.

Changed zebra-print to pangolin on Cindy's jacket.

Wednesday 2nd October

GASP AND FAINT! Something most strange and wonderful happened today. A girl in my year, who I don't know that well, came over at morning break while I was waiting for Tina and handed me an envelope. Thought she'd made a mistake, but it had my name on. I went straight to the bogs, locked myself in a cubicle and stared at the envelope thinking it might be hate mail off Julie and Sam. Not having made my life a misery for a while, they were due an appearance. I opened it, unfolded the piece of paper inside and studied the neat handwriting done in pink ... yes, *pink* biro.

This is it here:

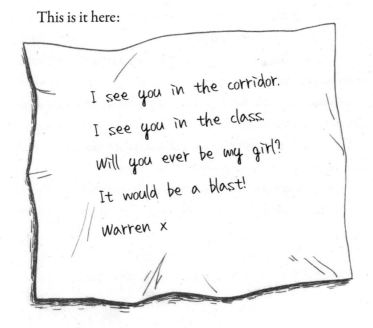

I see you in the corridor.
I see you in the class.
Will you ever be my girl?
It would be a blast!

Warren x

It was a terrible love poem. I looked at the bottom of the note and it was signed by Warren!!! NO WAY!

It had to be tall, handsome, floppy-fringed Warren. The only other Warren I know smells of farts and can't string two words together. I felt uncomfortably hot. I was blushing again . . . pfffffffffffffffffff!

Later, Tina asked where I'd got to at break time, then accused me of acting odd all day (cos I had been – VERY). Didn't dare tell her that the boy she was allegedly in love with wants *me* to be his girl! She would bloody kill me. She's the one who's been chasing him after all. But at the same time, it wasn't me who went after Warren – he was the one who asked *me* out. (Not sure why though, maybe he likes the fact I have goats?)

Oh god what do I dooooo?! Tina is my best (and only) mate. Do I sacrifice our friendship over a gorgeous hunk? Had to say something to someone or I would have imploded, so I told Bonny when I got home. She thought I was making it up, then I reminded her that she thought Tina was made up and she turned out to be real. Bonny was still unconvinced, so I showed her the note.

'Tsk, anyone could have written that,' she sneered. She is *such* Devil Spawn.

1.50 am: Head's been spinning all night. Can't get to sleep. How can it be . . . that a boy as handsome and popular as Warren would want to go out with a weirdo like me?

Thursday 3rd October

Woke up knackered but with funny feeling in stomach. I'd read, reread and agonised all night over Warren's love poem. Was it a joke? Bonny reckons it was. Well it could be. After all, he is veritable bronzed Adonis and I am just a short, fat-calved Chinglish girl.

Felt a bit amazing so I put on electric-blue mascara today and added extra volume to hair.

At school, word had got round like lightning about Warren asking me out. I only knew cos Penny 'Princess' Simpson, who normally carries a barge pole around people like me, said to my face, 'Is it true?'

'What?' I said.

'That you're going out with Warren?'

Going out with him? Flippin' 'eck. The next thing you know we'll be married with kids. I have no idea how the rumour started. The girl who delivered the note might have read it (but she would have had to steam the envelope open somehow). Otherwise Warren might have said something. That's if he really *did* write the note. It could still be Julie and Sam being morons.

Before I knew it, a crowd had formed around me and Penny.

'Jo, did he really write you a love letter?'

'What did it say?'

'What's he like?'

'What the hell's he doing asking *you* out?' (I ignored

that particular remark.)

Suddenly everyone was my friend – oh how the tide turns!! I kept my mouth shut, just in case it was a prank, but couldn't help basking in the limelight for just a few seconds, before flouncing off to a possible romantic liaison with Warren. Actually I went to find Tina so I could tell her my version of the story before the news got to her. But someone from her maths class told me she'd gone home with a migraine.

After English, when I got up to leave, someone was blocking my way. It was Warren!

'Hi,' he said, dashingly.

'Hi,' I replied, looking everywhere but at him.

'Fancy coming to the cinema with me?'

'Eh? What? Where? I mean *why*?'

'To . . . see *a film*?' he said, looking confused. 'There's a good one with Madonna in.'

'Uh, yeah, OK.'

'Cool.'

Then he smiled and sauntered off.

Oh.

My.

God.

Did I just get asked out? Flippin' 'eck. I think I did.

Decided to call Tina after school cos:

1) Keeping secrets is not good between friends
2) Could not contain self
3) AM QUEEN SMUGGY McSMUG OF THE
   KINGDOM OF SMUGDOM!

'Allroight Tiaana!' I said, trying to disguise my smugness.
'Oh it's *you*,' she answered curtly.
Oh crap. She knew.
'Yeah, um, I just wanted to tell you . . .'
'DON'T BOTHER!' she snapped.
Then she went berserk, calling me a turncoat, a Judas,
a backstabbing two-faced rat, and loads of other things I
couldn't quite hear cos I had to hold the phone away from
my ear. Apparently that's why she had gone home, not cos of
a headache, but cos she was so mad. Wow. I was not expecting
that. It's not my fault Warren likes me better than her – gosh!
I'm sure she'll calm down once she's got over the shock.

Cindy has suddenly lost her appeal. Art stuff banished
under bed.

Friday 11th October

It's taking ages waiting for this flippin' Madonna film
to come out but . . . date next week! It'll be so different
from just having quick chats in the school corridor, or
swapping notes in class. Maybe we'll even get to hold hands!

La la la la la, life is good, Disney bluebirds are twittering around my head and not the teeniest thing bothers me. Not Tina being jealous, not being a failed artist, not living in a takeaway, not even my fat barrel calves, which Warren has clearly seen past. Even when Grandma complained about the char siu being too dry for the ninety-seventh time, I laughed lightheartedly and said, 'Stick some gravy on it, Granny!' cos life really isn't all that difficult you know.

Simon asked why I was in such a good mood, but it's not the sort of thing you tell your older brother so I made up some story about being a platinum member of the Nik Kershaw fan club.

Mum and Dad haven't noticed my exceptionally fantastic mood, even though I have been skipping around and singing out loud all day. No surprise there.

But Tina has ignored me all week! OK, I'll admit falling out with Tina IS bothering me. Thought I'd be OK but I miss talking to her. It was a crappy thing I did, but it was Warren who asked ME out, so that's different isn't it? (I don't really know as *Mizz* have never done an article covering this scenario.) If it was the other way round, I'm sure Tina would have done the same, and I would have been fine about it (I think). Oh god, I am so confused!

Wednesday 16th October

Tina still avoiding me. I hate not talking. How long will she keep this up for? Maybe I should apologise and cancel the date? But then Warren will think I'm a knob for doing so. I know, maybe I should go on one date, just to see what it's like, then break up and apologise to Tina. Oh why do I have to choose between bestest mate and most gorgeous boy in known universe?!!

Only three days till date!

Thursday 17th October
Two days!

Friday 18th October
One day!

Saturday 19th October

9.17 am: Going on first ever date later – EEEEEEEEEEEEK! I have never even been friends with a boy platonically, let alone been out with one. What do I wear? What do I say? How do I toss my hair?

Decided to wear V-neck jumper (makes torso look less 'blocky') and boots with heel (gives illusion of height) as seen in *Mizz*.

11.30 am: Got dressed, did hair. Aargh! Hair would not behave. Used whole can of hairspray.

12.05 pm: As I was leaving, Bonny wished me luck with 'make believe' boyfriend. La la la, didn't listen. Devil Spawn was not going to ruin my day.

12.45 pm: Met Warren outside cinema. He said I looked nice (swoon). Was strange seeing him out of school uniform, he looked much older. Went inside, bought popcorn, found seat, sat down. Thought dating malarkey was all very formal.

3.25 pm: Film finished. Was all right, but Madonna should really stick to her day job in my opinion. Also, was awkward sitting in dark not speaking for two hours then coming out in broad daylight all blinded and stuff. Didn't know what to do afterwards, so I shook Warren's hand as if at a job interview.

'How did it go then?' asked Bonny when I got back.

'All right, I think,' I replied.

'Did you know you've got popcorn stuck to your face?' she said, pointing at my left cheek.

NOOOOOOOO!

Hope Warren didn't notice, or if he did, hope he's the sort of person who finds that kind of thing endearing. Wanted to tell Tina about the date, but I couldn't cos she is still blanking me.

Monday 21st October

Warren stopped and chatted with me for ages in the corridor today, GASP! He still likes me despite popcorn and handshake faux pas.

Saw Tina sitting outside science block and wanted to go over and speak but she was with some girl so I chickened out. What would I have said to her anyway? Plus she's probably still so mad she might have punched me in the face.

The unknown girl was Gothy too, but in a novice kind of way (hair crimped wrong, eyeliner uneven). Maybe Tina is trying to replace me with someone more like her. I felt crushed by this thought, cos it meant I was never up to scratch.

Novice Goth leaned over and whispered something to Tina, then they both looked at me, sniggering. There were a zillion things they could have been ridiculing me about, but it couldn't have been the fact that I was now officially *Warren's girlfriend* – ha!

If this is what she wants, Tina is welcome to Novice Goth, at least I have Warren. Wonder when we will go on our next swoonsome date?

Thursday 24th October

Warren spent his whole lunch hour with me in the canteen today. He must really like me. No one else does, but who cares when I have such an amazing boyfriend?

When I got home I found out Baarbara had been caught stealing red-hoofed. Even our goats are kleptomaniacs!

Mum was shouting at her in Chinese. I asked what had happened and Mum said that Baarbara had chewed through the last of the fence post, escaped and sneaked through the kitchen into the shop. Mum heard a '*ping*', and when she went to investigate, Baarbara was standing there munching away on twenty pounds' worth of fivers!

MUNCH
MUNCH

PING!

She had accidentally opened the till with her hoof and helped herself to a snack. She hadn't touched the coins – she obviously has expensive taste.

'You stupid animal, what's wrong with you!' yelled Mum, batting her over the head with a rolled-up copy of the *Sun*. Baarbara stopped chewing for a second, looked around dazed and responded with, 'Baaaaaaaaaaaaa.'

Ha ha ha! Wait till Warren hears about this. Wish I could tell Tina too, she would find all this well hilarious.

Friday 25th October

Came back from school to find Baarbara gone!

Dad said we couldn't trust her now she knew how to open the till. He said she could have embezzled thousands from us already without our knowing. He didn't want her to go, but the goats were brought in to entertain him, not give him grief. He's not angry about it though. He never gets as angry with animals as he does with us kids (UR). He has fixed the fence with some gaffer tape and flimsy twine.

The English bloke who delivers our beansprouts every week now has Baarbara. Dad asked if he could take her back with him to his sheep farm, so he did. At least she has gone to a good home. Mind you, I'm not sure Beansprout Man will stretch to giving her Jammie Dodgers . . . or goatybacks for that matter.

'She was my favourite!' wailed Bonny.

'We've still got Billy,' I said.

'I don't like Billy.'

'Why?'

'Cos he eats his own poo,' she said.

9.45 pm: Billy has spent the whole night bleating like a nutcase! Bonny tried to shut him up by feeding him chocolate bourbons, but he doesn't want them, he wants his sister.

Tuesday 29th October

Have second date!

Warren cheered me up about Baarbara by asking if I wanted to go to bonfire night down the park next week. What did he *think*, dur? He could have asked if I wanted to tour the cesspits of Britain with him and I would still have said yes! He seemed genuinely concerned for my loss. Was special moment to be appreciated by goat owners only.

Wish I could have told Tina, cos she liked Baarbara best too. Can't believe she's still not speaking, it's all getting rather immature now.

The girls at school are so jealous of me, it's unreal! I don't have to worry about being on my own without Tina either cos Penny Simpson and her entourage follow me about all day trying to get information about Warren. Even Julie and Sam are leaving me alone. But I reckon it's cos they want to be on the right side of Warren.

Wednesday 30th October

Billy went on rampage due to Baarbara being taken away. He chomped his way through Dad's shoddy D.I.Y., broke into the shed and ate half a sack of hops. Hops are used for brewing beer, so I have no idea what they were doing in our shed in the first place (UR).

Billy wasn't very well after that, poor sod. His bleat was

all weak and he had to go and lie down for the rest of the day. I felt like joining him, cos my head is so mixed up with thoughts of Warren (love) and Tina (guilt). Why is life so complicated? GAH!

Thursday 31st October – Halloween

The most horrifying Halloween-related thing happened today. The hops that Billy ate fermented in his stomach overnight, he bloated up . . . and EXPLODED!

Me and Bonny found him this morning when we went to give him his Weetabix. He was lying peacefully in a pile of his own innards. Dad had to borrow a spade off Mr Banga so he could dig a hole and bury him (Billy, not Mr Banga). Again, Dad wasn't angry, or sad (or disgusted) as he dragged Billy's body across the yard and laid it in the grave. Maybe the goats had been too manic, even for Dad. It was a bit of a jump from a hamster after all. Me and Bonny weren't particularly sad either – more in shock than anything else. I think the comical nature of the death helped take the sting out of it.

Mrs Burke watched over the fence and said she was glad as the bleating had been disturbing her beauty sleep.

Grandad said we should have pierced a hole in Billy's stomach to let the gas out. That may be obvious to him as I'm sure he used to deal with hordes of sick, bloated farm animals back in Communist China.

Friday 1st November

We are goatless (sob). And I am friendless (double sob). Jill came up to me at school and expressed her obvious horror over what happened to Billy. Grandma had been to their house to get a jar of preserved tofu and told them all about it. I didn't want to elaborate, especially as Sunita was there all wide-eyed, clearly desperate to hear the whole story. 'So what happened?' she asked.

'He ate some hops and exploded,' I answered sharply.

'I heard the other one got sent away too,' said Jill. 'You don't have much luck with pets do you? Maybe you should get an aquarium like us.'

Yeah, and maybe you can get knotted, I thought. Couldn't she tell I was in mourning? Plus fish made crap pets.

On the way home I went to Banga's to buy copious chocolate, binge eat, then fall into pit of despair and self-loathing. 'Cheer up, it might never happen,' said Mrs Banga.

'It did happen, one of our goats got sent away and the other one exploded,' I told her.

'What?!' cried Gurdeep.

'I don't want to talk about it.'

'Here, have a bag of Jelly Babies,' said Mrs Banga sympathetically.

That made me feel worse, cos Jelly Babies were the goats' favourite.

Tuesday 5th November – Bonfire Night

Went to bonfire with Warren. Wore heels again even though they stuck in the mud, but every centimetre helps as far as I am concerned.

Told him about Billy and he was appalled. It was the first case of exploding goat he had come across. He was ever so nice and bought me a toffee apple.

As we walked away from the stall, I saw Tina! She was with Novice Goth. It was my chance to make up. I would break the ice with the mad goat stories. I told Warren I'd be back in a sec, took a deep breath and marched right up to her.

'Hi, Tina,' I said, handing over the toffee apple, 'I got this for you.'

Tina did some sort of secret nod to Novice Goth who instantly obeyed and went to gawp at Guy Fawkes burning on the bonfire.

'No you didn't, Warren got it for *you*. I just saw him,' Tina said.

'Ah . . . yeah . . . well,' I squirmed.

She glanced over at him.

'Having a good time are you?'

My attempt at a truce was going from bad to worse.

'Hey, Tina, if I could go back in time, I . . .' I was going to say I wouldn't have done it, but then realised that was another lie. ' . . . I'm *sorry*,' I blurted. Phew. At least that was true.

She huffed. 'Look, as it was Warren who asked you out, I've decided it's not your fault.'

'Oh, really?'

'Really.'

What? She was letting me off the hook! True friend! True friend!

'Friends again then?' I squeaked.

'Yeah, but if you do it again I *will* slap you. And to be honest,' she said, looking over her shoulder at Novice Goth, 'she is WELL boring.'

YESSSSSSS!

Wednesday 6th November

Life is excellent! Tina is my friend once more and I am hopelessly in love with Warren!

Thursday 21st November

Me and Warren were hanging out in the canteen as usual today. I offered him a pickled onion Monster Munch and he touched my hand for longer than was necessary! Does this officially constitute hand-holding?

Monday 2nd December

Warren has arranged for us to go to town this weekend as he has something to say to me. I will absolutely die if he tells me he loves me too!

I cannot believe of all other long-limbed, doe-eyed, thick-tressed girls Warren could have chosen from (like 'Princess' Simpson for instance), he picked plain little *MOI*! I can only put it down to my scintillating conversation and wit.

As we are now best mates again, I told Tina and this time there was no falling out. (Apparently, she has her eye on some Goth lad in the fifth year and Warren is old news.)

Wednesday 4th December

Warren is spending Christmas in South Africa. I wonder if he'll take me with him? We could stay there, get goats and herd them together forever. It will be ever so romantic. And I will never have to think about arranged marriages, escaping the takeaway or any of that other crappy stuff ever again. It will be expensive what with airfare and considerable supply of Jammie Dodgers, but maybe I could save money by making Christmas presents this year instead of buying them? I am hoping homemade tissue-box covers feature highly on people's wish lists.

I am so committed to a future with Warren that I have even chucked my beloved Nik Kershaw poster in the bin.

Thursday 5th December

Am saving up for South Africa (even though Warren is still unaware of the fact I am going with him). Started on homemade gifts today. I was looking for Sellotape and scissors, but could only find tiger balm and an abacus. That is what happens when you live in a Chinese takeaway. I didn't have anything to cut string with, so I used the meat cleaver.

BIG MISTAKE.

As I went to chop the string, I missed and . . . *WHAM!* The tip of my left index finger came flying off! It was only the top of the nail and a sliver of flesh, but the pain was gruesome.

I stemmed the blood with a dishcloth and showed it to Mum, who looked at it, wandered off and came back with a bottle of soya sauce (UR). Now my guess is I should have been rushed to hospital to have stitches, but instead Mum sprinkled soya sauce on to the wound (which did nothing except sting like hell and make more mess) and wrapped it in kitchen towel. I shouldn't have been surprised. Mum and Dad think Western medicine is witchcraft so the only remedies they use are:

1) Soya sauce as general cure-all
2) Rubbing ginger so hard on a bruise that you get another bruise on top of original bruise
3) Dabbing wee on chilblains
4) For everything else: 'Get over it!'

Friday 6th December

Whereabouts of fingertip still unknown. Hope it hasn't ended up in someone's chow mein.

Saturday 7th December

10.51 am: Out with Warren later – nervous and excited! Am planning on telling him my plans to elope with him to South Africa, as we are now good as engaged (sorry, Wong, ha ha!).

We had Knickerbocker Glories at Wimpy and I got brain freeze. Also my finger was still throbbing from the home-crafting injury.

'Are you all right?' said Warren, spotting my bandage.

'Yep,' I winced.

'Thanks for coming today.'

He's so polite and will one day make a very good husband to me.

'Er . . . no probs,' I replied.

'Listen, Jo, I'm sorry, but I've been meaning to tell you something.'

OH.

MY.

GOD.

Any sentence that began with 'I'm sorry' meant utterly

bad news to follow. He had seen through my thin disguise of hairspray, make-up and illusionary attire and realised that:

1) I am too short
2) My calves are too fat
3) I am failed artist
4) I live in a Chinese takeaway
5) I may or may not smell of soya sauce
6) I. AM. A. LOSER.
7) (And worst goat owner ever)

'I, well, you see . . .' he mumbled.

'It's all right,' I butted in. 'I know what you're going to say.'

'You *do*?'

'Don't worry, I won't hate you for it.'

'You *won't*?'

'No.'

'Oh, thanks, Jo. I knew you'd understand.'

'That's okaaay.'

'Let me buy you another Knickerbocker Glory.'

NOOOOOOO! Dumped clean. Ugh.

After another brain freeze, we parted ways and agreed to be friends, just like they do in the stupid flippin' Hollywood movies.

I felt OK on the bus, I was used to rejection, especially off Mum and Dad. But when I got home, I started crying. But crying like I've never done before. Not the sort where I want my parents to go away. The sort where I want my boyfriend *not* to go away. But the pain was just the same.

Sunday 8th December

Have retrieved crumpled-up Nik Kershaw poster from bin and stuck it bitterly back on wall.

Spent all last night sobbing into sleeve like jilted Hollywood damsel. Bonny asked why my eyes were all red this morning and I said I was allergic to the duck down in my (100% polyester) pillow.

'And why is Nik Kershaw back up?' she asked.

'Cos I felt like it,' I said.

'Has something happened with Warren?'

'Maybe.'

'But how? He's not even real?'

'He IS real!'

'Well how come I've never . . .'

'OH GIVE IT A REST WILL YA!' I shouted.

Then I went over to her Smurfs video box, took out her Benson & Hedges and scrunched the whole pack into sawdust. And that's when Bonny knew I wasn't lying.

Monday 9th December

At break time I wanted to tell Tina about being dumped but she already knew, as the rumours had spread around school faster than when Warren asked me out.

'What a sod, he could have waited till after Christmas!' she said, giving me a hug outside the main block.

'What difference would that have made?'

'So you could have had a happy one for once.'

'Fair point.'

My eyes stung and I felt self-conscious as we stood there. Penny and her princess posse, so eager to be mates before, were now walking past giving me dirty looks. Oh how fickle fame is.

'Did he give you a reason?' said Tina.

'No,' I replied. Why should he? I had seven of my own, I thought.

'That's the problem with the good-looking ones,' she

said. 'It's all about ticking girls off their list.' Tina was trying to make me feel better, but nothing will right now.

After school, I went to Banga's to buy chocolate to wallow in and guess what?

Gurdeep has got a boyfriend!

Gurdeep!!

With her sticky-up hair and green lips!!! How can this be fair when I am tragically alone and drowning in a sea of my own tears?

Except . . . her hair doesn't actually stick up any more, and she gave up the ice pops ages ago. In fact, she looks quite presentable these days. Pretty, even. (Bet her Turkish Delight's still stale though.) Apparently, she met a boy called Raj during her trip to Delhi. He's a friend of the family and their mums arranged for them to meet.

Ugh, that's like me with David Wong. How can she be OK with *that*?

Tuesday 10th December

Wanted to sit down with Tina and draw a spider diagram on why Warren dumped me. But she wasn't interested cos she's started going out with Gary Tomlin, the Goth lad in the year above. I've seen him about, he's a bit of a loner too. She couldn't stop going on about him. Can't really complain, can I, considering what I put her through.

Beansprout Man arrived tonight with photos of Baarbara headbutting his sheep. Everybody stood about laughing except me. Couldn't they see I was busy being sad right now?

Friday 20th December

School Christmas holidays finally! Have spent last couple of weeks hiding in art room at break times to avoid bumping into Warren and/or being ridiculed by Penny, Julie and Sam etc. Has been awkward as hell.

Tuesday 24th December – Christmas Eve

Sadness momentarily replaced with abject confusion when Dad went out and came back with a dog (UR)! He looked very pleased with it. She is a fully grown Alsatian who he got off Kev, Mandy's dodgy older brother. We know Dad's been missing the goats, but it's as if he isn't happy unless there's some mad animal causing mayhem somewhere in the background. Maybe they're the only things that bring him happiness? I must admit they can be quite funny. And I suppose it's nice to see Dad can care for a living creature, even if they aren't his own kids.

'What's her name?' I asked.

'Lucky,' said Dad.

I remembered what Jill said about us being unlucky with pets – how ironic was that?

'She's hungry,' said Mum. 'Go next door and get Jammie Dodger.' (Jammie Dodger was said in English – obviously no equivalent in Chinese.)

Lucky is not very bright. I threw a ball and she just gawped at me gormlessly. We don't have anywhere for her to sleep, so she lies behind the plastic strip curtain between the kitchen and shop. Oh god, customers will think she is going in the food.

A customer came in and threatened to call the hygiene inspectors, cos of an 'animal in the food preparation area'. Dad told the busybody that she was guarding against drunk and disorderlies, but sent her upstairs just in case he got reported.

Later, when I went upstairs, Bonny was practising make-up on the dog. She had gold eyeshadow and sparkly red lipstick on one side of her snout. She looked very festive and pleased to be involved, so I patted her and she licked me. I think I'm warming to her.

Went to bed and prayed we don't have lobster for Christmas dinner tomorrow.

OVEN-READY TURKEY
WITH CRISPY ROAST
SPUDS... IF ONLY !

Wednesday 25th December Christmas Day

Grandparents arrived with a live chicken in a sack (UR). I knew I should have been more specific and prayed for an oven-ready turkey.

Lucky went mad barking while Grandma untied the sack, stuck her hand in and grabbed the chicken by the legs. (According to Simon, Grandma grew up naked on a pig farm in Guangdong province during the revolution, so nothing phases her.) Then she struggled over to the sink with it still upside down, plonked it on the draining board and hacked off its head. AAAARRGGGHHHH! She didn't even warn us!

Then while she was draining the blood out of the chicken's neck, it struggled free and zigzagged its way out into the garden, with Lucky barking behind. Up till now, I'd only heard rumours that headless chickens could still run about, but now I can say I have seen it with my very own eyes.

Couldn't bring myself to eat it after that. At least it took my mind off Warren.

'Merry Christmas, everybody!'

Thursday 26th December — Boxing Day

Went to Grandparents' with Bonny. Jill and Katy were there. Jill said she was sorry about what happened with Warren in front of EVERYONE, which was MORTIFYING, cos a) No one except me, her and Bonny knew I had a boyfriend and b) Simon heard! (Grandparents didn't understand but it was still embarrassing.)

After Jill and Katy left, I was talking to Simon and we agreed that this year's was the worst Christmas ever. Then I thought about the year my yellow teddy bear chair went missing – that came a close second. Simon asked Grandma in Chinese if she remembered that incident and she replied, 'Oh, didn't you know? Your mum wrapped it back up again and gave it to (someone's name I didn't know's) kid.'

I went pale. What? They sacrificed their *own child's* Christmas present to give to someone else's?

'Why?' Simon asked.

Yes WHY?! I thought (as I was speechless).

'Oh, they were cousins of your mum's from down south,' said Grandma, trying to recollect. 'It was a surprise visit and they didn't have anything to give to their daughter May, who was four or something at the time, so they gave her the chair. It was a nice chair.'

Yes. It *was* a NICE CHAIR! Well I hope May enjoyed MY NICE CHAIR! The worst thing was, Mum and Dad pretended the chair had never even existed in the first place. Why would they do that? Why do they hate me so much?

Tuesday 31st December — New Year's Eve

There is a reason why we don't keep loose objects in the shop. It's so they can't be used as missiles.

We were expecting the usual New Year's Eve drunkards and sure enough, after the pub shut, two came in and started having a go at Mum. So far, so predictable. But then one of them pulled up a carpet tile, which I had not predicted and was very resourceful, I thought. He threw it at her like a furry ninja star and it missed and hit his cretin friend instead, HA HA!

Mum started shouting at them in Chinese, which always makes me cringe cos it gives them more reason to have a go at us. 'Ahhh, *ching, chong, chang*!' they shouted back.

'Why don't you f**k off back to your own country if you can't speak English!'

Dad hid in the kitchen as usual, pretending it wasn't happening and Uncle Han wasn't here to protect us this time, so Mum made me call the police. I didn't want to, but it was getting out of hand. I dialled 999 and got put through.

'Hello, Coventry City police station. What seems to be the problem?'

I wasn't sure what to say. Was this serious enough to warrant a call to the police?

I was shaking as I said, 'There's two drunk men in our takeaway throwing stuff about and shouting at my mum. Can someone come round?'

Amazingly, they asked for our address and said they'd send someone immediately. I had to almost shout over the noise, so they could probably hear it was for real.

Thankfully, that was the end of the drama, cos the drunks had legged it before the police arrived. After they took notes and left, it was almost closing time, so Mum shut the shop while Dad sullenly glued the carpet tile back down.

What a crap end to a crap year.

We narrowly escaped a punch-up, I got totally dumped, nearly destroyed friendship with only friend, got rejected by *Take Hart*, didn't even make it to the top three in art competition, got squashed by a horse, lost two goats and have not even grown a <u>single inch</u>.

Wednesday 1st January – New Year's Day

Am still 4' 10" – Aargh!

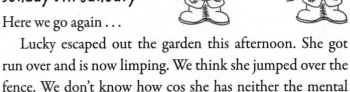

ME

A GNOME

Sunday 5th January

Here we go again . . .

Lucky escaped out the garden this afternoon. She got run over and is now limping. We think she jumped over the fence. We don't know how cos she has neither the mental dexterity or physical agility to do so.

One of our regular customers recognised her wandering the street. He brought her back, and started whinging on about how irresponsible we all were. She still had a red lipstick stain round her mouth from Bonny's Christmas makeover, which thankfully he didn't notice.

We are terrible pet owners, it's true. Dad does not understand that dogs need training and all that other necessary stuff. I told him to take Lucky to the vet, and he replied, 'Nooo, nooo, just rub ginger. She all right.'

Monday 6th January

Bumped into Warren going into double maths, the worst combination possible. He was very considerate though and kept his distance (in case I threw myself around his ankles and made a scene probably).

All the girls are still giving me the evils. Princess

Simpson came up to me and said sarcastically, 'Got bored of you quick, didn't he?' And as I was going into science, Julie shoved me into the life-size anatomical skeleton on purpose, causing several phalanges to fall off. Jill and Sunita are trying to look after me, but they're just as scared of the bullies as I am.

Wish Tina was about, but she's off being Gothy with Gaz at every available opportunity. Is she doing it on purpose after I spent so much time with Warren? Nah, she's not that petty. Although, I wouldn't blame her.

Took my mind off it by worrying about Lucky's leg. Tried to take a look when I got home, but she thought it was an amusing game and started bounding around the garden with a daft expression on her face. I got Bonny to shoo her over so I could do a rugby tackle, but she kept running off. It wasn't very amusing for me cos I kept slipping on the ice. Then one of Bonny's false nails snapped, so we gave up.

Came to conclusion: Lucky's leg is FINE.

PHALANGES

Saturday 11th January — My birthday (age 15)

Tina is with Goth Gaz all weekend, so I will not get a cake this year (sob). They spend practically every minute doing the *NME* crossword in his bedroom, which is painted black to 'resemble the inside of a coffin', Tina told me. Sounds ghastly if you ask me. I am not jealous or anything (much), but I hardly see her any more – and that's not a friendship!

Bonny bought me a new poster of Nik Kershaw to replace the crumpled-up one I rescued out the bin, and to help me get over Warren. It's the classic picture of him wearing a reflective jumpsuit plus snood, so I should have been made up. Instead I just stared at his floppy fringe, which reminded me of Warren, and then felt all sad again.

Tried doing some fashion designing but nothing came out. Hope I haven't lost the ability to draw! Didn't want to mope all day, so decided to take Lucky to the park for some much-needed training.

1.20 pm: Arrived at park. Let Lucky off lead.

1.21 pm: Told her to sit. She acted all goofy.

1.22pm: Told her to sit. She spotted a cocker spaniel and sprinted off.

1.23 pm: Lucky trampled on spaniel as if soft cushion. Angry owner bashed Lucky with handbag.

1.24 pm: Ran over to check spaniel not dead. Woman shouted at me for having uncontrollable dangerous animal running amok in public space. I apologised and put lead back on Lucky.

1.25 pm: Training over.

On the way home I bumped into Gurdeep. She was with a boy wearing a blue turban. 'This is Raj, my boyfriend,' she said.

Great. Everybody is getting all cosy and coupled up, apart from saddo me. She flicked her hair, which has become long and lush like Sunita's. And she was wearing one of those traditional Indian trouser suits in fuchsia pink. She looked so glam, I hardly recognised her.

'Hi, Raj,' I said.

'What you been up to?' said Gurdeep.

'Teaching Lucky to sit.'

'Did it work?'

'No,' I replied, emphatically.

Then she told Lucky to sit, and she did, the stupid flippin' mutt!

Sunday 12th January

Fancied doing something different with my hair after seeing Gurdeep's yesterday. Maybe it will attract Warren's attention and he will want me back again. I cut a fringe with the craft scissors but couldn't work out why it was so wonky. And how the heck was it so short?! This will now attract attention for all the WRONG reasons. Totally. Regretting. It.

Monday 13th January

Collared Tina in the canteen with Gaz. I'd never seen him up close before. He was deathly pale, like a corpse, with backcombed black hair like Tina's but shaved at the sides. I could also make out a slight hint of eyeliner. He didn't say hello or smile once. What a miserable bugger. But that is the whole point of being a Goth I suppose.

Asked Tina if she could sort out my obvious hair emergency but she said she was busy all week. She told me to flatten my fringe with gel to create more length and that it would grow out soon anyway. She didn't seem very concerned. Plus I wasn't expecting a present or anything, but she didn't even mention my birthday! She is being extremely slack on best friend front.

Saturday 1st February

Me and Bonny heard an almighty bang in the kitchen, so we ran downstairs to see what had happened. We found Dad standing there with some kind of indefinable brown stuff dripping on to his head from the ceiling. We thought he'd had an accident with his Irish stew, but apparently it was dog food.

Dad thought Lucky might appreciate a hot meal for a change, and had put an unopened tin of Chunkie on top of the hob and forgot about it. Half an hour later it exploded, splattering offal everywhere. No wonder Lucky is trying to escape, this place is a flippin' loony bin! I hope Julie and Sam don't hear about this, they will have a field day.

INDEFINABLE
BROWN STUFF

Simon said that what Dad did was very dangerous. 'My mate knew someone who put a tin of baked beans on a campfire,' he said. 'He ended up in hospital and it took four days to pick the beans out of his face.' Well, at least he can say he has 'bean' there, done that – ha ha!

Sunday 2nd February

Me and Bonny went to Poshos' for lunch, where it is always peaceful, safe and normal. They asked about Lucky. Not out of interest, but concern. I think they are being Kwan pet vigilantes. We told them she was remarkably intelligent and well behaved and didn't mention the exploding can of Chunkie.

When we got back, Mum was brandishing a dish mop at Lucky for eating the slab of pork that had been defrosting on the table, while Dad wrote out a notice saying there would be no char siu tonight. Why are our pets such reprobates?

Thursday 20th February

Tina and Gaz are like conjoined twins. I feel like I can't see her without an appointment these days. Thing is, I can't moan on after hanging out with Warren so much last year. At least my fringe no longer looks like it has been through a bacon slicer.

Warren came over at break today and commented on how nice my hair was. My attention-attracting fringe trick has finally worked – yessss! He regrets dumping me and will ask me out again, I know it.

Got home to find Lucky has been sent away to the same place as Baarbara! Beansprout Man's sheep farm is turning into a penitentiary for criminal pets! Mum seems relieved, after all it means no more pilfering of expensive stock. Grandma and Grandad were glad she had gone too, but I think they were only concerned about getting their char siu requirements fulfilled.

'I'm sad about Lucky,' said Bonny. 'I think Dad is too.'

'No he's not, otherwise he wouldn't have sent her away,' I replied.

'He loved her enough to warm up her food.'

'Hmm. Suppose so . . .' I said.

'Are *you* sad?' asked Bonny.

'Very.'

'Why?'

'Cos she'll be headbutted to death by Baarbara, that's why.'

When I thought more about it, I wondered if Bonny might be right. Dad does seem more subdued today. I hope he doesn't start getting all moody again.

Thursday 13th March

Was leaving English class when Warren approached me again. I called Tina after school. (Gaz wasn't with her so she was free to talk.) I reported it was twice in one week Warren had been all pally now. She reckoned he does wants me back, cos he hasn't been out with anyone since we split up. But when there's a queue of girls the length of the equator gagging to be within stroking distance of his highlights, why would he want me?

I took the opportunity to ask if Tina was free to go for a burger in town sometime, seeing as we hadn't had quality mates' time together in months. 'Yeah, maybe...' she replied. I was unconvinced, but didn't want to bug her cos I certainly wasn't in the running for 'most loyal friend' award.

When I got home, Mum told me Grandma had put corn flour in the mop water instead of bicarbonate of soda and glued herself to the floor. Mum thinks she's going senile. I just think she couldn't read the packet. She said Grandma needs a break and asked if I could help with the mopping every day till she comes back. I am quite happy to mop, it's not exactly strenuous and I'll get paid, so I can buy that portfolio case at last. Maybe the prospect of filling it will give me the incentive to get back into fashion designing!

Saturday 15th March

Bought *Mizz*. There was an article in it about Yoko Ono's life as an artist. It was a sign from above! I got out my pad and started sketching a Yoko-inspired range.

Friday 21st March

Spent entire week designing floaty white garments. I forgot how good drawing was for taking your mind off troubles and stuff.

Saturday 22nd March

Got paid for mopping, including an advance for the whole of next month (to keep me sweet probably!) so went into town. Was testing zip functionality on various portfolio cases in WHSmith when Warren walked in with a mate who wasn't from our school. (Good job my fringe was behaving today.) He was very gallant and came over and introduced me to him. His name was Tony and he was tall and good-looking too, except he had short gelled dark brown hair with a spiky fringe. He looked a bit like Dave Gahan from Depeche Mode. They were such a handsome pair, I was hoping someone might walk past and see me with them and start spreading rumours again.

I smiled at Tony, but he mumbled something to Warren
about getting some Tipp-Ex and sauntered off, which I
found quite rude. After an awkward exchange of words
about ballpoint pen nibs, Warren said goodbye without
asking me out like I'd hoped.

Felt disappointed, bought portfolio, felt better, went
home, felt disappointed again, stared at Nik Kershaw, felt
better again.

Sunday 23rd March

Spent most of day admiring my new art case and feeling all grown up and professional. I bought that with my own wages, I did! I put my best designs in some of the sleeves. It looks totally brill. Better get on with filling it.

Wednesday 16th April

Bonny found a baby sparrow in the alleyway while she was having a fag with Mandy (I know cos I was spying out of our bedroom window). It must have fallen out of its nest. She brought it in for Dad and he could not contain his glee. It was like Lucky had reincarnated into a more manageable, pocket-sized version, which wouldn't run into the road or require warmed-up cans of offal. Bonny looked smug too, for putting a smile on Dad's face for the first time since Lucky got sent away.

We took turns holding it, apart from Mum, who claimed it had fleas. I had a closer look and couldn't see any, just a worse view of its bulgy eyes and crusty beak gaping open for food. The last time I held a bird was with Uncle Han back in Nottingham. I won't be tying string to this one though, as I am now a responsible adult.

Dad fed it boiled rice and put it in an empty mushroom box lined with strips of Kleenex tissue. He put the cardboard lid back on and punched some holes in the top with a pen. Grandad kept tutting and shaking his head at all the nonsense. I bet he didn't have time for such frivolity in his day.

Simon once told me Grandma and Grandad helped Chairman Mao kill millions of sparrows in China for being pests and nearly made them extinct! Between that and Uncle Han trapping them, it was lucky they hadn't. Then later on I discovered something *even more* disturbing! While I was fetching salted black beans for Mum off the kitchen shelf, I found a strange tin. The picture on the label was done in watercolours and showed a flock of small birds flying over fields. I asked Mum what it was. She said it was for dinner, then opened it up to show me. Inside was what looked like a dozen miniscule roast chickens, all squished together in gunky brown gravy. It was gross!

'UGH, what are they?' I asked, trying not to barf.

'Sparrows,' said Mum.

What exactly have the Chinese got against the poor bloody things?! Maybe Dad's trying to make up for it by taking in Bonny's fledgling.

P.S. Wish Mum would stop feeding us every imaginable horror she can think of.

Tuesday 29th April

Dad has been tending to the scrawny bird like his own precious newborn. It has grown feathers and flies around the kitchen now. I found poo in my hair earlier. That bird is crapping everywhere! Simon said the takeaway could get shut down if the hygiene inspector finds out. I can't believe Dad is putting his business on the line for his ridiculous feathered ~~fiend~~ friend.

Tina wants to bring Goth Gaz to come and see our latest attraction. So it's OK to ignore me, but when my home becomes some kind of zoo/amusement park, she's over like a shot!

I designed a cloak made of feathers. Grandma might find this interesting, as she could make more use of all those chickens she decapitates.

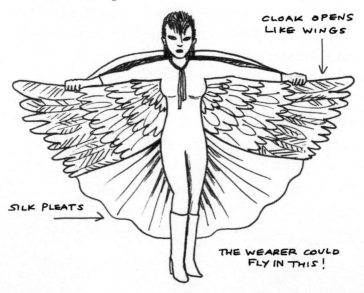

CLOAK OPENS LIKE WINGS

SILK PLEATS

THE WEARER COULD FLY IN THIS!

Sunday 4th May

Mum told us Auntie Yip is coming to stay at Grandparents' for two weeks soon. We haven't seen Mum this happy in ages. She likes a natter with her youngest sister, mainly cos it keeps her up to date with what's going on outside the walls of the takeaway kitchen. She is nearly as happy as Dad is with his sparrow. Apart from mine and Bonny's general teen/pre-teen angst, we are almost a happy family and I am optimistic about the future for once.

Dad is the jolliest he's been in ages. Which means everyone else is more relaxed. It's nice at home at the moment. The sparrow has taken to sitting on his shoulder while he cooks. I hope it doesn't fall into someone's foo yung. We would definitely get reported to the hygiene inspectors for that. Tina and Gaz came round to see it this afternoon.

'What's it called?' Tina asked.

'Sparrow,' said Bonny, original as ever.

'Cool,' Gaz replied, timidly holding out a prawn cracker, which Sparrow started pecking at like a drill.

'He likes you,' Tina said to him.

I didn't think I'd like Gaz, as I partly blamed him for the reason my friendship with Tina wasn't the way it used to be. But I have since discovered he is just painfully shy, and I know how *that* feels. Maybe I can like him after all.

When Simon came over for dinner, we showed him the new addition to the family. He thought a bird was better than hamsters, but not goats or dog. I'm glad we have established a place for it in the hierarchy of mad Kwan pets.

Sunday 18th May

Me and Bonny had Victoria sponge cake at Poshos' while Uncle read the *Daily Mail* and Auntie potted up parsley. They are more English than most English people! I forgot to tell Bonny not to mention Sparrow, cos it was my job to try and maintain our illusion of not being complete losers with animals, but it was too late:

'Dad's got a new bird,' piped Bonny.

'What? Like a *girlfriend*?' said Katy, eyes wide.

I kicked Bonny under the table and she glared at me.

'What you mean?' asked Auntie.

'I found it in the alleyway,' said Bonny, 'and now it sits on Dad's shoulder the whole time.'

'That's ace,' said Jill.

'So . . . not a girlfriend, then,' said Katy, regretfully.

Then everyone choked down their cake in awkward silence.

Oh why can't we just be normal?!

Thursday 22nd May

A reporter came in tonight to write a feature on Dad and Sparrow. Kev had called the *Coventry Evening Telegraph* thinking it would make a good story. Mum found the whole fiasco entertaining, even though she couldn't quite understand what was going on. Bonny, Mandy and Kev were behaving as if it was the biggest story breaking for years, but I was dreading the prospect of everyone in school, town even, knowing it was MY dad with HIS pet bird. I bet Warren will be glad he dumped me when he finds out.

The reporter asked questions like: 'Where do you keep it at night?'

'In mushroom box,' Dad replied, informatively.

'And what do you feed it?'

'Rice, fermented cabbage, sometimes moon cake,' declared Dad.

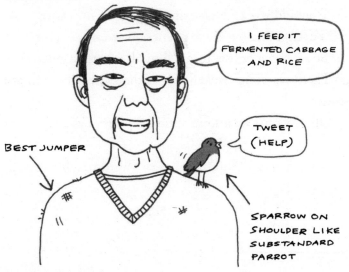

'Hmmm, fermented moon cake,' said the reporter, pondering and scribbling it down.

Afterwards, he took some pictures of Sparrow perched on Dad's shoulder, which made him look like a Chinese Captain Cook with a substandard parrot.

It is going to be in tomorrow's paper – ugh.

Friday 23rd May

Dad and Sparrow are on page twelve of tonight's paper. Their heads are almost life-size! (CRINGE.) The article takes up half the page, so there can't be much news about at the moment. The headline reads 'A Happy Gathering!'

Dad showed the article to every customer that came in saying, 'Look, we famous! We famous!' He ended up cutting it out and sticking it to the wall underneath the pop shelf behind the counter where everyone on earth, from space even, could see it. He has never been that enthusiastic about anything before in his life. Mrs Burke came round later to have a look at Sparrow, as she'd also seen it in the paper.

'Mrs Burke, we famous!' Dad announced as she walked in.

'Yes I know, Dennis, I can hear you through the wall,' she replied.

Monday 26th May

Kept head down at school hoping nobody saw Friday's article about Dad and the stupid bird. I almost made it to lunchtime when Julie yelled out, 'Hey, Kwan, one sparrow chop suey with flied lice please!' Followed by raucous laughter from Sam.

Great.

'Oi! Shut your traps or I'll shut 'em for you!'

Tina came marching over and the bullies shuffled off. She had non-regulation black lipstick on today, which made her look more menacing than usual. Apart from being a hairdresser, she also wants to be a militant and fight for peace and justice. Her and Gaz read about them in the *NME*. It is good to know she's still watching out for me.

'Hey, Jo, I saw the photo of your dad in the paper. It's so cool!' she said.

'Not for me it isn't,' I replied, glumly.

SPARROW CHOP SUEY AND 'FLIED' LICE IS A STUPID IDEA AS THERE'D BE HARDLY ANY MEAT AND YOU'D NEED A TRILLION LICE!

(AND IT WOULD TASTE GROSS)

CLOSE-UP OF LICE

'Aargh, forget about them airheads,' she sneered, nodding at Julie and Sam walking off towards the dinner hall. 'C'mon, let's get a pasty.'

'Where's Gaz?' I asked as we headed off.

'He's not in today.'

'Oh, nothing bad I hope?' I said, secretly hoping he was wiped out with pleurisy so I could have Tina to myself for a while.

'Nah, just having a tooth out.'

Never mind, a whole lunch hour with Tina was better than nothing.

Sunday 1st June

Auntie Yip is here! I knew she was coming to dinner cos I saw Mum opening a tin of Spam with a big smile on her face. She'd even made her favourite lotus bean soup. It's probably the only time Mum stops feeling second best, when Auntie's around.

Auntie was telling us about her wedding in August. She was ever so cheerful and optimistic about the future. Wonder if Mum was ever like that? Before work and kids made her all haggard. Note: Never work/have kids.

'I bought some new clothes for Jo and Bonny,' said Auntie.

'Good idea,' said Mum, tugging at my favourite old man's cardigan from Oxfam. 'I don't know why she wears these rags, she looks like a tramp.'

Mum has a habit of speaking as if the person she's slagging off isn't in the room.

'Ah, jeh' (big sister) 'don't be mean,' said Auntie in Chinese. 'You should be proud of your lovely daughters. I see Jo's really good at art.' I'd shown her my half-filled portfolio while Mum was preparing food. Was nice to hear someone in the family appreciating my talent.

'Look how fresh this soup is,' cooed Mum, as if she hadn't heard a word Auntie had said, while ladling it delicately into bowls. It did smell good . . . but how come soup gets more attention than us kids? Even Sparrow gets more than us!

Auntie thinks it's dirty having a bird in the kitchen. Good job she never saw the state of the goats or dog.

Monday 9th June

Still getting grief for Dad's stupid picture. I can't keep relying on Tina to save me. I am reduced to wandering around on my own at break times searching for suitable places to hide. I suppose I *could* make a new friend . . . but I don't like anyone else (most of them are bullies anyway). I wanted to call Simon to ask what he thought about the picture, but he's in the middle of writing an essay on power-supply decoupling on a circuit board, so he's disturbed enough.

Auntie Yip called me after school and asked if I wanted my ears pierced. Tina has hers done twice in each one and it looks well cool. If I had mine done maybe the following will happen:

1) Warren will ask me out . . . again
2) Everyone will think I'm amazing for being his girlfriend . . . again
3) I will be most popular girl in school . . . again.
   And maybe I'll make a new best friend?!

'Yeah OK, I'll come over!' I said to Auntie.

Grandma and Grandad were back to sprinkling prawn shells in the garden when I went over (don't think they even used that proper fertiliser I once got them for Christmas). I followed Auntie upstairs to the box room where she sat me down on the bed. When I saw no evidence of ear-piercing equipment, alarm bells started ringing.

'Are you ready?' she said.

'Errrr . . . yeah?'

She put her thumb and forefinger either side of my left earlobe.

'Have you done this before?' I asked, a tad late.

'Yes, course I have,' she replied reassuringly, and pinched her long nails together as hard as she could.

'AAAARRRGGGGGGHHHHHHHHH!!!!!' I shrieked. 'What are you *doing*?!'

'Piercing your ears,' she said.

'You don't do it like that!' I wailed, clutching my throbbing earlobe.

'Sorry, does it hurt?'

Hurt? She was trying to pierce my flesh with her bare hands (massive UR)!

I forget she is related to Mum.

Wednesday 11th June

So much for the idea of Warren asking me out again. I am now hideously marred for life.

Bumped into Tina and Gaz coming out the canteen. Tina asked what was wrong with my ear. (I had tried to hide it with a supposed 'flesh'-coloured plaster that didn't match any shade of skin I knew of, least of all mine.) I told her about Auntie's shoddy D.I.Y. ear piercing and showed her my wound, expecting some kind of sympathy or advice relating to skin infections. But instead she told me not to do my nose as I clearly didn't take well to skin punctures and it would be impossible to disguise a giant scab in the middle of my face, which wasn't very helpful.

Bonny thought it was hilarious. She said she's going to get hers done at the market, which is no more hygienic than unsterilised fingernails, I assured her.

Despite inflicting flesh wounds, the place is still much better with Auntie around. Even Mum and Dad are more chatty now there's something to talk about other than gas bills and noodles.

I took my portfolio in to show Miss Waterfall and told her my idea of sending it to *Mizz* in order to secure work experience after school. She told me I had a good chance of getting noticed with my unique designs and agreed it was an excellent idea. Yessss!

Monday 16th June

Dad hasn't used his snooker cue since he got it last year, so tonight when the takeaway was quiet, he went off to the social club with Kev. WOW – I didn't mean for him to go during opening hours!

I was worried as Dad has never left Mum in charge before. How would she cope serving *and* cooking? Thankfully Auntie offered to come round and help and Simon came as well, for dinner. He hasn't been over for weeks cos of revision. But he has finished his A level mock exams now.

When Simon left after dinner, I overheard Auntie talking to Mum about the butcher's. They talk too quick in Chinese so I could only catch bits. But I tuned right in for this . . .

'Make sure he doesn't start gambling again. You don't want the same thing happening here,' said Auntie, sounding strangely ominous.

'Nooo, snooker's not gambling is it?' said Mum. 'Don't worry, we won't go bankrupt. Business in the takeaway is good.'

I knew the word 'gambling' as I'd heard Mum and Dad say it before, but 'bankrupt'? I don't have the foggiest how to say that in Chinese, but I've been piecing all the words together and remembering the looks on their faces, and it's the only thing it could have meant, or that makes any sense. God. So Dad was gambling in Hull, and went bankrupt . . . and that's why we had to leave? Bloody hell.

'Yeah, well, just keep an eye on him, jeh,' said Auntie.

'Ah, let him have his fun, because soon he won't be able to, will he?' Mum smiled wryly. Then they both started cackling. What was *that* all about (UR)?!!

Tuesday 17th June

Auntie leaves tomorrow, so she came over for dinner with Grandparents and Simon. I wanted to tell Simon about Dad going bankrupt, but I didn't want to stress him out after he'd stressed so long over his mocks.

Wish Auntie could stay. Mum hasn't been this happy since going out once a week to play mah-jong with Auntie and her mates in Nottingham. She never goes out now. The only friends that seem to come round these days are the Wongs.

Auntie said something to me in Chinese but it was totally incomprehensible, so I replied, 'Huh?'

'Ah, jeh, your daughter's Chinese is terrible!' said Auntie.

Mum shot me a look. 'Yes, she's useless.' Auntie was simply stating a fact, but Mum was mocking me. I felt ashamed. Just like when Tina's mum couldn't believe I didn't know the Chinese word for 'hello'.

'*Good luck with your art*,' Auntie articulated in English, amused. She was probably flummoxed as to how we all communicated as a family. Not as flummoxed as I am, that's for sure.

As the adults chatted, I got the gist that Auntie met her fiancé, a chef, at the restaurant where she works. They're getting married at a big Chinese restaurant in Birmingham city centre. It really does seem that all Chinese people either work in a restaurant or takeaway. I wonder if Simon will be the first one to break the mould by going to uni and becoming a computer engineer? Maybe in England he will. I can't imagine everyone in China works in the Chinese food industry, otherwise who would fix leaking taps, drive fork-lift trucks or sell shoes?

Hey, maybe I could find Mum a job selling shoes? Even she could do that. The hours would be better, she might get some decent footwear and maybe even learn English. How amazing would it be, if I could communicate with her like I can with Auntie?

Wednesday 18th June

Went to Grandparents' after dinner to get our wedding invites off Auntie, and Smiffy was coming out the door. I reckoned he must have been to see Simon.

'All right?' I said.

'Mint,' he said, looking pleased with himself.

'What's up?' I asked.

'Check out this bad boy!' he said, pointing to the silver stud in his ear.

He'd had his ear pierced by Auntie Yip's fingernails!

Smiffy is rock-hard.

Saturday 21st June

Mum asked me and Bonny if we wanted to learn Chinese. 'Then you can be more like Jill and Katy and have a proper conversation with your mother,' she said.

I wish she would stop comparing us to Poshos. They weren't dragged up like us for a start. Their parents actually bothered to speak to them when they were little – when you're *meant* to learn languages. Doing it now would be like getting to grips with a bassoon concerto, and I'm not even sure what a bassoon is . . . or a concerto.

Auntie must have put her up to it and I appreciate the thought, but the time for learning Chinese has way, way gone. Anyway, I don't want to be any more Chinese than

I already am cos it's the Chinese part of me that I've been bullied for all my life.

'No thanks,' I said to Mum.

'Hmph, useless daughter,' she tutted back. 'What about you, Ling Ling?'

Bonny looked up with a scowl on her face.

'I'd rather stick my head in a wasp's nest,' she said.

Sunday 22nd June

Mum was down about Auntie leaving, plus I felt bad about not wanting to learn Chinese, so on the way back from Poshos', me and Bonny bought her a deep-fried pizza from the chippy and a Mother's Day card from Banga's. OK, so Mother's Day was months ago, but Banga's was flogging old stock cheap and anyway Mum thinks the world is flat and held up by elephants, so it makes no difference to her. We settled for a card with a pink teddy bear on holding three balloons that spelled out M-U-M.

'Happy Mother's Day,' we said, handing it to her. She stopped scrubbing the hob to open the card. Recognising the letters on the front, she smiled and said in English, 'Ahhh "Mum", yeah "Mum" is me. Fenk you,' and placed the card on the cleanest patch on the shelf. It's funny how Mum keeps banging on about us learning Chinese, yet her English is bloody dire! Anyhow, I think we cheered her up, but it was hard to tell.

Monday 23rd June

While waiting to go into science, I decided to tell Tina about the butcher's going bankrupt cos of Dad's gambling.

'... And that's how we ended up in the crappy takeaway,' I said.

'Serious?' said Tina. 'Does he still gamble?'

'No,' I replied, remembering what Mum had said to Auntie.

'Good,' said Tina.

'Yeah, good,' I replied, more as a reassurance to myself.

Tina glanced over her shoulder, then back at me.

'Hey, I've got something to tell you too,' she said in hushed tones.

'What?'

'You will absolutely die when I tell you.'

'*What*?' I said.

'It's just something I heard,' she whispered.

I stared blankly at her.

'You don't know, do you?'

'Well I will when you *tell* me,' I said.

'It's Warren. There's a rumour going round that he might be . . . *gay*.'

'WHAT?!'

Everyone stared at us.

'Keep it down,' hushed Tina.

'That's stupid!' I hissed.

'That's what I've heard.' Tina could hardly contain her mirth.

I could understand her enjoying this, seeing as I'd stolen Warren from her, but she could have dialled it down a BIT.

'Who said?' I asked.

'Penny told Lizzy who told Helen who told me.'

Hmph, so it MUST be true then.

Tuesday 24th June

Can't believe what Tina told me about Warren! I mean, he seems just like any other bloke to me. Mind you, I've never met anyone gay in real life before. I know Boy George is, cos anyone can tell a mile off (except for Mrs Burke who calls him 'That lovely lass what sang about chameleons'.) And Warren is not at all camp, like the guys in Spandau Ballet or Duran Duran (even though they are not gay).

But when I thought about it, I realised there were a few clues I should have picked up on, such as:

1) The love poem he gave me was written in *pink* biro
2) He chose a *Madonna* film for our first date
3) He didn't try to snog me once the whole time we were seeing each other, or even hold hands for that matter!

OK, now I was speculating and being just as bad as the gossipmongers who had started this rumour in the first place. What if it were true though? Was he worried about catching AIDS? The ads on telly say you can DIE from it if you're not careful! Oh god, now I'm being ridiculous! And why would he have gone out with me at all, if he was gay? As a cover maybe, to stop people suspecting?

Just thought, that Tony I saw Warren with in WHSmith might have been his boyfriend! Anyway, hope they leave him alone, rumours or not. Bullies can be merciless.

Got grief from Julie and Sam all day at school. It was bad enough when I got straight-off dumped, but now it was: 'Hey, Kwan, we heard you turned Warren queer!'

At break, Tina came over with Goth Gaz and asked if I wanted to hang around with them; then Jill and Sunita came over and said the same. I was grateful, but they were only doing it cos they felt sorry for me. I was fine feeling sorry on my own in the art room, where I drew a self portrait with Kevin Keegan calves. Is that why he went out with me, cos I was the closest thing to a bloke without actually going out with one? Maybe he didn't even know he was gay when he asked me out? He's probably not even gay at all! I AM SO CONFUSED.

Thursday 26th June

OH MY GOD OF ALL GODS. As if my head isn't already in tatters.

Beansprout Man came in today and I heard him say to Mum, 'How far along are you, Mrs Kwan? It's hard to tell with them overalls on. Four months, is it?'

'Nearly five months,' said Mum. Then she laughed uncomfortably and busied herself putting the beansprouts away.

NO WAY!

Mum is *PREGGERS* (humongous UR)!! How come I never noticed? How come Mum hadn't told us?

That means . . . that means . . . Mum and Dad *DID IT*! The whole idea is utterly and incomprehensibly gross. Mum and Dad hardly talk to each other, never mind touch each other. And when would they have found the time?

MUM IS PREGGERS!!

OVERALL HID BUMP FOR 4 MONTHS!

GAMMY NAILS FROM YEARS OF DEEP FAT FRYING

'LUCKY' JADE BRACELET

I can't think about it . . . I CAN'T! This must have been what Mum and Auntie were joking about together, when they said Dad won't have much time left to have fun. But it's not funny. There will be a ten-year gap between the baby and Bonny, and a seventeen-year gap with Simon. That is ridiculous. And also, how the flip are they meant to look after a baby? They barely have time for work and sleep, never mind their kids.

When Beansprout Man left, I got straight to it.

'Are you having a baby?' I asked Mum accusingly.

She looked embarrassed (talking personal things makes us queasy) and replied, 'Yes, it's due in November.'

I stomped upstairs and told Bonny.

'WHAT?!' she shrieked. 'That means Mum and Dad *DID IT!*'

'That's exactly what I thought,' I said, grimacing.

I couldn't bear to look at Dad all evening. The one time I did, he looked more cheerful than ever with his annoying sparrow chirping away on his shoulder.

I called Tina with the outrageous news and all she could say was, 'Oh, I luuurvve babies!' That's cos all she goes on about these days is having one with Goth Gaz. Doesn't she care how much madder having a baby would make my already mad madhouse?!!

Saturday 28th June

Bonny announced at Poshos' that we were expecting a baby brother or sister, and Auntie and Uncle nearly choked on their salmon baps.

'Your mum . . . having a *baby*?' said Auntie, gobsmacked.

'Awww, it'll be ace,' said Jill.

I wish she would stop saying everything is ace, cos EVERYTHING IS NOT ACE! And I knew she was being extra smarmy cos of the gay rumours about Warren.

'Yeah, yeah it will,' I answered, forcing a smile.

'Not sure how Mum's gonna look after it though,' said Bonny. 'She can hardly take care of us.'

I did the usual and kicked her under the table.

'Well, I'm sure it'll be fine,' said Auntie. 'You and Joanna' (I hate that name) 'will enjoy having a new baby in the family, they're such fun.'

Fun?

Yeah, so were the gormless goats, and the dumb dog, until they weren't, then they got conveniently sent away to the sheep farm. You can't do that with a baby if it starts malfunctioning.

Saturday 5th July

Sat in launderette watching everyone's pants go round and round, thinking how pants a new baby was going to be for ME. Cos let's face it, no one else was going to look after it were they?

Haven't even had a chance to sort my portfolio for *Mizz*, what with all the palaver going on. Everything around me was turning to excrement.

Was already feeling sorry for myself, walking back from the launderette, when the whinge-bag lads from school shouted, 'Oi, gay shagger!' at me, from across the street. Great.

I ignored them and kept walking. When I didn't take the bait, they had another go at me. 'Chinese girls are up for anything,' said one to the other loudly. Then they both laughed. What did they mean? I'd never heard that before. Nothing was ever mentioned in *Mizz* about it. I walked faster, then they crossed over to my side. Crap.

I could hear their footsteps. It didn't feel safe. I'm not sure even Tina would have had a back-up plan for this. Wish I'd stuck at kung fu. I almost got to the front door when the big one came over, pushed me and made me drop my bag of clothes everywhere. Then he stood back waiting for me to crouch down to pick them up. I was dead meat.

'Hey, Jo, you all right?'

The bullies turned.

It was Smiffy!

He came charging out of nowhere and punched the big one straight in the eye – WHOOMPH!

Down he went like a sack of spuds. The little one didn't even stop to help him. We watched them scarper, one running, the other stumbling, holding his face.

'You OK?' Smiffy asked again, brushing himself down.

'Yeah . . . thanks,' I said, shocked.

'Mint,' he said and strutted off, all full of himself.

I stuffed the clothes back in the bag, ran into the shop, locked the door and shut my eyes. That was CLOSE! If they were picking on me like that for the gay rumours, I wonder what kind of torment Warren must be getting? I hope he's OK.

Will I ever be able to walk the streets on my own again? I will while Smiffy's around. When people hear about what he did to those morons, no one will bother me.

Sunday 6th July

Told Simon about Smiffy smacking the bully. He said he knew and was glad, 'Cos they deserve to have severe amounts of pain inflicted on them or even better, death.' He hates bullying more than I do. Wonder if he got it at school? Nah . . . not if he was best mates with Smiffy. He was probably referring to Dad. He got totally bullied by Dad. Like we all did, and still do.

I sensed his simmering rage, so I changed the subject. 'Bet you don't know this though,' I said, raising my eyebrows in suspense.

'What?' said Simon grumpily.

'Mum's having a BABY.'

'Sod off!' he said, making a disgusted face.

'Yep. God's honest truth.'

'That's dumb, where they gonna put it?'

I shrugged. 'I dunno, in the goat shed?'

Simon didn't laugh.

'They're idiots. Don't they think before doing anything?' he scowled.

'What do you mean?'

'That kid'll end up just like us.'

I hadn't thought that far ahead, but put that way Simon was right. What is the point of bringing a child into this world just so it can have the crappest experience imaginable?

'How can they have another kid when they don't care about us? They're not bothered if we do well in school or not, or what our plans are for the future. All they care about is their stupid takeaway.'

True. We've been disappointed by them ever since the infants, when everyone else's parents went to school plays, fairs and parents' evenings. It was as if we never had parents at all. And now there is another Kwan on the way about to go through the same misfortune.

Friday 11th July

Simon was round for dinner tonight. Halfway through, Mum turned to him and said in Chinese: 'You know I'm having a baby?'

'Yeah,' Simon grunted, uncomfortably.

'And the takeaway's getting busy . . .' Mum continued.

Simon didn't look up, he was suspicious. I could tell he knew she was going ask him for something – most likely to help out in the takeaway. The thought of it makes him feel sicker than it makes me. He is dead set on getting a normal Western job like I am.

'Well,' Mum went on, 'it'd be great if you could start helping out occasionally.'

Eeek. She'd said it. Me and Bonny squirmed. Simon looked on the brink of an outburst.

'We'd pay you,' said Mum in a lighter tone, hoping that would change his mind.

More silence. Then . . .

'I've just finished my exams. Gimme a break!' Simon hissed. I think the comment Mum made ages ago about him being able to buy clothes instead of stealing them was also on his mind.

'Can't you spare a few hours a week?' Mum went on, a bit more irritated this time.

Me and Bonny glanced at each other, willing it to stop.

'No!' he snapped.

Then Dad intervened. He scraped back his chair and stood up.

'You do what we tell you!'

Simon was stony-faced. He slammed down his bowl, spraying rice everywhere, and stood up too. He was taller than Dad. He was seventeen and not the defenceless little kid that got sent away any more. 'I said, NO!' he boomed.

I knew this could explode into something much, much worse. We all did, we'd all been there before, in the wrong place at the wrong time, when Dad was in destructive-mode.

'Don't be silly, sit down!' Mum said, flapping her hands at them both.

Simon glowered and left. Then Bonny ran away to Mandy's. Mum mumbled sadly, 'What kind of kids have I raised?' and went to serve a customer who'd just wandered in, while Dad went to switch the extractor fan on, swearing under his breath.

I trembled as I washed the chopsticks later. While Dad was in the loo, I asked Mum why they couldn't have done something other than run a Chinese takeaway.

'I don't know how to do anything else,' she answered feebly.

'Dad's clever, he could have,' I said.

She ignored that, thought for a moment and replied simply, 'When we're dead, the takeaway's yours.'

'I *don't want* the takeaway,' I answered, offended.

'Well then you can marry David Wong from Wong's Garden and inherit his parents' takeaway.'

'You were forced to marry Dad and look what happened to you!' I wanted to scream, but I couldn't cos:

1) It would have been well cruel
2) I didn't know how to say it in Chinese (story of my life)

Why are they always forcing us to do stuff anyway? And why do they think the only future for us is in a Chinese takeaway?

I have come upstairs to be on my own. I swore I wasn't going to put the crap bits of my life in this diary, but I am SO angry and I need to get it out my system!

Sunday 13th July

The last two days have been utterly dire. Dad was already furious about Simon, and now Sparrow has flown away!!! It hopped off his shoulder while he was frying rice and disappeared out the back door. It probably couldn't stand the tense atmosphere any more and I don't blame it. Dad has been smashing the wok and not uttering a single word apart from to swear every now and again, with a face that says 'Cross me and you die!' Me, Bonny and Grandparents have been on edge all day. I am sure my blood pressure is off the scale.

Wish I really was a yenzi – I could fly away right now.

Tuesday 15th July

The hygiene inspector came round without warning! The veins in Dad's temples were almost bursting and Mum was looking nervous. The inspector said he was 'acting on concerns raised by customers'. I knew putting an article in the paper telling everyone there was a bird flapping around our kitchen was a bad idea. Thank god it buggered off in time, that's all I can say.

The inspector checked inside the fridges, freezers and around the hob, while writing things on his clipboard with a serious expression. After half an hour, he told us he would be in contact to let us know what course of action to take and left.

Bonny came downstairs a minute later and said, 'Was that the hygiene man?'

'Yeah why?' I said.

'Cos I left my mud foot scrub in one of the salad drawers.'

Great. If Dad gets closed down cos of that, he really will blow his flippin' top. We need to rally round to keep Dad's anger in check at the moment cos it's very likely to explode.

When I started this diary, it was supposed to be for putting GOOD stuff in, but I am now finally facing the fact that GOOD stuff doesn't exist. This is my lot, like it or not, and now it's time to own up. So here goes . . .

Up till now I haven't been honest. All the worst bits about Dad have been left out on purpose, to make my life sound better than it actually is. But who am I kidding? It's only me that reads this bloody thing anyway! So from now on I've decided EVERYTHING goes in – even the gruesome stuff. Then hopefully one day, I will look back and congratulate myself for getting through this mess.

Friday 18th July

Grandad's got gout (UR)! I thought only eighteenth-century aristocrats who drank too much sherry got gout?

GOUT

It means he can't come in to help, so Mum asked if I could do his jobs while he recovers. Ugh, I'm already doing Grandma's mopping and now I have to prepare food as well. I know I'm getting paid, but personally I would rather not work at all and wear bread bags for shoes.

Mum is probably asking me cos Simon nearly bit her head off when she approached him. Why can't Bonny do it? Surely even she can swish a mop back and forth? I decided not to argue in the end, cos of how Dad is right now, but I will make a note to go to the school library to find a cure for Grandad's gout. I can't be doing his chores forever, I have other important matters to attend to. Summer holidays are almost here and I need to fill my portfolio, so I can become a fashion designer and get out of this flippin' place!

Saturday 19th July

One of my new chores is onions! They are TORTURE. I have to peel and slice five, and peel and chop five more into cubes. Mum insisted on me using the meat cleaver I nearly chopped my finger off with (UR), and the whole thing was made more treacherous due to the stinging tears blinding my eyes.

Later, Bonny asked why my eyes were all watery and I couldn't answer as I wasn't sure if it was the onions, or if I was crying cos I completely hate my life right now.

Must find cure for Grandad's gout.

Monday 21st July

Went to library. There was nothing in any of the medical encyclopedias that referenced gout. The closest thing I could find was 'swollen foot', which requires an ice pack to reduce inflammation, so I went to Banga's and bought a bag of Birds Eye garden peas. I will put in freezer and take it to Grandad's soon.

Also the maggots are back! Flippin' typical after Sparrow has just flown off. It could have been useful for once instead of just perching on Dad's shoulder like some kind of stupid novelty epaulette. I spent a resentful twenty minutes pouring kettles of boiling water over maggots, when I could have been doing something useful, like honing my skills as a fashion designer, to ensure a maggot-free future.

Friday 25th July

Summer holidays start today.

    Pros: No more homework, or hiding from bullies

    Cons: Am now child slave

Lately, cos Tina's not around much, I think about Yoko Ono whenever things get crap. She appears in a flowing white gown and smiles down on me like Jesus . . . but female . . . and oriental. Is it a message to say everything will be OK? Whatever it is, it's quite comforting.

Mum has just given me thirty quid for a week's work! Everything WILL be OK, thanks, Yoko! If I grin and bear it for long enough, I won't even need a job after school. I will just buy a smallish, second-hand canal barge and retire.

Saturday 26th July

Started another new chore, which involves chopping four cartons of mushrooms. Two into slices and two into chunks, like the onions. Why can't it be one or the other (UR)? I mean, realistically, what drunken bum is going to lodge a complaint about whether their mushrooms are sliced or chunked? As far as they're concerned, it all goes down the same hole. Still, I can't make a fuss as Dad's still in a dodgy mood.

I reminded Mum to make char siu for Grandparents so I could take it over to them this weekend. Not out of the kindness of my own heart, but so I can go over and see if there's any remote chance they can return to work. I gave Grandad the peas for his gout, but he didn't want them and passed the bag to Grandma, who sprinkled them on the flower bed. Nope. They're not fit for work.

At six o'clock, Simon walked into the shop and straight into the kitchen.

'Oh, you've just missed dinner,' I said.

He glared at Mum and Dad, who were shovelling water chestnuts into tubs.

'I'm working, ain't I?'

'What?' I said.

'I'm working Friday and Saturday nights now.'

'Why?'

'Cos Grandad told me to.'

Oh bloody hell, if Simon's caved in, there's no hope for any of us now. Although he only probably agreed cos he respects Grandad, who is like his surrogate dad really. Even if we did get the occasional hiding off him at least he was fair – unlike Dad. I reckon Mum must have spoken to Grandma, she must have spoken to Grandad, who then had a word with Simon.

As soon as the shop opened, Simon was thrown in at the deep end. I knew what that was like. It was worse for him though cos as well as learning how to cook on the job, he also had to decipher Mum's scrawly Chinese characters.

Dad and Simon never said a word to each other all night, even though they had to stand next to each other at the woks. They were smashing them about quite a lot, as if they were having a slanging match in wok language.

After my chores, I went upstairs to go through my portfolio. I desperately need to get the damn thing done! As I was working out how many more pictures I needed, it suddenly seemed insignificant compared to all the other things going on in my life. I couldn't concentrate for feeling guilty about Simon working, while I had escaped upstairs. So I pushed it back under the bed to collect more dust.

Saturday 2nd August

Ugh GROSS! Now I have to do prawns!

Was Grandad really made to do all this? Surely it's a violation of human rights? Dad wasn't about, so I dared to say no to Mum. But she pleaded and rubbed her swollen belly. I have been made to feel guilty a lot lately.

In the end I agreed, but she hadn't told me there were over a hundred of them! Halfway through prising off their shells, my hands started to itch, then the brine made the itching sting like hell. I didn't think it could get worse than the onions, but I was wrong. I tried to think of Yoko, but I couldn't focus. Shame the prawns were already decapitated, I would love to have ripped their stinking heads off and stamped on them for good measure. Oh god, I am turning into Dad!

When I finished, Mum said, 'Now gut them.'

WHAA? She never mentioned scraping their disgusting stringy innards out!

Mum demonstrated, then it was my turn.

PRAWNS!!!

1. GET STINKY PRAWN

SHARP STINGY BIT THAT CUTS YOUR HAND

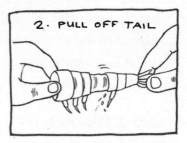

2. PULL OFF TAIL

3. PRISE OFF REST OF SHELL

4. SLICE ALONG SPINE

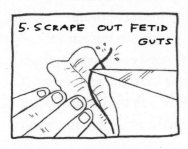

5. SCRAPE OUT FETID GUTS

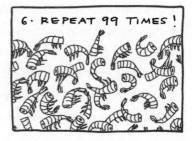

6. REPEAT 99 TIMES!

I tried not to vomit while I breathed in the vile stench. I really wanted to walk out and never come back. How can a person be made to do this against their will? Then I thought about Mum – that's her life all over. I couldn't just bugger off. Like it or not, I am stuck.

Bonny got in at eleven. She had been at Mandy's all night. (Wish *I* could still come and go as I pleased.) I showed her my rashy hands and she told me to put TCP on. I went to find the first-aid kit, before remembering we don't have one. I am NOT resorting to soya sauce.

Tuesday 12th August

OH. MY. GOD. Kev came in and dragged Dad off to snooker, leaving me and six-months-up-the-duff Mum on our own – and this time there was no Auntie Yip to save us! Given the choice, I would have preferred Dad in the takeaway with his godawful mood than me and Mum being left on our own. I crapped my pants cos if Dad wasn't there, who would do the cooking?

'You'll have to serve while I cook,' said Mum.

'No way!' I said.

I would rather have stuck my hand in the deep fat fryer than face the public. 'I'll cook, *you* serve.'

Then I realised I didn't know how to cook and if I didn't serve either, it meant Mum would have to run the whole shop on her own. UGHHHHH. She looked so waddly and helpless and desperate. Ever since I discovered she was second best, I felt I needed to be nicer to her. 'Oh, OK,' I grumbled, but felt sick to the stomach.

When I complained about Dad slipping off, Mum said, 'Let him have his fun,' and I remembered what she'd said to Auntie Yip again, about him not being able to have any after the baby was born. But what about Mum's fun? Or mine, for that matter. She only sticks up for him cos of the whole second-best thing.

I stood behind the counter, heart thumping. I could just about see over the top. I hadn't a clue what I was doing. I didn't know what was on the menu, how much everything was, what to write on the pad, or which buttons to press on the till to make it add up. Anyway, I couldn't stand there flapping, I just had to get on with it.

The first customers came in five minutes later.

Crap.

It was the Barnsley twins from the fifth year at school. I didn't know them that well but they recognised me. I hope they don't tell anyone they saw me. The last thing I need is another excuse to get bullied. They asked for two chicken curries with fried rice, which I was relieved about cos it was simple. I abbreviated it to 'CHK curry (FR)', to make it easy for me to write and Mum to understand. There were only three customers while Dad was gone and they were all easy, thankfully.

I only have myself to blame about the snooker, cos it was me who told Dad about it in the first place. Wish I'd kept my flippin' mouth shut. It was supposed to improve his mood, but when he got back he was in a worse mood than when he left (UR)!

Sunday 17th August

10.36 am: Was woken up last night by Mum and Dad arguing at closing time. It sounded like Dad was looking for something and was blaming me and Bonny for losing it. Then the shouting stopped and I heard footsteps coming up the stairs. The bedroom door burst open and Dad marched in. I held my breath.

'WHERE IS IT?!' he shouted at me.

'Where's what?!' I whimpered.

I could tell he was on the verge of one of his attacks.

Bonny woke up looking confused.

'MY ACCOUNTS BOOK!'

'I don't know what you're talking about,' I said. I didn't. I didn't even know what one was. I tensed up, ready for what was coming. He loomed over me, grabbed my hair and pulled me out of bed. The pain seared through my scalp.

'HOW MANY TIMES HAVE I TOLD YOU NOT TO TOUCH MY STUFF!?' he said, punching me in the back. I opened my mouth but no words came out, cos of the shock. When he realised I didn't know about his stupid book after all, he left and went downstairs.

I was shaking.

'Are you OK?' whispered Bonny, from under her duvet.

'Yeah,' I replied, crawling back into bed. But I wasn't. I just didn't want her to be as petrified as I was right then.

IS IT SAFE TO COME OUT YET?

BONNY   HEDGEHOG

Of course Bonny's seen it all before. She's been at the receiving end of Dad's violent outbursts, along with the rest of us. I don't think she remembers the worst time though.

That was back at the Golden Empire when she was only two. I walked in and found Dad booting her down the aisle to the kitchen. She was rolled up like a hedgehog and Mum was screaming at him to stop. It was shocking to see such a tiny little body being kicked like a football. I wondered what she could possibly have done to deserve it?! No one saw me, so I ran upstairs and hid in the stock room till dark.

The next day she seemed right as rain, playing with her toys as if nothing had happened. How is a two-year-old supposed to react to that anyway?

Why are people so cruel?

Mum came up soon after. I was pretty sore, so I thought she was checking to see if I was OK, but instead she said, 'Well . . . did you take your dad's accounts book? Because if you did, you'd better put it back right now.'

I was already angry, but that made me want to explode with rage.

This morning I woke up with a wheezy chest. Think I have a cold coming on. Great.

Bonny felt sorry for me and invited me over to Mandy's, but I said the passive smoking would probably make my wheezing worse.

I have a purple bruise on my shoulder. What is wrong with Dad? Shouldn't he be more caring now a baby is coming along? Is he still sad about Sparrow, or mad about Simon? But if so, why did he take it out on me? I mean, I was the one who helped Mum run the shop while he went off to play snooker. What more does he want, the stupid sod?

He hasn't had a go at me like that since Hull. I hoped it wouldn't happen again, but it has.

I am sick of being on hyper alert and being caught off guard, like I was last night. Although in a twisted kind of way, actually getting beaten up is better than the torturous, drawn-out threat of it. It is so tiring.

Called Tina, but her mum picked up and told me she was out with Gaz.

Tuesday 26th August

Dad went to snooker, and to be honest I was glad he wasn't around.

Mum told me what a good job I was doing serving, then asked if I could do Friday and Saturday nights till closing, same as Simon. She didn't even ask how I was after Dad hit me. Why didn't Mum help me that night? Maybe she is more scared of him than we are. I don't feel like her daughter, just some kind of handy skivvy she happened to give birth to.

'No,' I said, using Simon's approach. 'Get someone else to do it!'

'No, you have to!'

'Why?' My chest felt tight.

'You're my most well-behaved child. You'll be good and help us, won't you?' And she patted her belly again.

Thing is, I knew she was trying to manipulate me, but she didn't have a choice. There was no one else she could turn to right now. Yes, I was hard done by, but she was stuck in the kitchen all day, every day, with a baby on the way and a husband who walked all over her.

'Oh *all right*,' I replied through clenched teeth. But what could I do?

Later, Simon came over to drop off a bag of home-grown cabbages from Grandparents and saw me standing behind the counter.

'What you doing there?'

'Dad's at snooker and I have to serve till he gets back.'

'*What?* Just say no!' he snapped.

'*You* didn't!' I retorted.

'Yeah, but you're just letting Dad bugger off whenever he likes!'

'Well what am I supposed to do?'

'Tell him where to go!' said Simon.

I got upset when he said that cos he didn't understand:

1) How hard it was for a fifteen-year-old girl to stand up to an abusive dad

2) That living in the takeaway meant I couldn't escape like him, back to the safety of his own room three streets away. There was nowhere for me to hide.

'Actually,' I said, 'Dad hit me the other week, so I don't really want to go winding him up right now.'

'What ... he *hit* you?' said Simon, his face darkening.

'Yeah,' I replied, wishing I hadn't brought it up, cos it was starting to make me angry too.

There was a pause, then he slammed the bag of cabbages

down on the counter. I stepped back and he said, 'You know why I went to live with our grandparents?'

My heart stopped.

Simon was about to reveal the biggest UR in my ENTIRE life.

'No.' The word came out slowly. I wasn't sure I wanted to know.

'So that he didn't kill me,' he replied, with a menacing stare.

I was shocked.

'Wh— why would he do that?'

It must have been bad if he'd kept it quiet all this time.

Then he told me the story.

'I'd bought some Silly Putty from the toy shop and shoved a whole load down the bog at the restaurant. I dunno why, I was just being a stupid kid. It ended up blocking the bog and it flooded the toilets just before opening time. Dad went mental. He dragged me out into the car park, swearing and shouting. Then he picked me up and hoisted me over his head. Grandad and Grandma and Mum were there, screaming at him to stop, but he was like possessed or something. I thought he was going to throw me down and smash my head open. But you know what he did instead?' he said furiously.

My mind boggled, what could be more horrific than that?

'What?'

'He ran over to the nettles on the other side of the car park and chucked me straight in them.'

'What?' I gasped. 'Those nettles were taller than us!'

Simon carried on, his voice breaking a bit this time.

'I was hysterical, thinking I was never going to get out, cos every time I moved it stung like hell, on my hands, my face, everywhere. Thought I was going to die.'

Poor Simon, I couldn't imagine the pain.

'Grandad had to pull me out in the end. I was in agony for ages after.'

I could see in his eyes he was imagining himself back there. I've never seen him like that, he's always so confident about himself.

It took a moment to sink in, and eventually I said, 'Oh my god, Dad's such a bastard. How could anyone do that to a *kid*?' Knowing that he'd done something similar to me and Bonny in the past. I was on the verge of telling Simon our stories, so he didn't have to suffer on his own. But now wasn't the time. It would have just made him even angrier.

Thursday 28th August

Is horrible being in the same room as Dad, especially after hearing what he'd done to Simon, so I've taken to leaving the room if he's in it, which is quite difficult when you have so few rooms and are forced to work with each other.

Gaz is on holiday so I went to meet Tina in town, even though this chest infection or whatever it is made me feel like staying in bed. I didn't tell her about Dad hitting me. I did tell her about having to work though.

'That's bull crap,' she said. 'And probably illegal.'

'Do you reckon?'

'Yeah. Why don't you call ChildLine?' she suggested.

'What's that?'

'It's a thing set up for kids with problems who don't know who else to talk to. They might know your rights. My mum told me about it once. Why don't you speak to her?'

I know Tina's mum is a social worker, but it's kind of embarrassing having people know about your business when you don't want them to. 'Yeah maybe, thanks,' I said.

259

Afterwards, I asked Bonny if she'd heard of ChildLine. Surprisingly she already knew quite a lot about it from Mandy. Apparently you can call anonymously. I need to talk to someone. But what about the trouble if Dad found out, and the grief that Mum and I would get? It's not worth it. This is truly the biggest drag ever and I honestly feel like throwing myself under the first bus that comes along.

Friday 29th August

Was good hanging out with Tina yesterday. We had a laugh, it made me forget about all the crap in my life, and I was almost back to my old self again. Shame I hardly see her any more.

Felt better so I went to town to buy outfit for Auntie Yip's wedding with some of my wages. I got a blue blouse, baggy grey trousers and a plum scarf to go over one shoulder, Spandau Ballet-style (I will be best-dressed child slave in town). Auntie's wedding is this Sunday. Can't wait!

Worked till closing for the first time tonight. Not easy. It got so busy at pub chucking-out time, Mum had to help me sort out all the drunks. God knows how she manages, when even I can't understand half of what they're slurring.

It's nearly end of summer holidays and I have managed to do sod all on my portfolio. Will I ever make it out of here? (Sob.)

Saturday 30th August

Mum is paying me double for weekends. That's no consolation, it just makes it feel permanent! Also, Dad has built a wooden platform for me to stand on so I can see over the counter better. He thinks I'll be here forever as well. *Think again, Dad!*

At least I have got used to serving now. Most customers are OK, but you do get the odd fruitcake. Tonight a man walked in with a neck brace and a bright orange fake hand. I noticed he had a left hand on his right wrist, so effectively he had two left hands.

'What do you recommend?' he asked.

I wanted to say a right hand on his right wrist but instead I said, 'Special chow mein.'

'That's them wormy things innit?' he said, making a face.

'Noodles,' I said, correcting him.

'I'm not having them, they bung you up!' he said, as if I was the nutter!

'Well don't flippin' have them then, you freak!' I wanted to say, but didn't cos I know my boundaries, unlike freak man. Honestly, sometimes I think I'm just a sitting target for every racist remark going. It's especially hard to avoid when you're standing behind a Chinese takeaway counter.

I told Bonny about him later and it turns out he's Mandy's mum's boyfriend. That says it all.

Sunday 31st August

Went to Auntie Yip's wedding today. Was feeling better about everything, so did my hair and make-up properly for first time in ages.

The party took place in a Chinese restaurant in Birmingham next to the Bull Ring shopping centre. It was the kind of restaurant that only Chinese people go to, cos it specialises in delicacies such as tripe, intestines and that perennial favourite, chicken's feet.

The room was decorated with red tablecloths and carnations and Auntie wore a traditional red cheongsam, just like Mum did at her wedding. I wonder if Auntie's marriage was arranged too? She looked genuinely happy . . . so maybe not.

It was weird seeing her husband for the first time. He was tall for a Chinese man, about five feet nine. He came over and said hello. I was surprised to find his English was really good, just like Auntie's. They will do well in life, like the Poshos. And not like some other people who can't even go to the grocer's and ask for a pound of apples after living in England for twenty years, naming no names.

David Wong and his parents were there. Luckily they were sat at the far end and I had strategically positioned myself behind a floral arrangement so they couldn't see me. David had done something strange to his hair. It was parted far too low down on one side and looked greasier than normal. His skin had suffered a recent breakout of acne and he was wearing a big black bow tie. Ugh – I had a horrible thought that if my portfolio idea didn't work out, I might have to end up marrying David after all, just to get away from my miserable life in the takeaway. But then figured I would just end up being miserable in *his* takeaway, so I pinched myself and swore I would never do that.

Everyone looked like they were having the best times of their lives. Bonny was with Katy, helping themselves to juice and nibbles, and Jill was chatting and laughing to some adults in Cantonese. Wished I could have joined in, but how could I when I don't know how to have a conversation, never mind understand all the traditional stuff going on?

There were other kids around the same age as me dotted about with their parents, looking normal. Why couldn't we be like that? Then it struck me. At school I was different for being Chinese . . . but I was also different here, among the Chinese community, for having a dysfunctional family. I was doubly different.

I studied the framed silk tapestries on the wall, trying to look like I had a purpose (like I do at school break times), when really I was just dying of shame inside.

Uncle Han turned up with his new fiancée, who'd flown over from Hong Kong. She spoke less English than Mum, so she's trapped in a prison of non-Englishness, like her. If either of them ever ended up at an English wedding they'd feel exactly as I do right now. Like an alien.

Everyone commented on Mum's massive belly. She wasn't wearing her normal baggy overalls, so it was really obvious. And all the blokes congratulated Dad. (What, on impregnating her??? Yeah, well done, Dad.)

We left the party just before the best bit, when the bride and groom go round to each table and collect 'fung-bao' (lucky red packets of money). Of course we did. We had to go back and open the flippin' shop.

Called Tina and told her about the horrible thought I'd had about David Wong. She told me to 'Breathe deeply and repeat after me: Wong is wrong, Wong is wrong . . .'

So from now on, whenever I weaken, that will be my mantra.

Wednesday 3rd September

First day back at school – UGH!

Fifth and final year – YESSSS!

This is now my list of chores – UGH!

1) Mop floor
2) Peel and chop onions
3) Chop mushrooms
4) Peel and gut prawns
5) Clean counter and arcade machines
6) Get all food out the fridges
7) Serve customers

Please get well soon, Grandma and Grandad!

Thursday 4th September

Knew it wouldn't be long before Julie and Sam staked me out. In between lessons, they cornered me and said they'd seen me serving in the 'Chinky'. At first I thought the Barnsley twins must have told them, but then figured it would be hard for anyone to miss me cos our shop window is so massive I might as well be standing in the street with a sandwich board on saying '*Look at me, everyone!*'

'So?' I said, trying my best to act unconcerned. I knew I had to start fighting my own battles at some point, even though I was withering inside. It was daft to hope Tina and

Smiffy could materialise like guardian angels every time I was in trouble.

'So can you get us some free grub then?' said Julie, chewing gum like Mandy does, all sloppy and open-mouthed.

'No,' I replied.

'We'll put a brick through if you don't,' said Sam, her face looming close.

WE'LL PUT A BRICK THROUGH!

CHEWING ALL OPEN-MOUTHED

Just then, I heard, 'Is this a party? Am I invited?'

It was Warren!

'Oh hi, Warren,' said Julie, nervously. 'We were just asking Jo about ... you know, about ...'

' ... That new Studio Line hair mousse,' said Sam innocently.

'Oh, I use that, it's great!' said Warren.

Could he be gay? I thought. Hard to tell when every boy uses mousse right now.

'You got it in now?' asked Julie, completely forgetting she was there to make my life hell.

'Yeah, feel,' he said, bending down so they could touch his exquisitely sculpted fringe.

I stared at them dumbfounded as they giggled away. Idiots.

The bell went so Julie and Sam said goodbye to Warren.

'Never mind those bimbos,' Warren said to me.

'Thanks,' I replied, dying of embarrassment.

He touched me on the arm. I felt a tingle. Did I still love him? I certainly could have done with a hug.

'Any time,' he said, smiling warmly.

Oh Warren, Warren, Warren. We were so close to herding goats together in South Africa. Why did you have to go and leave me? Even if you are gay, you were the closest thing to love I have ever known.

Monday 22nd September

Came home from school and Mum wasn't there. I thought for a horrible moment that Dad had sent her to the sheep farm with all the other rejects. Instead Grandma was back helping in the kitchen. 'Where's Mum?' I asked.

'In hospital,' said Bonny.

'What for?'

'She's having a baby, you plum!'

'But it's not due yet,' I said, slightly manically. I felt my chest tighten and the wheezing started again. Wish this infection would just sod off. We hadn't prepared for this. Who would fry the pork balls, roast the char siu, order the beansprouts, etc? Not me! Had Mum left notes? I felt panic rise at the thought of running the shop with angry Dad and dippy old Grandma.

'When is she back?' I asked Bonny.

'I dunno do I?' she replied defensively.

This situation was just as unnerving for her as it was for us lot that had to work in the takeaway. She's used to Mum being around too, holding things together.

'Do you reckon the baby will be OK?' I said, still jittery. 'I mean, it wasn't meant to happen till November.'

'I'm not an expert, ask Dad!' she said, and marched off upstairs.

I guess Bonny was the worst person to ask. She is only ten and her expert subjects are a) Fags b) Make-up and c) Ra-ra skirts. I couldn't ask Grandma cos I knew I'd muddle my Chinese. And I didn't want to ask Dad, but there was no one else I *could* ask. He was frying rice at the far end of the kitchen. I shouted over to him, 'When's Mum back?'

Dad replied without looking up or smiling, 'Er . . . maybe few days.' He didn't sound sure and seemed just as nervous as me about Mum not being here. After all, she is the backbone of The Happy Gathering.

I know it's bad but I was more scared about Mum not running the shop than I was of the baby being premature.

Why couldn't we just shut for a few days?

'Well don't just stand there, peel the bloody prawns!' Grandma ordered.

Phew! Thank god someone's taking responsibility – even if it is a batty octogenarian with half her marbles missing.

Tuesday 23rd September

Have new baby brother!!!

Last night Mum gave birth to a premature five pound five ounce boy. If he knew what he was in for, he probably wouldn't have been so eager to come out and join us.

Went to Banga's and bought Lucozade and grapes for Mum (cos that's what I've seen people do in English soap operas). Mrs Banga gave me a bag of samosas and Mrs Burke gave me a card for her. Me and Bonny took the day off school (skived), so Dad could drive us to the hospital to see them.

It was strange seeing Mum in an environment other than a takeaway kitchen. She looked out of place. I was half expecting her to be lying there with her overalls on, but she was wearing a pink nightie, which made her look almost like a real mum. At least she's getting a break from the greasy takeaway kitchen. She asked what we should call our new brother. He looked so tiny and scrawny and helpless. Like the fledgling Bonny brought home that time. I couldn't think of anything apart from 'Poor Sod', so kept my mouth shut.

MUM LOOKS ALMOST LIKE A REAL MUM!

BURP

She brings him home in two days, but the place won't be decorated with balloons and bunting like a normal home would. We don't do those things. It will be full of dirty pans and greasy woks. Dad, Simon, Grandma and me are running the shop, and only just keeping up. I'm serving till closing time every night. Hate it.

Bonny doesn't know what to make of the baby.

'He doesn't do much, does he?' she said.

Then I reminded her that this is just how she was when she arrived back in Nottingham, all those years ago.

Thursday 25th September

Told Tina about the baby yesterday and she was made up. She wants to see him but my life is too mental right now (as predicted), so I told her it might be better when things calmed down a bit (maybe never, the way things are going).

271

Mum and baby are home now. The baby has a Chinese name, 'Taozi' which means 'Little Peach' (even though he looks more like a shrivelled-up prune). Dad seems to have cheered up a bit. Maybe the baby is like a substitute pet to him? OK, so it's not small and fluffy and won't perch on his shoulder, but it still adds comedy value with all the burping and farting (like Bonny when she was a baby, as I am now reminding her at every opportunity).

But . . . surprise! Dad is leaving all the baby duties to Mum, and in turn she is leaving most of them to me.

'Why can't Bonny help?' I asked, infuriated.

'Because you're the older sister. You're expected to look after the younger ones, just like I did with your aunties and uncles.'

Yeah, maybe in China . . . and maybe in your life, not *mine*, I wanted to say. I already had a million things to do. But Mum had more. I couldn't let her down now.

She has put the baby in a Chinese sling (a flimsy square of cloth tied round her back and knotted at the front) and is furiously frying pork balls as I write. Mum's back to work full force, even though she has just been in labour for nine hours and expelled a whole living being from her body. The woman is insane.

Friday 26th September

Woke up wheezing really badly, so didn't go to school. Has been stressful with work, school and now childcare too. When I told Mum I didn't feel well she squinted at me and said, 'Wheezy chest? That means you're full of yin. I'll make some pig trotter soup to warm you up.'

NOOOOOOOOO! If yin is wheezy chest, why does yang have to be flippin' pig trotter soup? This could only happen to me.

As I was home all day and probably wouldn't be disturbed for being ill, it was the perfect opportunity to get my portfolio out and do some work on it. But what actually happened was I fed the baby and changed his stinking nappies and saw to him whenever he screamed his head off, which was every ten seconds. Mum and Dad would love it if I skived off permanently from now on, cos it would mean they could get on with their work uninterrupted.

What was the point of having a baby (UR)?!

Monday 29th September

Felt better this morning but couldn't be bothered to go to school again. Even babysitting is better than having to go to crappy lessons and dodge bullies all day.

Tuesday 30th September

Wagged it again. One more day won't hurt. I'll go in tomorrow.

Friday 3rd October

Skived all week! No one has been in touch from school, so think I'm in the clear. I'll go back in on Monday. Everything will be fine.

Took the baby to see Mrs Burke who thought he was 'adorable'. She didn't have her specs on and hasn't heard him scream yet, so we'll see if he's still adorable *then*. Mrs Burke has knitted him a jumper. It was very kind of her, even though it has two and a half sleeves.

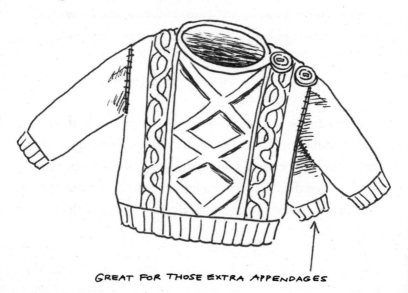

GREAT FOR THOSE EXTRA APPENDAGES

The baby was asleep when I got back so I quietly slipped my portfolio out from under the bed and started sorting through it. Half an hour later he started screeching in his carrycot downstairs. 'YENZI!' shouted Mum. 'Come and sort out the baby!' UGGGGGGGHHHHH. Back it went under the bed (the portfolio, not the baby, I wish).

At four the phone rang and Mum picked up, she said it was for me. I thought it might be school wondering where I was, so I motioned to Mum I wasn't here. Hopefully that will be the end of it.

Kev, of all people, has suggested the English name 'Larry' for the baby and Dad agreed. (How is Kev allowed to name our family members?) Mum can't say it cos she can't pronounce her 'r's, so to her he is now 'Lally'. I told Bonny that if he grows up to be as tormented as we are, he will be known as Doolally Lally. Oh how we laughed. Not.

Monday 6th October

8 am: Am dressed and ready for school but can't be bothered to go. Eliminating it from my life has simplified things a lot. I don't have to spend ages doing my hair and make-up, wait for buses, or write essays on tedious subjects like combustion engines. But the best thing is, I don't have to deal with Julie and Sam.

There was a knock on the door at ten o'clock while I was in the middle of mixing formula milk for Larry. It was a man wearing a grey suit and tie.

'Hello?' I said, answering the door.

'Are Mr and Mrs Kwan in?' he asked.

'They're in bed,' I said, trying to work out who he was.

'Can you tell them I need to speak to them, please? I'm the school truancy officer. Are you Joanna?'

Crap. The wagman.

'Yes,' I admitted.

Dad is going to go APE.

'I've come to see why you haven't been in.'

Then Dad appeared. We must have woken him up.

'Hello, what is the problem?' he said.

'I'm the school truancy officer. I've come to check if Joanna's all right. Why hasn't she been going to school?'

'Ah,' said Dad, 'she has very bad assmer. Yeah, she not well.'

Oh. My. God. Where the hell did *that* come from? I mean:

1) He was defending my absence from school
2) He was lying to an official
3) How did he know I had assmer? (Note: look up spelling for assmer.)

I played along, wheezing feebly. The wagman accepted Dad's explanation, took some notes and left without a fuss.

276

I thought I was going to get a proper hiding off Dad, but he was as calm as anything and it was never mentioned again. Sometimes it pays to have parents who don't give a toss about your education.

Tuesday 7th October

Didn't want the wagman hassling Dad again, so I dragged myself to school. Everyone looked at me as if I had bubonic plague, cos nobody likes a skiver. Doesn't matter, it's not as if I have any friends anyway. Am behind on coursework too. Took a sick note in which read:

> Dear Sir,
>
> Joanna has been off with severe assmer.
>
> Mrs Kwan

I decided Dad's diagnosis of asthma was the most credible. I didn't have a snotty nose or sore throat, so it couldn't have been a cold. And it was on and off, so it couldn't have been a chest infection. I wrote the note myself and forged the signature, cos Mum looked far too busy to hold a pen, plus I am not sure if she can write her name in English. I didn't know how to spell asthma cos I forgot to look it up (bit late, but have now!). Anyway, thought the bad spelling gave my note a ring of authenticity and it worked, cos I handed it to my form tutor, who read it and nodded silently.

Yeesssss! Totally got away with it.

Tina asked if I was OK at lunch. I told her I wasn't sure what had been wrong with me and described the symptoms. She reckoned it definitely was asthma cos her cousin has it. She said I should see a doctor and get an inhaler. I don't want an inhaler. I want a cure for child abuse and slavery.

Saturday 18th October

Mum keeps Larry upstairs in the carrycot all on his own while we work downstairs. Every now and then, me, Mum or Bonny (if she's around and can be bothered), has to pop upstairs to make sure he hasn't fallen out of bed or swallowed his socks, or something. Even I, a non child psychologist, know it can't be good for a baby being left on its own like that.

During a break between customers, me, Simon and Bonny, who was home cos Mandy was at some family do, went up to check on him. Simon hasn't really seen Larry all that much since he was born.

'He's an ugly sod isn't he?' he said.

'Yeah, he takes after you,' I quipped.

'He doesn't look like Mum or Dad,' said Bonny.

'Er, you were born with curly hair, remember? *Weirdo*.'

'He's a mutant,' said Simon.

'Awww, don't be horrible,' said Bonny.

'Hey, Bonny, why don't you stay in and look after him tonight?' I asked hopefully.

'Take a hike! He's *Mum's* baby, not mine.'

'Now who's being horrible?' I said.

Damn, thought I'd roped her in there.

'He's just another drone destined to work in this craphole,' said Simon.

I couldn't help agreeing with him. Poor thing. He looked so cute dribbling and gurgling. We all started off that way.

'Well at least Dad's stopped going to snooker,' I said, hoping to lighten the mood. 'I think he's trying to make an effort since Larry came along.'

'Nah, he'll be back in no time,' said Simon.

Simon hates Dad more than ever for making him work weekends. They still haven't said a single word to each other since their row.

Tuesday 21st October

Hello? Nobody has given me instructions for Larry. I *think* I've been feeding him properly, but I am not sure his eyes, nose and mouth are supposed to disappear into billowing folds of face fat. He looks like a giant, pink marshmallow. Surely is not right?

JABBA THE TOT

Wednesday 29th October

Got my calculator out to check how many hours I was now working. Checked three times (as my maths is dire) and found it is 31 hours per week!

Weekdays and Sundays – 4pm till 7pm = 15 hrs a week

Fridays and Saturdays – 4pm till midnight = 16 hrs a week

Total = 31 hours a week

OK, so I am getting paid. But like I said before, I would rather be poor than a slave. I am virtually holding down a full-time job . . . on top of school . . . and childminding! It is criminal!

May need to call that ChildLine thingy that Tina told me about.

Friday 7th November

Enough is enough! Today I was so overwhelmed I managed to put the nappies in the fridge and onions in the cot. Thank god they weren't peeled, Larry bawls enough as it is. Calling ChildLine still seemed quite an extreme thing to do, so I called Tina instead, to affirm.

'I'm working 31 hours a week on top of revising British monarchs of the seventeenth century while wiping a shitty arse!'

'Yep call them,' she affirmed.

I put the receiver down, picked up again . . . and hesitated. My hand was shaking. The full impact of what I was about to do hit me. What if this turned out to be deadly serious? What if they had to get in touch with Dad? He'd know for sure that I'd dobbed him in and all hell would break loose! It won't just be a bruising I get this time either. He'll probably want to kill me, like he did when he chucked Simon in the nettles.

The only escape now is my portfolio. *Portfolio, portfolio, portfolio!* I am starting to sound like a broken record. No wonder so many artists go mad.

Saturday 8th November

Before Larry's afternoon feed, I forced myself to look at my portfolio. I had to stop wallowing in self-pity and take positive action!

Larry was asleep, Mum and Dad were downstairs and Bonny was at Mandy's. I had two whole hours to myself. As I flicked through and lingered on each page, I was surprised at how fresh they still looked. Then suddenly, I don't know where it came from, I felt a kind of spark inside! Something made me decide that on Monday I would ask Miss Waterfall for that help she offered me over a year ago.

Simon can sod off with his remarks about art not being a real job. Yoko did it. And anyway, Simon isn't right about absolutely everything. I mean, he only got a B in his geography O level. AND got caught for nicking trousers down his trousers!

Called Tina to tell her ChildLine was off, so I'm reverting back to portfolio plan. She sounded irritated and claimed she was in the middle of doing 'homework' with Gaz. It must have been funny as there was lots of giggling going on.

Monday 10th November

Dreamed about Yoko last night. She was doing all my chores while I sat back drinking a fancy cocktail with an umbrella in. She didn't seem overly chuffed.

Showed Miss Waterfall my portfolio and reminded her of my plan to send it to *Mizz*. She thinks I'm insanely ambitious when in fact I'm merely a child slave planning a breakout. She said even though it wasn't completely full, it was good enough as it was. She even gave up her lunch hour to help me pack it for sending off. She is most amazing art teacher ever!

During lunch I wrote a letter to go with it, which read:

Dear Head of Fashion,

I am one of the most ardent and loyal readers of your fabulous magazine. Thanks to you I have accumulated a wealth of impressive fashion knowledge. I am up to date with the current trends, but also know a lot about the history and technical aspects.

So, if you require any work experience staff next year, I would love to have the opportunity to come along and offer my skills.

Also, please find enclosed a selection of my latest trend predictions for the spring/summer '87 runway.

Don't 'Mizz' out, hire me!

Yours eagerly,
Jo Kwan

P.S. Please consider using models of shorter stature in your mag, as being 4'10" myself, I find there are only so many ways you can roll up trouser legs.

Hope I didn't come across too desperate, even though TOTALLY AM. Called Tina just now to read the letter out loud to her. She was on her way out to the cinema with Gaz, so I had to rush and didn't feel she was really listening. Am I getting too tedious and boring?

Wednesday 26th November

No response from *Mizz*. Will be so mad if lost in post. Those drawings were originals, so there will be no way of replacing them. I will have a complete nervous breakdown if I have to start from scratch. Plus I paid one pound extra for Special Delivery – that's like, an *hour's* worth of prawn-gutting!

If this plan fails then I only have my O levels to fall back on next year. Am dreading them. The only one I'm sure to pass is art. But with only one O level under my belt, I am certain to face a future of misery in the takeaway. Only *Mizz* can save me now!

Monday 1st December

Nothing from *Mizz* AND I have lost an expensive case AND it's nearly Christmas. It will be the worst one yet – worse than last year when I got dumped by Warren . . . and the year my teddy bear chair was donated to a random mystery child. I wish Bob Geldof would release a charity single for ME.

Things are getting desperate and it's hard not to show it. I grabbed Tina at break and ranted to her about *Mizz*. She wasn't very sympathetic.

'Stop flapping, you only sent the parcel a few days ago.'

I didn't, it was THREE WEEKS ago.

I wonder if I'm starting to get on her nerves?

Tuesday 2nd December

Bonny came in with Mandy, who somehow managed to sell Dad a box of Christmas decorations. He must be in a good mood! Me and Bonny put them up and I didn't even care they were nicked cos at least it was taking my mind off *Mizz* for a change.

Mandy must have spread the news about Dad's unusually good mood, cos Kev came in later and sold him a second-hand pram. Dad told me to take Larry for a walk over to Grandparents' in it. I felt self-conscious going down the street with the pram. What if someone thought the baby was mine? That would've been *well* embarrassing! Actually no one would have thought that cos I still look ten. There would've been a greater chance of them recognising the pram as stolen, and wrestling it off me. I probably would have let them have it. And Larry, while they were at it.

Friday 12th December

Still nothing from *Mizz*. I needed to speak to Tina about it but she hasn't been on the bus the last week or so. Wonder if she's all right?

Monday 15th December

Saw Tina at the school gates this morning and asked why she hadn't been on the bus. She told me she'd been getting a lift in with Gaz off his dad. I told her about *Mizz* and then she told me I had to 'Bleedin' calm down about it' and that was one of the reasons she'd been avoiding me. Oh. I was right, I *had* been annoying her. The last thing I want is to fall out with her again, so I will back off and keep my gob zipped. But who can I talk to now? I only have Yoko, and she's also starting to get miffed with me. And she's not even real.

COUGH

Thursday 25th December – Christmas Day

9.56 am: It's our annual day off. Hold on, I will see if I can muster some enthusiasm.

Greeeaaat.

FESTIVE FAG →

1.32 pm: Am stuck here with my mad-as-ever family. Bonny is outside having a festive fag with Mandy, Dad is watching *Scrooge* (how apt) in his flip-flops, Larry is regurgitating a banana and yet another lobster is being murdered by Mum. Why can't we just have turkey (UR)?!

Simon is having turkey with all the trimmings at Smiffy's, lucky sod.

4.25 pm: Dad is still in a good mood. Actually everybody is, what with not having to work. (Makes you wonder why we don't do it more often, *sigh*.) Larry is getting loads of attention for a change. He did look a bit startled though, cos he's normally staring at the ceiling on his own, in silence. Grandma said he is still far too round for a three-month-old, so I joked that we never usually have a big fat pudding for Christmas, but we got one this year, ha ha! Grandad's gout is better so I hope he can come back to work soon. That would be the best present ever for me (besides a reply from *Mizz*).

Took Larry over to see Mrs Burke this evening. He had the jumper on that she knitted him. It fits surprisingly

well considering the extra half a sleeve poking out from under his left armpit. Gurdeep came round with Raj later and gave us a wholesale box of Wagon Wheels from her parents. We ate them while playing the Space Invader till midnight. Wish every day could be like this.

1987

Thursday 1st January – New Year's Day

New Year's resolution: Forget growing taller, forget spots, forget boyfriends.

JUST. GET. OUT. OF. HERE.

SCREAAAM!

Monday 5th January

Back to school. Was on my own as usual but at least there was no sign of Julie and Sam. Spent my breaks in the art room doodling and wondering what happened to *Mizz*. Jill and Sunita found me and gave me some late Christmas presents: soap and shampoo. It was nice of them but then I got all paranoid cos I thought:

1) They knew about Dad hitting me (if this is true then I am mortified)
2) They felt sorry for me getting bullied the whole time
3) They knew about me being child slave
4) They thought the reasons I've been skiving was cos of above
5) They knew about my misery over *Mizz*
6) Do I still smell of soya sauce?

Surely these are not normal problems for an average teenage girl? To top it all off, my final exams are coming up, and with them guaranteed academic failure and a future stuck in the takeaway for sure. WHERE ARE YOU *MIZZ*? Can't believe I spent months and months and months working on that bloody damn portfolio . . . for absolutely sod all! It's probably time to let go of that stupid fantasy now. Why is my life so shite?

Friday 9th January

Dad went to snooker! On a FRIDAY, one of the BUSIEST NIGHTS of the week!

Simon was right. It was just a matter of time before he went back. Sod. Mum said he wouldn't be having fun after the baby was born, but since when did she call the shots? *NEVER*. She's been married to him for about twenty years, she should know him by now.

When Dad came back a couple of hours before closing time, he had a face like someone had just snapped his cue in half. Woks were crashed about all night and he had a go at us all, for UR. I looked at Mum for some explanation, but she shook her head discreetly as if to say 'Don't even go there.'

During a break between customers, me and Simon went outside.

'What the hell's wrong with Dad this time?' I said, exasperated.

'Don't you know?' said Simon.

'Know what?'

'Grandma said he's started betting on snooker.'

Oh no, he's started gambling again. Crap.

I'd forgotten to tell Simon about the conversation between Mum and Auntie Yip about Dad gambling and going bankrupt in Hull. So I thought now was a good time.

'Yeah, I know all *that*,' said Simon, after I spat it all out.

'How?' I asked, shocked at the amount I didn't know even though *I* was the one that lived under the same roof as Dad.

'Grandma told me.'

That figured. Grandma must know and tell Simon everything.

'Why didn't you tell me?' I asked.

'You're the one who lives with Dad, I thought you already knew.'

I scoffed at the farce.

'Pff, I know sod all. Tell me more, then,' I said.

'Well,' he said. 'Don't quote me on this, it's second-hand info which I didn't fully understand in the first place.'

Just like every other bit of info we get off our relatives, I thought.

'Dad used to go to the casino in Nottingham,' said Simon. 'That's when he first went bankrupt and you moved to Hull. Then he started gambling on the horses, which made him bankrupt again, and that's why you came to Coventry.'

'And now it's the snooker,' I said.

'He's gonna go bust again, I'm telling you,' said Simon, kicking a hole in the old goat hut.

I was filled with dread. If Dad went bust again, we'd have to move. I couldn't face it. The least he could do was wait till I finished school so I didn't have to get bullied at a new one. Plus how small will the next place be if we keep downsizing each time? At this rate we'll be living in a flippin' shed!

When we went back in, no one spoke for the rest of the night, apart from to shout out orders. Bonny noticed there was something up when she came in later, but I didn't tell her why. What was the point of spoiling her night as well?

Saturday 10th January

Oh god. Simon turned up late for work cos he'd been studying, which made Dad start smashing the woks again.

'If I flunk my A levels, I'll kick Dad's teeth in,' Simon hissed, on our break. His face hardened, as if he meant it. And I believed he could. There is one thing I know Simon would definitely revenge Dad for, and that was the nettle incident.

It's my birthday tomorrow.

Sunday 11th January — My birthday (age 16)

Sweet sixteen? Bitter, more like. I can safely say I do not have anything to celebrate. This is cos I have:

1) Mental parents
2) Nicotine-addicted criminal sister
3) Seriously angry older brother
4) Pooey, pukey little brother
5) An on-off friend who is more off than on
6) And worst of all, zero prospect of anything changing.

Monday 12th January

Was in art room contemplating building a fire using all my artwork then throwing self on to it, when Tina walked in.

'Thought I'd find you here,' she said.

'Oh hi,' I grumbled, ignoring her and going back to planning my own death.

'I . . . I just wanted to say sorry,' she said, sitting down next to me carefully. She could sense I was not in the mood.

'Whatever,' I huffed.

I didn't have the energy to make up with her right then.

'I know I've been a useless mate,' she said.

I turned to face her.

'So what's changed?'

'Well, I forgot your birthday yesterday . . . sorry. Then I realised how selfish and wrapped up in Gaz I've been for ages.'

Awkward silence.

'I knew something was going on when you were skipping school last year too.' Her voice went weak. 'I . . . I should've asked if you were all right, but I didn't.' She wrung her hands. 'You must bloody hate me.'

Must say I was impressed by her heartfelt apology. 'Oh, I managed,' I said with a slight lump in my throat.

'Yeah but still . . .' she jumped in.

'I'd have done the same to you, so . . .'

We looked at each other and Tina held out her hand and said, 'Hey. Let's forget about it and be proper mates again.'

I hesitated, then shook it. 'OK,' I sighed. 'I know how your brain turns to mush when you get a new fella. I've been there, remember?' I nudged her with my elbow and we managed a chuckle. What a relief. For ages there was this sort of barrier between us and now it was gone. Then she placed a paper bag on the table. I knew what it was, a chocolate swiss roll, just like the one she got me on my birthday after we first met.

I know Tina has missed me, cos she only has one true friend too. So good to know I'm not on my own again.

'Oh, and I got you this as well,' she said, taking a rolled-up magazine out of her coat pocket. 'Sorry didn't have time to wrap it.'

It was the latest copy of *Mizz*.

'Thanks. I haven't bought this in ages,' I replied, trying

not to think about the grudge I still held against it. Pathetic, I know.

'But look at *this*,' said Tina with a cheesy grin. She flicked to the centrespread and stabbed the page with her finger.

I scanned through. My heart skipped a beat. It was a *competition*. The first prize was a place on the Fashion Styling course at the London College of Fashion.

OH.

MY.

GOD.

'Thought you'd like it,' said Tina, noticing my face light up. 'You gonna give it a shot then?'

'Yeah, might as well, why not?' I answered nonchalantly. I didn't want Tina thinking I was going to get all worked up and annoying again. But inside I was screaming with excitement.

My heart pounded the rest of the way home. Then I ran upstairs, shut the door and read the entry rules properly. There was a line drawing of a girl's face, which had to be filled in with an original make-up design. Was that it? Easy! I'm a fashion guru after all! Will make a start tomorrow. What with Tina talking to me again and now this – it has been the best day EVEEEEEER!!!

Tuesday 13th January

Raced home, did chores and started scribbling. What could I fill the blank face with? I was blank about the blankness. I wrote down some ideas:

1) Sun-kissed Beach Babe
2) Shimmering Mermaid
3) Bronzed Temptress
4) Rainbow Angel
5) Sultry Rocker

No, no, no, they were all too boring and conventional, I'd seen those looks a million times before. Then I remembered I was doing a project on Marcel Duchamp in art. I liked his cubist style and in particular a painting called 'Nude Descending a Staircase'. It was different, daring and made you look twice. I flicked through *Mizz* for more ideas and stopped at an article about skiing. Yes! That was it! The movement of the skier, the spray of the snow and her red suit all looked great against the bluey-white background. It was all there.

I sketched out my skier in the style of Marcel Duchamp. It looked brill, so I copied it over on to the girl's face on the entry form and coloured it with pencil crayon. I was just finishing off when Bonny got in at half nine.

'What you doing?' she said.

'Er, just some homework for art,' I answered, covering it up.

She's still in our bedroom now so I had another peek at my picture. It is SO good. Am dead excited. Am calling it 'Skier Descending a Ski Slope'.

Here's the original sketch:

Wednesday 14th January

Met Tina on the bus this morning. I waved the envelope with my entry in. 'I've finished!'

'Already? Wow, what? Show me!' she said.

I got it out and explained the idea.

'That's dead imaginative . . . and original. You're bound to get shortlisted.'

Yessss! Tina loved it and that was good enough for me. We went to the post office at lunchtime and crossed our fingers as the lady behind the counter stamped the envelope 'Special Delivery' and placed it in the sack. Hopefully I'll get a flippin' response this time!

This is it . . . this is it . . . this is it . . . this is it . . . this is it . . . this is it . . . this is it . . . this is it . . . this is it . . .

Sunday 18th January

Went to Poshos' for lunch. Me and Bonny haven't been for ages cos going back home again each time was starting to depress us. But now I am in best mood ever, so nothing can get me down! Not Jill being predicted seven As in her O levels, Sunita being predicted eight As in hers, or Katy playing violin for the school orchestra and winning a trampoline proficiency award. (Bonny was bit jealous of Katy though.)

I didn't tell anyone about the competition. Nobody must interfere, especially not Devil Spawn.

Thursday 22nd January

Has been over a week since I sent my entry to *Mizz*, and is only two weeks till closing date! I daren't tell Tina how worried I am. Am scared we'll break up again and I need her right now. Tried to visualise Yoko instead, but all I saw was a blur. Collared Miss Waterfall at afternoon break and told her my predicament. She reminded me I still had plenty of time and not to worry, as that achieved nothing but indigestion and migraine. She is so wise.

When I got home I went and stared at Nik Kershaw for comfort, but he still reminded me of Warren, so I did mopping to take my mind off it all.

Dad is still in a right mood. He's been swearing and muttering under his breath all day. Wonder how much money he's losing? Wonder how far off he is from bankruptcy?

Must stay positive.

Saturday 24th January

While Bonny was painting my nails, she asked why I had been acting all weird lately.

'Have you got a new boyfriend?'

'No way!' I said, a bit too high-pitched.

She looked at me suspiciously and said, 'Something's up and you're not telling me.' Then she splodged my fingers with too much *Fearsome Fuchsia* on purpose.

It's not as if Bonny will sabotage my chances of winning, it's just she will ask if I've won every five minutes, then laugh in my face if I don't. And that would finish me off.

Mum and Dad haven't noticed my good mood. They're too busy frying chicken balls and dealing with a screaming jellyhead of a baby.

Sunday 1st February

Today has been the worst day of my life.

Around seven o'clock, Dad told me to call Simon round to help so he could play snooker. I was dreading it cos I knew Simon was fixing his computer and he's only supposed to do Fridays and Saturdays.

Sure enough when I called, he went berserk.

'Tell Dad to take a f**kin' jump!' Simon yelled down the receiver.

'Don't shoot the messenger,' I pleaded.

'You didn't *have* to call me!'

'What, and get battered again? No thanks.'

He slammed down the phone.

'Is he coming?' said Dad, fetching his cue out of the cupboard.

'Er ... yes,' I replied.

But I wasn't really sure, I just didn't want him to get mad.

Simon arrived half an hour after Dad left. (He was angrier than I've ever seen him, which is saying something.) I was still glad he came though, cos it got well hectic in the kitchen.

It was nine when Dad finally returned. He marched through the counter hatch, into the kitchen and started shouting at us (UR). There were two blokes waiting for food – they could see everything through the plastic strip curtain. Dad seemed drunk but I've never seen him touch alcohol, so my guess was he'd lost a bet.

We ignored him, hoping he would calm down. Mum said something in Chinese like, 'What's the matter with you, Kwan Yun?' It was a perfectly reasonable question, but cos Dad was SO MAD, it made him storm over to the solid oak butcher's block and overturn it in one rage-fuelled hurl. It must have weighed a ton.

We stared in shock at the upside-down block, surrounded by the scattered knives spilled all over the floor.

Then something else unexpected happened. Dad picked up one of the knives, grabbed Mum in a headlock and put the knife to her throat. I froze. Mum looked remarkably composed, like she had been expecting it all along.

Oh god, oh god, this was it, Dad was actually going to kill her this time.

I glanced over at the customers, wondering if they could stop it, but they were leaning on the counter enjoying a right old gawp. Tossers.

Then Simon lunged. He leaped on Dad, who wasn't used to anyone fighting back, grabbed his knife-arm and pulled Mum away. He pushed Dad to the ground and started kicking him over and over again.

Thwump,

thwump,

thwump,

thwump . . .

'HELP!' screamed Mum to anyone. 'CALL THE POLICE!'

It had to be me.

My heart was pounding so loud I thought it was going to explode out of my chest. What do I say? It wasn't just drunks causing trouble this time, it was my brother trying to KILL my dad, after my dad just tried to KILL my mum! It was insane! Would they even believe me?

I ran out to the counter and dialled 999. My hands were shaking so much I could hardly dial. Mum was still screaming in the background. For all I knew, Dad could be dead by now.

The two customers watched on. It was a weird feeling

I had right then, but I was actually embarrassed and ashamed about them witnessing how completely mental my family were. These things always happened in private, and that's how I preferred it. At least then I could pretend to some extent that we were normal.

'Hello, you're through to Coventry City police station. Can you tell us what the problem is?' said the voice at the other end.

'Yes . . . er.'

My voice cracked, I couldn't speak. I swallowed.

'My brother's kicking my dad in. Can you . . . can you come over now please, I don't know what to do.'

My jaw juddered. Dad might be dead.

'Can I take your address?'

I tried to be as calm as possible so I could give them the information.

'All right, don't worry, we'll be over straight away.'

'Thanks.'

Relief! Someone was coming to stop it all! I hoped it wasn't too late.

But when I went back in the kitchen, Simon had legged it and Dad had gone upstairs. I had no choice but to sort things out in the shop. I was in a daze, refunding customers and locking the door while all the pandemonium was going on. Our family was already hanging by a thread, but this had finally annihilated it.

Dad wouldn't come down when the police got here and I could hear Larry crying upstairs. Then the ambulance arrived. It was ten minutes before he showed himself.

Wow.

He looked like the Elephant Man. His face was mangled up and swollen twice the size, and he seemed shrunken and feeble, not like him at all. The paramedics tried to convince him that he should go to hospital for X-rays, but he stubbornly refused. Didn't they know about his soya sauce cure-all? Or that you could make bruises go away by rubbing ginger on them? DUR!

Not sure where Simon had gone, but I was secretly glad Dad got what he deserved. After all the abuse he'd dished out, someone had had the guts to stand up to him at last.

I wonder if Mum felt the same? Surely this would be the perfect time for her to leave him. She could go and live with her sisters in Vancouver and start a new life.

By all accounts they are way more clued-up than her. They will look after Mum, find her an easier job and show her what it is like to be happy. I wouldn't go with her though. No way! I'd want a quiet life of my own. Can't think where though. Grandparents' isn't far enough. Bonny will probably get adopted by Mandy's family – she pretty much is already. Anyway, it's never going to happen is it? Mum would rather risk her life being stuck with Dad, than have to learn English so she can look after herself.

After the police and paramedics had gone, Mum and Dad reopened the shop and carried on as if nothing had happened (UR!). Dad carried on cooking looking like Joseph Merrick, and Mum didn't even cry. She is either an android or devoid of tear ducts. Or maybe she was just in severe shock like I was?

I went upstairs and left them to it – the shop was closing soon anyway. But the image of Simon kicking Dad kept replaying in my mind. He could have killed him. I wanted Dad to be taught a lesson as much as Simon, but I'm not sure I wanted him bumped off.

Somewhere around half ten, Bonny burst into our bedroom. She'd come back from Mandy's and seen Dad's face. 'What the freakin' hell happened?!' she said.

I sighed heavily. 'Simon went berserk and kicked the crap out of Dad.'

'Why?'

I didn't feel like explaining, but she would have gone on till she got an answer, so I kept it simple.

'Dad asked Simon to take over while he went to play snooker. Then he came back and started shouting at us . . . then do you know what he did?' My heart quickened as I recalled the incident. 'He nearly slashed Mum's throat open.'

'*What?!*' Bonny gasped.

'Then Simon flipped and kicked the crap out of him.'

Bonny pursed her lips for a second then said bitterly, 'Good! Serves him right.'

Secretly, we had all been waiting for this moment.

Monday 2nd February

Felt sick when I woke up. Was that real, what happened last night?

Saw Dad's dragon drawing in bin. Bonny has ripped it into a million pieces.

Didn't want to go to school, but didn't want to be at home either. They were equally awful places to be. I needed to talk to Tina about it, so I went to school. Wasn't sure if it would make or break our friendship, but I blurted it all out to her anyway in the art room at lunchtime.

Surprisingly she didn't run away. Think she was in shock too.

'Oh my god. Are you . . . *OK*?' she said, when she'd recovered.

'Not really.'

My asthma was back, but she didn't need to know that as well.

'Are Bonny and your mum *OK*? How about Larry?'

'Dunno.'

'What about Simon?'

'Dunno.'

I was numb.

'I might try calling him after school,' I mumbled.

Tina shook her head. I think she wanted to hug me but didn't know if it was the right thing to do just then. Probably not.

'Has this kind of thing happened before?' she asked, terrified for me.

I didn't want to say yes, but the incident in Hull was just as horrendous in my mind, only in a different way.

'Yeah . . .' I said.

Tina stared straight at me. 'What? *When?!*'

She already knew about last night. What difference would it make if I told her more? She was the only person I trusted to share these things with, so she might as well know everything.

'It was back in Hull,' I began. 'I'd been out with some kids from the estate . . .'

311

. . . They asked if I wanted to join their sports day in a field nearby and I was dead chuffed cos I hadn't made any friends yet. They were dead nice. I won a chocolate medal for the egg and spoon race.

Anyway, it was about seven when I got home. Dad was waiting for me on the landing and I could tell from where I stood that I was in for a hiding.

He said, *'Where have you been all day?!'*

'With . . . with my friends,' I whimpered.

'I needed to go out. You should have watched the shop!' he shouted.

I was confused. How was I supposed to watch the shop? I was only ten!

'What about Mum?' I said to him.

'You know she can't speak English!'

Then he grabbed me by the hair. I still couldn't work out what I'd done wrong.

He started dragging me across the hallway. I thought he was going to take me into the kitchen where all the knives were, and stab me to death. I was absolutely crapping myself. Mum wasn't around, not that she could have saved me. No one's strong enough to stop Dad when he gets like that.

I got pulled into the toilet instead. I couldn't think why, but I knew anything involving the bog wasn't going to be good. He forced my head over the bowl (which I noticed was clean, thank god), then shoved it right in and flushed. He held me down till I started spluttering. I thought I was going to drown! Then he let go and left me kneeling there, soaking wet, wondering what the hell just happened.

I felt disgusting. Like shit. Cos only shit gets flushed down the bog, doesn't it?

'So,' I said to Tina now, taking a deep breath. 'I guess Dad kind of deserved what Simon did to him.'

There was a sniff.

I looked up and Tina was crying.

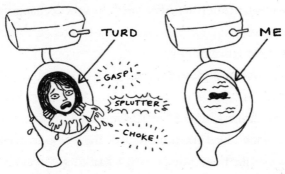

When I got home Dad was in the kitchen. He still looked like the Elephant Man. It wasn't a dream.

Tuesday 3rd February

Was thinking about when Simon told me Dad had been betting on the horses in Hull. The day I got my head flushed, Dad must have wanted to go to the bookies and that's why he asked me to mind the shop. Then maybe his horse won and cos he didn't make it to the bookies he'd lost out on a load of dosh and blamed it on me. Yeah, that made sense.

Saw Tina on the bus this morning and this time it was me asking her if *she* was OK after ending up in tears yesterday.

'Yeah,' she said. 'Couldn't believe what you told me, Jo. Still can't.'

I shrugged. 'Welcome to my world.'

'How's your dad now?'

'Er hold on, let's think. Yep, still a moron.'

There wasn't much she could say to that.

'Have you heard from *Mizz* yet?' she asked, changing the subject quickly.

'No,' I replied, gloomily.

'Don't worry, there's still time.'

'Yeah.'

To be honest, I couldn't have cared less, cos what happened with Dad and Simon made me feel so scraped out inside, just like those vile prawns I had to gut every night. Mum was no help. Not sure what I was expecting her to do though. Maybe a normal Mum might ask if me and Bonny are OK. But why would she do that when we don't check on her? How do you say in Chinese 'Are you OK after almost getting your throat sliced?'

Back home after school Mum and Dad were still pretending everything was normal (well, as normal as our family can be). Bonny has been unusually quiet since the fight, so I asked if she was all right.

'Yeah, Mandy's got flu so I'm not going round tonight.'

'No, I meant you. Are *you* all right?'

'Yeah, why shouldn't I be?'

I wanted to say, 'Cos our family time bomb has just exploded and destroyed everything.' But I could tell she didn't want to talk, so I left her alone.

EVERYONE TRYING
TO ACT NORMAL
EVEN THOUGH DAD
LOOKS LIKE
JOSEPH MERRICK

MUM'S SPRING
ROLL MOUNTAIN

Grandad came round later and casually told us that Simon had gone to stay at Uncle Han and his fiancée's in Derby. He didn't seem bothered about our family crisis, or the state of his son's head. He had obviously seen worse atrocities in Communist China.

What about Simon's A levels? What if he doesn't get to do them? He will be sick as a dog.

Dad's face is a mess. My whole life is a mess!

Wednesday 4th February

Asthma back with a vengeance so I skived.

Dragged myself out of bed and staggered to Grandparents' to ask when Simon was coming back. Grandad said never, due to some kind of police protection order. I wonder what a protection order is? Will Simon be arrested . . . sent to prison? Will his trouser-stealing episode count against him? Horrified, I found myself thinking like Mum. *What will Poshos and our friends think? Oh, such shame on the family!* And what about Julie and Sam – what will they do to me when they find out?

Tina called after school to see if I was all right. I told her to tell the wagman my asthma was playing up if he asked, but not to tell him anything else. I told her about the protection order too, but she didn't know what it was either.

Dragged myself back to bed and wished I could die quietly.

Thursday 5th February

Asthma better today, but didn't feel like going to school. The whole place probably knows what happened by now, and I bet Julie and Sam are waiting to pounce on me at the first opportunity. No one will understand the hell I am going through.

Usually on skive days, I get dressed and hide in the garden

till Bonny's gone, so she can't see me, but today Mrs Burke spotted me and started yapping on about her varicose veins. She was probably the only person in the known universe who didn't know what had happened. Bonny heard and came marching out. She found me behind the old goat hut.

'I'm not going in either then,' she huffed.

'Fine, do what you want, I'm past caring,' I replied. And to her glee, she went trotting off to Mandy's, where her mum would no doubt have welcomed her with open arms (unlike our mum) and offered hot buttered toast (as opposed to nothing at all here).

Tina called again. She'd asked her mum about the protection order and her mum said that it's when 'the authorities have a right to move a child away from a place where they believe they might be harmed'. Tina didn't tell her mum this was about me – thank god. She hasn't seen the wagman either.

When Bonny got back, I decided to tell her about the police protection order, but she seemed more bothered about the police coming round our house than Simon being sent away.

Dad's face is black and blue and puffed up like a haggis. He can only see out of one eye. Isn't he ashamed of what he did? None of us talk about what happened.

Larry cried all day. I know how he feels.

Wonder how Simon is?

Friday 6th February

Skived again, but didn't want to be in the house with Mum and Dad cos every time I look at them, I want them to vanish into a bottomless void.

I managed to sneak out of the house without Larry and couldn't think where to go, so I went to Mrs Burke's.

'I heard about your dad,' she said, swigging ale. I reckon Bonny told her. 'It's me medicine,' she said pointing at the bottle on the table. 'Do you want some?'

'No thanks.'

'How you feeling, love?' she said.

'I think I'm depressed,' I answered.

'Oh, my Arthur had depression.' (That was Mrs Burke's husband.) 'He wouldn't change his underpants for six months. Does your mum know?'

'About Arthur's underpants?'

'No, you daft sod, about your depression.'

'No.'

As if she'd care.

'You better get yourself to the doctor's,' she said.

If I couldn't face going to the doctor's about my asthma, how could I go about this? I'd never felt this low before though, so I thought maybe I should.

'Yeah, you're right,' I said.

It's funny how old Mrs Burke cares more for me than all of my family put together. So out of respect for her, I went, registered myself and made an appointment for next week. Ugh, I am such an utter failure.

Monday 9th February

Skived.

Tina called at half twelve to tell me the wagman had been asking if she'd seen me around. I said, 'If he asks again, I'm off to the doc's.'

'Why?' she asked.

'To see if they can stop me wanting to kill myself . . .

or even worse, from marrying David Wong – anything to get me out of here.'

'NO!!!' she shrieked. 'Remember your mantra; Wong is wrong, Wong is wrong... Come round to mine after school.'

Tina has been really supportive throughout this ordeal, but going round to hers won't help. I'm going to feel depressed wherever I am.

Tuesday 10th February

Skived.

Saw doctor at 11 am. She asked me what the matter was. I didn't tell her about Dad, just in case the police got involved and stuff. I just told her that I felt down. I didn't know what to expect but found the whole experience rather unhelpful.

'Are you sleeping OK?' she asked.

'Apart from intermittently waking up thinking I'm having a nightmare, but actually it's my real life,' I answered.

There was a pause.

'Are you eating well?' she said.

'If a diet of chicken's feet and chocolate counts, then yes.'

She looked at me straight-faced, then scribbled a prescription and slid it across the desk. She didn't say what it was, but she was the expert so I didn't question it.

On the way to the chemist, I saw Bonny and Mandy

walking down a side street together. Bonny's been bunking off again. I said she could last time, so I can't blame her. I don't know what is right or wrong any more, to be honest. My head's in a right state.

Before opening time I heard Mum on the phone to Auntie Yip. I couldn't make out what it was about but assumed it was the fight. Mum still hasn't mentioned it to me or Bonny, even though we're the ones who have to live with it.

At bedtime, I took the box of tablets out of my drawer. The label was written in medical language. Whatever they were, I'm sure the doc knew what she was doing. I popped one out of the pack and swallowed it. Hoping that when I wake up, I will have transformed into a normal human being.

Wednesday 11th February

Woke up feeling like a tranquillised slug.

Took another tablet before school. Tina was worrying about me on the bus. 'It's OK,' I said. 'I'll just take them till I feel better.'

My French teacher asked me to stay behind after class. Thought I was in trouble cos my marks have been straight Ds all year. But apparently I had fallen asleep during lesson and hadn't even realised! I wanted to suggest maybe learning past participles of irregular verbs rendered me unconscious, but couldn't find the words, so instead I said, 'The doctor's given me some pills.'

I got them out of my bag and showed her. She frowned and took me to see the headmaster. Thought I was really in trouble then. She explained everything to the head and he said, 'Is everything all right at the moment, Joanna?'

'Er, yeah,' I lied. I wanted to avoid involving the police and making things worse.

'I've noticed your attendance has been slipping again,' he said. 'Is something bothering you?'

'Um . . . no,' I replied, unconvincingly.

'Everything OK at home?' he asked.

As soon as he said that, my chest and throat tightened. I felt like crying.

Did he know what had happened? He couldn't. I stared at the desk and shook my head. 'Yeah, everything's fine,' I mumbled.

'Have Julie and Sam been bothering you?' said my French teacher.

How did she know they'd been bullying me? And why did she never do anything to stop them?

'No,' I said, wishing the whole scenario would end so my godawful crappy life wasn't under the spotlight.

'Well, whatever the problem is, you will let us know, won't you? We can always help,' the head said sympathetically.

Right. OK then, off the top of my head I can think of three things that would help:

P.S. Still not heard from Simon – hope he is OK.

Saturday 14th February

Mum sent me to Banga's for a bottle of bleach. I did wonder for a second if she wanted to drink it and end it all, but then remembered her life's mission was to stuff spring rolls for all eternity, so there was nothing to worry about. Bumped into Smiffy coming out with some cider.

'Hey, Jo,' he said, looking irate. 'If your dad ever lays a finger on you, tell me and I'll smack him, OK?'

'Er, OK,' I replied as he headed off down the street.

Wow, that was nice of him.

I mean Tina's cool, and so is Miss Waterfall, and Mrs Burke. But if Dad did ever lay a finger on me again, they wouldn't be able to knock him out like Smiffy the rock-hard brickie could. I hope to hell it won't come to that, but I felt a bit better knowing I had someone watching my back.

As I went into the shop Mrs Banga asked, 'Is your Dad OK?'

Flippin' all of Coventry knew!

'What do you mean?' I said, not really wanting to talk about it.

'I heard about the fight.'

'Oh yeah, that.'

'How's your brother, is he OK?' she said.

Aargh, leave me alone!

'Oh yeah, he's fine,' I said quickly.

I paid for the bleach and tried to leave, then Gurdeep appeared.

SILKY HAIR

LOOKS LIKE A DISNEY PRINCESS!

GORGEOUS DRESS

OWL be your VALENTINE

MASSIVE CARD!!!

SPARKLY BANGLES

'Look what I got off Raj,' she said, holding up an absurdly oversized Valentine's card, with a soppy owl on saying *'Owl be your Valentine'*.

'Ha, that's nice,' I replied, and hurried out the door so I could go and drink the bleach myself.

Sunday 15th February

Went round to give Mrs Burke her chomato. She didn't look very well and was hobbling as she walked. It was probably her varicose veins playing up again. Either that or she'd had too much ale.

'How did it go at the doctor's, love?' she asked.

'All right. Don't you think you should go yourself?' I said, helping her into the armchair.

'I'm eighty-two now, you know,' she said, puffing and wheezing. 'There ain't no pills that'll fix me.'

'The doctor gave me some pills but they made me feel funny,' I said.

'Funny ha ha, or funny queer?' she asked.

'Queer, Mrs Burke, queer,' I said, rolling my eyes.

You can always count on Mrs Burke to lighten things up, even though she is decrepit and on her last legs.

'Have you got them with you?' she asked.

'No, they're at home.'

'Bring 'em over next time. Arthur might have took the same ones.'

'OK,' I said, holding up the chomato. 'Shall I put this on a plate for you?'

'No, leave it on the side. I can't chew any more, cos of me teeth.'

It turns out Mrs Burke has not been eating her chomato for the last year and four months. She just enjoys me popping round for company, god bless her cotton surgical stockings.

Monday 16th February

After school I dug the tablets out of my drawer and went over to Mrs Burke's to show her. 'Oh yes,' she said, 'they're what I called Arthur's "happy pills". They made him feel queer too. But at least they stopped him being miserable.' Probably cos they turned him into a flippin' zombie like they did with me. Chucked them in the bin when I got back.

Saturday 21st February

Haven't heard from Simon since he moved to Uncle's. Am worried. Grandad said he was doing all right, but I wanted to know for myself, so I wrote a letter, which went like this:

Hi Simon,

Hope you're OK. Grandad told me you were at Uncle's, so I got the address off him.

Can't believe what happened. You must have been mega pissed off to lose it like that! I don't blame you though. Me and Bonny are glad you taught him a lesson (even though it was a tad OTT). You should have seen Dad after you kicked him in, he looked like the Elephant Man! Now he just looks like a deformed haggis. He hasn't left the house yet. I think he's scared you might finish him off.

Everyone is acting like normal, even though Mum nearly had her throat cut! No one talks about what happened, including Grandma and Grandad. It's really weird. But our family ARE really weird.

Kev's helping in the kitchen now you've gone. He's a total idiot. He can't tell the difference between an onion and a potato, so I'm not sure how that's going to work out.

Smiffy said he's going to visit you soon.

Anyway, I hope all this hasn't buggered up your A levels. Write back when you can.

Sis x

Saturday 7th March

Letter back from Simon!

Hi Pongo,

Yeah I'm OK. I was wearing my most expensive pig-skin trainers when I kicked Dad in. They cost £100 and now they're ruined. He had it coming and deserved it. I'm done with the old man now, he's a useless piece of dog crap.

I've joined a sixth form college in Derby and finishing my A levels there.

Can you tell Smiffy to bring the rest of my tapes (especially Echo and the Bunnymen) — they wouldn't fit in my bag when I packed.

Bro

P.S. Get out of that dump!

Thanks, Simon, I don't know if you've been aware but I have been trying to plan my escape for the past two years. And stop calling me Pongo – it's well annoying! Anyway, it's good to see all this hasn't put him off doing his A levels. In fact, it has probably made him even more determined.

Me and Bonny went to Grandparents'. to deliver their char siu and collect the tapes Simon was asking for. They weren't in, which was unusual. I told Mum when I got back and she said they've started working at Poshos' takeaway. God, even his own parents can't stand being around Dad any more.

Sunday 8th March

Has been over a month since the 'incident'.

Dad hasn't been back to play snooker. These days he seems to walk around with an air of shame about him. He's not even been shouting or smashing woks about. Hopefully he's had time to reflect and think about what an utter moron he has been. I don't know how Mum puts up with it. If I was her I would have killed him long before now. Maybe by injecting his chicken's feet with rat poison or something.

It's not Mother's Day yet, but thought Mum needed cheering up, so me and Bonny got her a bunch of flowers.

'Tsk, don't buy flowers!' said Mum.

'Why?' we asked.

'Cos they just get in the way and die!' she said.

I wonder if she feels the same way about us?

Thursday 19th March

OH MY GOD!!!! BEST NEWS EVER!!!!!

Got back from school to find a letter waiting for me with a 'London College of Fashion' stamp on it! I ran upstairs clutching it to my chest, sat down on the bed and shut my eyes. I could almost hear the bugles calling, party poppers popping and a million angels chorusing at once, '*Ahhh, ahhh, ahhhhhhhh.*'

I stared at the envelope, then tore it open.

Here it is:

Dear Jo,

Congratulations. You have been shortlisted as a finalist to win a place on our BTEC OND Fashion Styling course.

The final will be held at the London College of Fashion on Monday 25th May at 1 pm.

Please acknowledge by return if you are able to attend and more details will follow shortly.

Yours sincerely,
Gloria Goldstein

Course Tutor

EEEEEEEEEEEK!!! YES! YES! YES! THANK YOU, GLORIOUS GLORIA!

I could have died happy right there and then. I jumped up and down as quietly as possible, cos Mum and Dad must not know there is anything going on and try to stop me.

Then Mum shouted up the stairs, 'YENZI! Come and peel the onions!'

'No problem, I'll be right down!' I chirped back. Blimey, when have I ever sounded so happy about peeling the sodding onions?

Think my depression is cured.

Friday 20th March

Grabbed Tina at break and showed her the letter. She was more made up than I was!

'This is *mad*, Jo! *Mad, mad, mad!*' she said, clutching my arms and shaking me.

'I know, *isn't* it? It's like ... not real.'

'It IS real, you better believe it. And I'll come to London with you if you want?'

'Will you?'

'YES!!!'

Then we both twirled around till our heads started spinning.

At lunchtime, I wrote a letter back to Gloria telling her that absolutely nothing on earth could stop me from going to the final, and posted it on our way to the Mini-Mart.

I still had ten minutes' spare at the end of lunch so decided to see if Miss Waterfall was in the art room. She was in there rinsing palettes. 'Hi, miss!' I said, suddenly getting a bit breathless.

'Oh hi, Jo, what's up?'

'I've got something to tell you.'

She sensed my excitement and turned to face me.

Did you get picked?

'YEESSS!' I squealed.

Miss dropped the palettes in the sink and gave me a big hug. 'Well done! You've worked hard for this, you deserve it.'

'Thanks,' I replied, blushing (hate hugs).

'And I'm glad to see you happy again, cos I know how glum it's made you lately, all this.'

She thinks my recent depression was due to not hearing back about the *Mizz* portfolio. I'm fine letting her think that. I don't want her to know about Dad. I want her to remember me as Jo the troubled artist, not Jo the troubled child of a dysfunctional family.

Before I went for lessons, Miss reminded me to check that I didn't have exams on the day of the competition – CRAP forgot it will be right in the middle of my O levels!

Got home, checked my exam timetable, all clear. Called Tina, so is hers – PHEW!

Tuesday 7th April

Eeeeek! Another letter from the London College of Fashion! I dashed upstairs, stroked the envelope like it was a delicate pedigree chinchilla, then ripped it open in a frenzy.

Here it is:

```
Dear Jo,

Thank you for confirming your
attendance. Please find directions
to the college enclosed and a brief
for the event. We look forward to
seeing you on the day.

Yours sincerely,
Gloria Goldstein

Course Tutor
```

I unfolded the map. The college was in the centre of London. Then I read the brief:

Theme: 'Nature'
We would like to see your interpretation of this theme using make-up on a live model. Two hours will be allocated. Model and make-up will be provided on the day.

I sped through my mopping, hoovering, chopping, slicing, peeling, gutting, serving and nappy-changing, then got all my art stuff out from under the bed. I sat down at the table in parents' room, spread out my pencils and got thinking. Hmmm, 'Nature'. I looked out the window. All I could see was the brick wall of the Talbot car factory across the road. Zilch inspiration there.

But then I spotted a plant growing out of a crack. Oh yeah. It was spring! Easy to forget when you live in a concrete city all year round.

After that, everything was a cinch. Decided to stick with the idea that got me through to the finals: make-up that defied convention! I did a delicate patchwork of leaves, buds and flowers, filled with pastel greens and pinks. It took till midnight and when it was done, it looked positively bursting with life. I am calling it 'New Beginnings'. And that's exactly what I want, for me!

This is my design:

Wednesday 8th April

Showed Tina and Miss Waterfall my design for the competition final. They approved!

Let's all do the conga, let's all do the conga, la la la la, hey! La la la la!

Thursday 9th April

Bonny is having a birthday party at Mandy's. Can't believe she is eleven already. It doesn't seem that long ago she was watching Care Bear videos, and now she has full-on smoker credentials and is going to senior school in September!

I have been invited, but turned it down cos everything will be smothered in cigarette smoke at Mandy's and that will include the sausage rolls and trifle.

Bonny was in the bathroom giving herself a home perm.

'Do you know what you're doing?' I asked, reeling at the stench of ammonia.

'I'm following the instructions, DUR!' she said.

'How's school?' I asked casually.

We don't do much 'proper' talking these days, so I wanted to check how she was, while I had the chance.

'What about it?' she said.

'Just asking.'

'Why?'

'Just making sure you've been going, that's all.'

Bonny sneered at me. 'What's it to you, anyway?'

I hoped she hadn't carried on skiving since I gave her permission a couple of months back. Otherwise, if her education goes downhill from here, and she turns out to be a massive dunce, then I will single-handedly be the one to blame. But how could I make her understand that the only way to escape the takeaway was to do well at school and leave Coventry altogether? Simon told me that after we arrived here. Now I had to pass that message on.

'You've got to get good grades,' I said.

'Why?' said Bonny.

'So you don't end up working here.'

'I'm not gonna, am I?' she said, pinning another roller in. 'Me and Mandy are going to run a nail salon, remember?'

I glanced at Bonny in the mirror. She was putting on her brave front again. Up till now she's been escaping to Mandy's, but how much longer can that last? If I won this competition, she'd be taking my place as child slave no matter what, and then she'd be doomed.

She was doomed anyway, cos her perm turned out frizzier than Gary Kemp's.

Saturday 18th April

I should be up to my eyeballs in Easter eggs, but instead I'm up to my eyeballs in onion juice and prawn intestines. And soon I'll have to start revising too, cos my flippin' O levels are coming up. Why do I have to do exams? Exams are not for creative types like me, they are for academics who end up doing complicated things I will never understand.

Saturday 16th May

O levels start on Monday. Christ alive, better do some revision!

Monday 18th May

Woke up, ate digestives, panicked.

My first exam is maths. MATHS! I HATE MATHS! Tina is the only one who isn't panicking. She has a job as a junior hairdresser lined up for when she leaves school. Tried to stay calm by thinking about the slim possibility of winning that scholarship to the London College of Fashion. Where there is possibility, there is hope.

9 am: Maths exam – nothing made sense. It might as well have been in Swahili. There was a booklet called 'Sines and Tangents' provided. Wasn't sure what it was for, but it did a grand job of propping up the wobbly table leg.

Wednesday 20th May

2 pm: History exam – was just a bunch of questions about boring old events and dead people! What good is this in the real world?!

Friday 22nd May

9 am: French exam – I have just discovered maths and French are the same thing, i.e. Swahili!

Competition day on Monday. If I don't win, I will climb into the lion enclosure at Twycross Zoo and get eaten alive (so I don't have to finish off my exams and rely on them for a better future). I confessed all this to Larry. He's the only one in the family who will listen without judgement, or at least cannot voice his judgements as he is unable to talk.

Monday 25th May

Hurray, hurray! It's competition day!

9.05 am: On the coach with Tina to grand ol' Londinium!
Have gelled hair, worn best pixie boots and done make-up
dead cool. After all, I will not be judged for creative skills
alone, but also for my bang-on-trend fashion sense. Tina is
dressed like Robert Smith. We already look like winners!

12.10 pm: Arrived at London Victoria coach station at
11.30, then hopped on the tube and got off at Oxford
Circus.

Am now at the London College of Fashion, in the loo
freshening up. How glamorous and exciting! (Not the loo,
the college.) The other seven finalists are already here. They
have their parents for support, and here I am with Tina. I'm
still the odd one out even though we're all here for the same
thing.

12.15 pm: They gave us tea and sandwiches, but I could
hardly eat from nerves. It is hard to tell if anyone will be
better or worse than me. It's strange to think the winner is
among us right now. Wish this was all over already!

12.45 pm: We have been brought into an extremely shiny
room with mirrored workspaces lined up against the wall. I
had a quick chat with Laura, my model. Was noticing how

340

pretty her eyes were when I suddenly thought mine look pretty too these days, especially with the right make-up.

Am checking I have everything I need:

1) The design, which I stuck in this diary – yes
2) Right colour make-up – yes
3) Nerves still intact, just about – yes

Gloria, the course tutor, came in and introduced herself. She isn't how I'd imagined. She has an oversized blonde bouffant and gaudy crimson lips. 'Welcome, and thank you all for coming to this *very* exciting event today,' she announced. Then I only heard snippets as she went on to talk about the college and the course cos I was too busy wondering whether I had butterflies or indigestion. '. . . So I hope you're all ready to go?' she said right at the end, checking her watch. Twitchy yeses and silent nods all round, Tina patted me on the back and grinned. 'Then you have two hours from . . . *now*!'

Well, here goes . . .

3.10 pm: Oh my god, just finished! What have I done? Everything was going so well! Aargh!

At 1 pm on the dot I started copying my design on to Laura's face with blue eyeliner as planned. I didn't feel nervous at all, I knew exactly what I was doing. The green eyeshadows were blended to make swirling leaves and the flower petals were filled in with lipstick. I worked without a break until I heard Gloria say 'One hour to go!' Had loads of time to paint the outlines using my watercolour brush dipped in mascara.

'Twenty minutes!'

That was my cue to put the finishing highlights on, using the white pearlised paint I'd brought along.

'Time's up, everyone!'

Phew! My masterpiece was done.

I inhaled deeply and stood back to admire my work. Then gazed around the room.

My face dropped in horror.

NOOOOOOOOOOO!

Everyone else had put make-up where it was supposed to go, you know, lipstick on lips, eyeshadow on eyes . . . like *normal* people do. But of course, I'm not normal, am I? How can I be? I was born from the loins of NOT NORMAL people! I gaped at Laura. I had gone completely astray with my wacky avant-garde collage.

Tina noticed my panic and whispered, 'Calm down, calm down,' through the side of her mouth, but I felt like puking, fainting and wailing all at the same time. Am in the loo now, trying to pull myself together. Tina is knocking on the cubicle door asking if I am all right.

3.28 pm: Just been to canteen for a drink, while Gloria and two other tutors judged our work. They didn't serve stiff whiskies, so I opted for Irn-Bru instead.

'Why didn't you stop me?' I said to Tina, as if it were her fault.

'Cos you were being *different*, and that's good, isn't it?' she replied hesitantly.

'That's easy for you to say!' I said, sensing a rant coming on.

Tina was taken aback.

'Being different works for you. There's loads of other Goths out there that get you. Even people who aren't Goths get you, cos you wear black and listen to morose music, you belong to a tribe. Where do I belong? Nowhere! Nobody gets me, cos nobody is like me. I'm on my own, an oddball, a freak!'

'You're not a freak,' said Tina with a pained look on her face.

'What am I, then?'

Silence.

'A talentless no-hoper, that's where "being different" gets me!' I hissed.

I was being cruel, but couldn't help it. I had just blown the best, maybe THE ONLY chance, of escaping the takeaway.

6.15 pm: Oh my god, oh my god, oh my bloody, flippin' god. Am on the coach home pinching myself every two seconds cos guess what? I only went and flippin' WON!

After my rant at Tina (which I am now extremely sorry about), we went back into the competition room. Gloria stepped forward with a piece of paper in her hand and hushed the crowd. By now I was feeling totally defeated.

'We have some very special talent in this room,' she said. 'So you can imagine it was very tough for us to come to a decision.'

Go on then, put me out of my misery, I thought.

'Second and third will win places on the Fashion Styling course, but the overall winner will receive a scholarship, sponsored by Miners Cosmetics for a whole year.'

There was a subdued 'ooooh' in the room. Could I come second or third? No. I was definitely doomed. Gloria cleared her throat. 'So, in third place . . . is Emma with her "Winter Wonderland" look! Well done, Emma.'

Emma and her mum squealed with delight. I clapped non-committally.

'Second place goes to . . . Josey, for her "Summer Party" look!'

Both of Josey's parents hugged her. I smiled through gritted teeth. I was done for.

'And now for the extremely well-deserved first prize, which goes to . . .'

Ah well, I thought, time to go home. Those prawns won't gut themselves . . .

'Jo Kwan, for her "New Beginnings"!

'A brilliantly inspired and unique design depicting springtime *blah blah blah ...*'

Her voice trailed off.

What was happening? Did she say my name? I heard clapping and cheering for someone, but was it for *me*? Then Tina picked me up and swept me off the floor ... so then I knew the someone must be me.

Wow!

Me.

I was the someone.

I *am someone*!

'Oh my god, you won, Jo, you bloody won!' said Tina, squeezing me so hard I couldn't breathe. 'Go and get your certificate then,' she said, pushing me forward. I remember walking slow motion towards Gloria who was beaming and holding out an envelope. I felt eyes boring into me as I accepted it. I felt like puking, fainting and wailing, but from sheer unadulterated joy this time. As I returned back to my spot next to Tina, I swear I spotted Yoko across the room for a split second, winking as if to say 'Well done'.

As everyone packed up to leave, Gloria came over and told me how much she was looking forward to having me as a student in September.

'You, a *student*! How grown up does that sound?' Tina is gushing next to me on the coach. 'I'm dead proud of you I am.' And I am dead proud of myself.

Tuesday 26th May

Woke up SMUG AS SMUG could be, went straight over to Bonny's bed and shook her awake. I hadn't told her yet. She wasn't back from Mandy's when I got home from Tina's last night, and I'd gone straight to bed, I was so knackered.

'What you doing?' she groaned, nudging me away.

'Bonny, I'm leaving home!' I said excitedly.

'What, *now*?'

'No, you plum, in September.'

'Why?'

She rubbed her eyes and sat up.

'I was in London yesterday and I've won a place to a college there.'

'What you on about?' she said.

So I told her every tiny detail. When I was done, Bonny looked at me with a crooked smile. I think she seemed pleased for me, but couldn't tell cos she didn't say much for the rest of the day.

Went to see Miss Waterfall at break to tell her the news. She was so chuffed she hopped up and down and her glasses nearly fell off. 'I'll miss having you,' she said.

'Thanks, miss. To be honest, your class was the only reason I went to flippin' school,' I replied.

She chuckled. 'Well good luck, and remember,' she said, more seriously, 'stay different. That's what makes you and your art unique.'

Wow.

That's exactly what Tina had said to me (before I went mad with her).

They were both right. I should be pleased I'm different. It won me first place after all.

Was dreading telling Mum and Dad the news. They were already one child slave down with Simon gone. How will they react when they find out their prize prawn-gutter is also going to abandon them? They wouldn't think twice about nailing down the windows and barricading me in. (Which is ironic, as only a few years back, they couldn't care less where I was.)

I decided to spring the news at dinner. I watched as Mum plonked the food down: boiled lotus root, steamed fish, fermented tofu . . . What were the right words? I didn't know. I never knew. All I knew was that I would open my mouth, something garbled would come out, and I'd have to hope for the best.

Everyone started eating. Mum told a story about how watery the beansprouts were in this week's delivery. Then there was a gap. Now . . . NOW!

'Er, Mum, Dad,' I spluttered.

Bonny looked petrified, she knew what was coming.

'I . . . I go live London,' I continued, in Chinese.

'*What?*' said Mum, scrunching her face. 'What rubbish are you telling us?'

I could hear alarm bells ringing in her head already: *Who'll mop the floors? Who'll look after Larry? Who'll serve the customers . . . ?* I didn't know how to say the next bit in bad Chinese, so I said it in English.

'I've won a scholarship to the London College of Fashion.'

Mum looked blank. Dad leaned forward and I thought for a moment I was going to get whacked.

'Is it real?' said Dad.

'Yeah, course it is!' I said, staggered he could think I was making it up (unbelievable UR). Mind you, they didn't give a toss about Simon's exam results so why would they give a fig about me winning a scholarship?

'Sounds like you're being ripped off to me. You're not going.'

'I am.'

'NO!' he said, in English. 'YOU STAY!'

Dad's face was dark and angry, just like it was in Hull, before he dragged me to the toilet and flushed my head down it.

I felt a cold sweat all over.

'Don't be silly. What's going on? What did she say?' said Mum to Dad, trying to diffuse another potential fight bomb. Bonny sat rigid, waiting for it to explode.

Simon had stood up to Dad and now I was going to do the same. I was *not* going to be dictated to any more. I couldn't if I wanted to get out of here. But instead of erupting like Simon did, I replied as calmly as I could.

'I. Am. Going.'

Dad seemed taken by surprise. His mouth opened and closed again. He was speechless for once.

Then Mum recognised the word 'going' and jumped in with what she thought *really* mattered. 'Who will help us if you go?' she said.

'I don't know, it's not my problem,' I replied coolly. Although I felt awful for leaving her and Bonny in this whole mess.

Everyone went silent, then Bonny threw down her chopsticks, ran up to our room and slammed the door.

She knows it will be her.

Wednesday 27th May

On the way to Mini-Mart today, I apologised to Tina for losing my rag about the 'being different' thing during the competition. Have been thinking about this a lot and wanted to say sorry properly.

'Don't be daft,' she said. 'It was a big day, you were under a lot of pressure.'

'Yeah, I know but . . .'

'Don't worry about it, honest. I'm just dead made up you won.'

'Thanks, Tina,' I replied sheepishly.

'I know, let's celebrate with a pasty, my treat!' she said.

She's so happy for me. I think secretly she wants the best for me after learning the crap I have to deal with from Dad.

Thursday 28th May

Heard Bonny crying in bed last night. I looked at the clock, it was quarter to midnight. I got up and went over. 'What's up?' I said.

'I don't want you to go,' she sniffed.

'I know. But I've got to.' (*Need* to, more like.)

'I don't want to work in the takeaway.'

My heart sank. She seemed so tough on the outside with her smoking and nicking and hanging about with Mandy. But right then she seemed so vulnerable. Well she IS. She's only a kid.

'Well that's why I've been telling you to do well at school, so you can get out of this dump when you're old enough,' I said, sounding exactly like Simon when he lectured me.

'But that's *ages* away!' she said, burying her face in the pillow.

She was right. But what was the alternative? Me staying? No chance. I felt bad about abandoning Mum but even worse about Bonny, cos she's only eleven, nowhere near ready for slogging away in a takeaway kitchen – how would she survive? The thought of Mandy's family looking after her was some comfort at least. And I would still be at the end of a phone if she ever needed me. It wasn't as if I was going to disappear off the face of the earth completely.

'It'll go dead fast,' I tried to reassure her.

'But I'm not talented like you, or brainy like Simon. What am I meant to do?'

'You don't need to be talented or brainy, just . . . just make sure you don't ever give up.'

'What's that mean?'

'You want that nail salon, don't you? Well, keep that vision in your mind, don't stop thinking about it, no matter what, and eventually you'll get it.'

It sounded simplistic, but it worked for me. Then I told her to stop snivelling, cos I was trying to get to sleep. She sat up a bit and latched on to my sleeve. 'Jo . . .'

'Yes?' I said.

'I'm scared.'

'Of what?'

'What if Dad goes off it again? You and Simon won't be there to help me.'

'He won't, don't worry.'

'How do you know?'

I thought back to the moment Dad emerged after the fight looking so frail. He never has fully returned to his former self – thank god.

'I just do. And anyway, Smiffy'll look after you. Trust me.'

Bonny sighed sadly and went back to sleep. Even though I'd like to, I can't always be around to protect her, I've got my flippin' self to take care of.

Saturday 30th May

Wanted Simon to hear the good news, so I wrote him a letter that went like this:

Hi Simon,

How you doing? It's weird not having you around. Has Smiffy been to see you yet? I hope you've made mates in Derby.

Guess what? I've won a scholarship to the London College of Fashion! I'm doing a Fashion Styling diploma in September! It was through a national competition in a mag. So it looks like art CAN be a proper job after all eh???

I've started packing already. I won't need much apart from art stuff and a few clothes. I'm getting a full grant so I can buy stuff when I get there.

I filled in the forms and got Dad to sign them. He thought the competition was some kind of hoax till he saw the official paperwork — berk. I got my digs sorted — it's a room in student accommodation in Streatham, south of the Thames.

You'll be off to uni soon too, won't you? We vowed we'd get away from the takeaway and here we are — the jammiest gits in town. Ha ha!

Anyway, I'll forward my address soon so you can visit.

Sis x

Tuesday 2nd June

Back to exams – UGH!

1 pm: Geography exam

Question: What is your view on the flood plain of the River Wye? Answer: I don't give a 'dam' – ha ha!

Actually I really don't give a damn, cos I'm off to fashion college in September! What a clever girl I am!

Thursday 11th June

10 am: English language exam – enjoyed this, think I've done all right, maybe B.

Monday 15th June

2 pm: Art exam – still life, light and shade in pastels. Loved it! Most likely A.

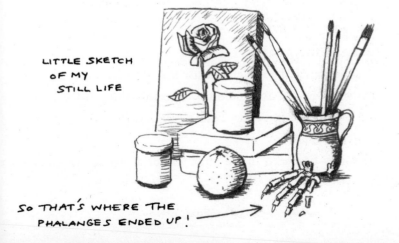

LITTLE SKETCH OF MY STILL LIFE

SO THAT'S WHERE THE PHALANGES ENDED UP!

Friday 19th June

Got a letter back from Simon!

Hey Pongo,

Nice one! That's a massive achievement, winning a national competition. I'm proud of you, sis. Yes we are indeed jammy.

I've got my digs and grant sorted too. I start Warwick Uni end of September.

Yeah, send me your address so I can visit.

Bro

If he does visit, he'd better stop calling me Pongo. Especially in front of my new college mates.

Tuesday 23rd June

Exams are over, thank the Lord!

Tina thinks she will get mostly Bs, Jill and Sunita reckon theirs will be As, and Simon is expecting three A level As and is all set for university. I don't even care that I'm the only non-boffin now!

Bonny has been home after school all week, which is

not like her. When I asked why, she said, 'Mandy's been grounded for shoplifting, so I can't go round.'

Well *quelle surprise.*

'What did she nick?' I asked.

'Corn plasters,' said Bonny.

'Unlucky.'

'Yeah.'

'Good job it wasn't you,' I said. 'You might have got more than just a grounding off Dad.'

Bonny was the only one out the three of us who hadn't been caught nicking yet.

'He didn't care when Simon got caught,' she huffed.

'Yeah, but Dad's a bit cuckoo, isn't he?'

Although he has been quieter since the fight with Simon, who knows what it'll take to wind him up again.

'Anyway, if he touches me Kev'll batter him,' said Bonny.

'How? He's best mates with Kev.'

'Mandy told Kev what happened with Simon and he said if the same thing happened to me, he'd stick up for me cos I'm a defenceless kid.'

Wow. So Kev isn't as thick as I originally thought.

I'm glad Kev (and Smiffy) will be there to protect her when I'm gone. It's a good job Bonny spends most of her time at Mandy's actually cos even though they are the roughest family in the street, at least I know she is safe there. Wonder how long Mandy's grounded for?

Thursday 25th June

When I got back from school today, there were several people wearing black standing outside Mrs Burke's house. I thought for a moment it might have been Tina with a group of Goths, but they were old and I didn't recognise any of them. Thought it was weird as I have never seen anyone visit Mrs Burke in the whole three years we've been here. She didn't have kids and her relatives live miles away in East London where she was originally from.

Mum was in the kitchen stuffing spring rolls. She looked up briefly and announced, 'The old woman next door's . . .' then she said the rough Chinese equivalent of 'snuffed it.'

'What?!' I replied.

'At least we won't have to give her free chicken any more,' she said.

'Hold on . . . Mrs Burke . . . dead?' I spluttered.

Then Bonny came bounding downstairs and shrilled, 'Have you heard – Mrs Burke had a stroke on Monday and died!'

No.

I couldn't believe it. I was only round on Sunday to see how she was.

Even though I had an inkling she didn't have long before she popped her clogs, I hadn't prepared myself for this. Naively I hoped she would be around forever.

I used to hate going round hers at first. Her stories were torturously boring. But then I got to like her cos she listened to me just as much as I listened to her, which is more than any of my family ever did. My eyes welled up. I went upstairs so Mum and Bonny couldn't see me crying. Why did she have to go? Now there is one less person I can turn to.

I will miss you, Mrs Burke.

? – 1987
HERE LIES
MRS BURKE

GOOD NEIGHBOUR
KIND FRIEND
DODGY CROCHETER
WILL BE MISSED

Sunday 28th June

Started getting the chicken out to do Mrs Burke's chomato, when I remembered she wasn't about any more. I had got so used to going round every Sunday. It's strange how I cried when she died, but not when Simon nearly detached Dad's head from his shoulders.

Bonny offered to take Grandparents' char siu round on her own today cos she saw I had chores to do. I have noticed a difference in her since she was banned from seeing Mandy. She has become almost . . . good. Maybe she is not well?

Saturday 4th July

Three weeks left till senior school officially ends, and my uniform has just started to fit. Sod's law, but I am growing at last, yessss!

Mum and Dad have not mentioned London since the announcement, but they are silently making preparations for when I am gone. Are they pleased, proud, sad, angry, panicking? I have no idea. Never have, never will, but at least they're not in denial!

So, Grandma and Grandad are back helping (they were at Poshos', who have now hired a professional cos they are normal and sensible and do things like that), and Kev is a full-time cook. Wonder what customers think when they see an Englishman tossing woks in the kitchen? No weirder than seeing the chef's son kicking the crap out of the chef, I guess.

Bonny's at senior school in September. The thought of it fills her with as much joy as the mopping she has now been roped into doing every night. I told her she was doing really well and she coughed a little on the bleach fumes, like a

Victorian scullery maid. Is that what I used to be like? Outrageous!

Later on I found her shoving random things from under her bed into a bin bag.

'What you doing?' I asked.

'Chucking away all this stuff I nicked,' said Bonny.

I knew it.

'Why?'

'Gonna stop stealing, stop smoking, do well at school and get as far away from here as possible, like you said.'

Wow, I was flattered she was taking my advice for a change. (Even though it's taken like, *eleven years*.) Anyway, glad she is taking positive steps now. Doing it this early on in life means she has a better chance than I did.

Sunday 5th July

Went to Banga's to buy what may be the last pack of kitchen rolls in a long time. I'd never noticed before, but as I walked in there was a strong scent of incense. Rose or something, really floral and fresh. When did that happen?

Raj was there helping Gurdeep stack shelves.

'Haven't seen you guys in a while,' I said.

'You won't see us at all next year,' said Gurdeep.

'Why's that?' I asked.

'Cos we're moving to India and getting engaged.'

'Wow, er, that's great.'

She looked happy too, and so grown up. I could see hardly any trace of that dopey little kid I first met three years ago.

'I'm moving away too, in a few months,' I told them.

'Really, where to?' asked Gurdeep.

'London.'

'What for?'

'College.'

'To be a student?' she said, looking surprised. 'Won't you be poor and starving?'

'Well I'll try not—'

'Tell you what,' she jumped in, 'send me your address and I'll post you some out-of-date stock. Don't worry, I'll make sure you get Turkish Delight, I know they're your favourite.' Then she winked.

Ah, so there was some of the good old Gurdeep left after all.

Monday 20th July

Since I won the scholarship and realised I really would be leaving, my asthma has completely disappeared. The walls of my prison have vanished, along with the strangulating, vice-like death grip on my chest. Funny that.

Me and Tina arranged a multiple celebration for:

1) The end of stinking school
2) My imminent escape to London
3) Her new job as a junior hairdresser

We went to Wimpy for our last burger and milkshake together.

'It's going to be crap when you're gone,' said Tina, wiping froth off her lips with her black lace fingerless gloves, the first Christmas present I ever bought her.

'Same here,' I said. 'You'll be OK though, you've got Gaz.'

Just like Gurdeep and Raj, Tina and Goth Gaz have all sorts of couply things planned for the future, so I knew she wasn't quite as upset as she was making out.

'Will you miss Coventry?' said Tina.

'Pffff, no!'

'You did have some good times though, didn't you?' she said.

'Did I?'

'Yeah, like Lucky . . . and Baarbara and Billy . . .'

Cor, I'd forgotten about them. That was like, a lifetime ago.

'Well that's about it,' I said.

'What about *me*?' she whined sarcastically.

'*You*? Oh you were the reason my life was worth living,' I joked, but actually there was a lot of truth in it.

'Will you call me every weekend?' she asked.

'Every day,' I said.

'What about every hour?'

'No way! You do my head in enough as it is!'

'Ha ha! I'm gonna miss you, eejit,' she said.

'I'll miss you too, dope.'

Then we both laughed and cried till our buns went soggy.

THE BLACK LACE FINGERLESS
GLOVES I GOT FOR TINA'S FIRST EVER
CHRISTMAS PRESENT

Sunday 26th July

Me and Bonny went to Poshos' for lunch today. I will not miss being reminded of how life could be in a perfect world every time I walk into their floral-scented hallway, that's for sure. Hadn't told them about London as I wanted to leave without a fuss.

'Jo! Congratulations!' said Jill, answering the door.

Eh, how did she know?

'My mum told me you'd won a place at a college in London,' she said.

'Who told her?' I asked.

'*Your* mum.'

Wow, I didn't think Mum would be so proud. Or had she been slagging me off for leaving them in the lurch? Yes, probably that.

'Er, thanks,' I said, coyly.

It was normally Jill getting all the gold stars and certificates, so being praised by her felt odd. I followed her into the not-best living room where Grandparents were sat.

'Where will you live?' Grandad blurted, who obviously knew about it as well.

'In student halls,' I replied, in English. Grandma didn't understand. I wilted. I still couldn't say the right words in Chinese like Jill and Katy, so Jill had to translate.

'What will you eat?' Grandma asked.

I could answer that in Chinese easily enough.

'Oh, er, soup, bread, noodles...'

'And char siu, you must eat char siu,' she said.

'Yes, char siu definitely, Grandma,' I said. 'And Bonny will bring yours round from now on.' I glared at Bonny to help me out.

'Yes, er, I bring char siu,' she said. Hmm... at least Bonny's Chinese will always be worse than mine.

Grandparents cannot understand why someone my age would leave the family home to be on their own in a big strange city. They said it was dangerous, which I think is bonkers considering the Communist horrors they must have been through. And didn't they know how completely and utterly ecstatic I was about the following:

1) No more working in takeaway
2) No more childminding
3) No more chicken's feet
4) No more Dad

I guess not.

'And be a good girl,' said Grandma, unexpectedly. 'Your brother's disgraced the family.'

Whaa?! No one had even mentioned the fight since it happened, and now Grandma was directing her disappointment in Simon... at *me*... in front of everybody! What about Dad? I wanted to say. He was the one that put a knife to Mum's throat. Simon saved her. Why were us kids always in the flippin' wrong? Then I realised everyone in the room must have heard the whole story. It was *SO mortifying*.

Then Auntie piped up, 'Your mum and dad disappointed.'

'They want you to stay and help in takeaway,' Uncle added.

Everyone stared at me. I stared at my quiche. Kill me now.

'But *we* think you very clever and should go London. Get better prospect and good job,' he continued, smiling.

PHEW! They weren't having a go at me after all! Forgot Posh Auntie and Uncle understood the importance of aspiring to something better, and they were being dead kind to me and Bonny by not mentioning the fight thing. We spent the rest of lunch talking about London and Jill's A levels and for once, I didn't feel like the outside loser looking in.

Thursday 30th July

Mum was talking to Auntie Yip on the phone and at the end of the call Mum passed the receiver over to me with a slight glower on her face and said, 'Auntie Yip wants to speak to you about something.'

'Hello, Auntie?' I said.

'Hey, Jo, your mum told me about you going to college in London,' she started. Here we go, I thought. Auntie was about to talk me out of it on Mum's behalf. 'What a clever girl you are!' she cheered. 'I knew you'd go far after you showed me those fashion pictures when I was down yours last time.' Wow. I honestly thought all Chinese people held the same views as Mum and Dad, but Poshos and Auntie have proved me wrong.

Tuesday 11th August

Oh my god, can't believe what turned up today. It was only my portfolio back from *Mizz*!!! I'd totally forgotten about it! The pictures inside still looked good. There was a note with it saying how sorry they were for the delay in sending it back as it had been 'mislaid by an intern', and how impressed they were by my work, but couldn't 'accommodate me right now'. What do I care? I'm doing something way, way better now! They are obviously a whole different department to the competition organisers, otherwise they would have known that – DUR.

GOD KNOWS WHERE
MY PORTFOLIO'S BEEN
FOR THE LAST NINE MONTHS!

Thursday 20th August

Got O-level results today. Thought I wouldn't be that bothered but was a teensy bit disappointed. Maybe cos since winning the scholarship, I think I am totally brill at everything, ha ha! Results are:

Art – A (of course)
English Language – B
History – C
Geography – C
French – D
Maths – U

Had to call Simon and ask what U was as I'd never heard of it before. He said, 'It stands for "Utter thicko",' which was exactly the type of answer I would expect from a smart-arse like him, so wasn't quite sure why I asked him in the first place. I called Tina and she told me it meant 'ungraded', i.e. I am *actually* an utter thicko. Tina got five Bs and a C, which is what she'd expected.

Saturday 22nd August

Tomorrow is THE BIG MOVE!

Went and treated myself to a brand new pair of Doc Martens boots. It's what anyone who's anyone is wearing these days.

Mum has offered to drive me to London (UR)! She is

doing double the amount of food prep today, so she can spare a few hours. This is strange as she has never done anything as thoughtful as this for me before, let alone driven anywhere outside of a one-mile radius of our home (due to not being able to read road signs).

It was a nice gesture but I felt uncomfortable. It is Auntie Yip's job to be thoughtful and kind – it doesn't suit Mum, it makes me think she's up to something. Is she making a last-ditch effort to be a proper parent? To make me think twice about what I'll be missing? If so, then I'm sad to say she's sixteen years too late! Eighteen, if you count Simon. Or maybe she doesn't want me to marry David Wong after all, so I don't end up like her. Or could it be she wants me to escape and live the life she couldn't? Hmph, wishful thinking on my part. If that were true, she'd never tell me anyway. All she said was:

'Will you come back for holidays?'

Why? Cos you'll miss me, or to guarantee that you get help in the takeaway over Christmas? I guess that'll have to remain a UR for now.

Sunday 23rd August

11.45 am: Put on my Doc Martens (they make me feel more confident, somehow) and said goodbye to Bonny. She had her brave face on.

'You forgot to pack Nik Kershaw,' she said, pointing at my

faded, snood-wearing pal on the wall. He got me through a
bad patch with Warren once, but I don't need him now.

'There's no room in my suitcase,' I answered apologetically.
'You can have him.'

'Nah, I've got Gary Kemp,' she said, holding up his
chump-faced, poodle-perm picture, and we laughed. The
conversation was pointless but it distracted us from what
was really happening.

I went up to Larry, who was smearing soggy rusk all
over the wall. Bonny wiped it up with the antimacassar Mrs
Burke gave me as a gift.

'Hey, Larry,' I said. He gazed at me inquisitively.
'Bonny's going to look after you now.' His face dropped
and he started bawling. 'Don't worry,' I said to Bonny. 'It's
just wind.'

I took one last look at Mum and Dad's bedroom, with its peeling seventies wallpaper and dirty laundry piled up everywhere. I felt bad cos I couldn't imagine Larry's life being any better than mine, Simon's or Bonny's – poor sod. There was that all-too familiar whiff of stale grease everywhere too. I won't miss that, but funnily enough, I will miss the char siu. Mum's char siu is bloody lovely, despite what Grandma thinks of it.

Then Mum shouted up the stairs:

'YENZI!'

But this time it wasn't cos I had to mop or murder maggots or serve a weirdo. How liberating was that?

'I READY!' she shouted again.

I grabbed my case, and gave Bonny a piece of paper with my student halls' number on. She smiled faintly. 'Call me whenever,' I insisted and gave her a hug, even though we don't do them. Downstairs, Dad was frying rice. I went to wave at him, but he was in that faraway world of his so I turned and left silently.

11.56 am: We are in the car and driving off. Gasp! I have escaped!! I have actually done it!!! It is super exciting. Mum hasn't a clue how to get to our destination and I don't even know if we'll get there alive, but I find that exciting too! Everything is suddenly VERY EXCITING! The clouds in the sky, the strangers walking by, the two-for-one cucumbers in Banga's shop window.

I glance back at the takeaway. God, I had the life squeezed out of me in that place. But now I'm free. I'm in charge.

And at the grand age of sixteen, I'm making sure that good stuff is finally about to happen.

AFTERWORD

I was asked to write an account of my childhood and immediately there was resistance. No way! No one must know who I was! And anyway: 1) Who would want to know about a working class girl growing up in a Chinese takeaway in Coventry? 2) Can I even write a novel? 3) What would my family think?*

I did it anyway, because I'm the sort of person who wanders off down unmarked paths, prods things with sticks and eats discarded sweets off the floor. I live dangerously.

At first I stuck to the warm fuzzy memories, because the not-so-nice ones were stored safely out of sight and that's how I liked it. But as I went on, I was encouraged to tell the truth where it needed to be told, otherwise my story wouldn't be authentic. Done right, the book could end up helping a ton of kids going through the same things I did. And stop them from eating mouldy foam bananas as adults, because they were so screwed up as kids.

Although the story is based on real life, it's woven together with fiction, because there are lots of gaps between

---

* 1) Everyone (according to James, my wise agent) 2) Still no idea 3) 'What the hell?!'

memories. So people like Mandy and Smiffy are your average sort of mates kicking about in the eighties, and Julie and Sam are your perennial type of bullies. They're not real. Tina is though, and she's still one of my best friends (she recalls the Onion Head incident avidly). My family do exist of course, which means Dad's goatybacks, Mum's deep-fried pizzas, Simon's trousers-down-trousers nicking, Bonny's Gary Kemp perm, Larry the human marshmallow, and all our unfortunate pets, are also real. You'll be pleased to know, just as I was at the time, that I actually did win a scholarship to the London College of Fashion and was featured in *Mizz* magazine. I kept the clipping for years, but sadly it got lost in the ensuing mad years. But like yin and yang, good can't exist without bad, so the not-so-nice memories came out of storage and made it into the book in the end. Everyone else's version of our lives in Coventry will be sad, funny and exquisite in their own way. This is mine.

ACKNOWLEDGEMENTS

With thanks to Chloe Sackur, Kate Grove, Charlie Sheppard, James and Lucy Catchpole and all my friends and family who gave their support throughout. The biggest thank you goes to Dave, who seems to have spent most of our relationship rolling his eyes at my ideas and antics, but remains resolutely patient (with a slight twitch).

If you've been affected by any of the issues featured in this book, you can get in touch with these charities. No problem is too big or small, and all calls, webchats, texts and emails are completely private and free.

ChildLine	**Childline Ireland**	**Kids Helpline Australia**
childline.org.uk	childline.ie	kidshelpline.com.au
0800 1111	1800 66 66 66	1800 55 1800
	Text 50101	

If you live in another country, check: childhelplineinternational.org to find the right helpline for you.

If you want to find out more about the issues in this book, including ways you can help, take a look at:

NSPCC
nspcc.org.uk
Protecting children and young people from abuse

Refuge
refuge.org.uk
Working against domestic violence

Mind
mind.org.uk
Providing advice and support for people experiencing a mental health problem

Young Minds
youngminds.org.uk
Mental health support for young people

Kidscape
kidscape.org.uk
Help with bullying to protect young people

Anti-Bullying Alliance
anti-bullyingalliance.org.uk
Organisations united against bullying

Stop Hate UK
stophateuk.org
Supporting people affected by hate crime, including racism